Also by Bob Kaster:

The Septuagenarian – An R-Rated Thriller

Bob Kaster

The Mansion

A Septuagenarian Thriller

By Bob Kaster

PROLOGUE

The Car

At about 8:00 AM two students on their way to class at Pineland Community College called the Pineland Police Department and reported that they had discovered an abandoned vehicle parked along the side of a country road just off of Interstate 5. The town of Pineland is approximately a 45-minute drive north of Sacramento. They reported that the vehicle was a new convertible but was trashed. It still had the new car sticker. Two Pineland police officers responding to the report found a new blue Mustang convertible parked partially in the ditch along the road. Its body and windows were smashed like they had been hit by a heavy instrument, maybe a crowbar. All four tires were flat. The convertible top had been ripped. No one was inside, but the interior was strewn with broken glass and debris ... and blood. The damage to the car did not result from an accident.

Without touching or disturbing anything, the officers called in their observations, and were soon joined by a detective and crime scene technicians from the Pineland Police Department. They were joined later by technicians from the California Department of Justice. This was an unusual crime scene, at least by Pineland's small-town standards. They spent several hours doing their work, before directing that the car be towed away.

Except for broken glass and blood, little was found in the interior and trunk of the vehicle. There were no personal effects or belongings of any kind. No suitcase, purse or handbag. No items of clothing. Nothing in the areas inside the car that usually accumulate stuff, such as cupholders and storage compartments in the doors. The glove box contained a packet with the usual items that come with a new car, including temporary ownership and registration documents and the fat binder of owners' manuals. Nothing else was in the car, not even a discarded gum wrapper.

The technicians also made a thorough examination of the area surrounding the car, with nearly equally negative results. The road was not paved but was covered with gravel. The tires on the driver's side were on the gravel road. The other two tires were off the road, on loose dirt and dust. There were no skid marks or other indications that the car had crashed at its present location. They concluded that the car had been driven there, parked, and then vandalized. The dirt and gravel surrounding the car had clearly been disturbed, although there were no rake marks. There were no footprints or other identifiable marks on the ground, and it appeared that whatever marks there might have been had been obliterated by use of something to push the dirt around, possibly a stick, not a rake. With one exception, no noteworthy objects were found. The one exception was a woman's necklace, a gold chain with a single diamond in a yellow gold heart-shaped setting, simple but expensive.

The blood inside the car had dried. It was not extensive, but had splattered and was on the front seat, dash, and steering wheel. The technicians took eight swabs of the blood from various locations and transmitted them to the California Department of Justice Bureau of Forensic Services Laboratory in Sacramento. They took two swabs from the necklace and transmitted them for analysis as well.

After testing the swabs, a DOJ Criminalist submitted reports indicating that two DNA profiles were recovered from the blood, and that the same two profiles were recovered from the necklace. One profile was confirmed to have come from a male, and the other from a female. The DNA profiles were entered into the Combined DNA Index System (CODIS), but there were no matches to any previously entered profiles.

CHAPTER 1

Hailey

Hailey Madison remembered the first ten years of her childhood as the happiest time of her life, at least until she met Ben. Children thrive in small rural towns. There is a sense of freedom that city kids can't enjoy. Children can walk or ride their bikes just about anywhere. In the summer, she spent many hours swimming at the public swimming pool and playing softball. She had friends who lived outside the city limits, on farms and ranches. She would go horseback riding with them for hours on the open range, guiding their horses wherever they wanted.

During her tenth year, her idyllic life ended when Uncle Phil moved to town. Uncle Phil was related to Hailey's father, some sort of a cousin. Hailey's father, although not wealthy by any means, had a successful small business. He was a franchisee of a national hardware chain and had his own store. He was well liked and respected in the community. Hailey's family consisted of her dad, mom, and her younger brother. The family chose to live in the small community, knowing they would never be wealthy, for the same reasons that Hailey loved her childhood, the down-home people, the laid-back lifestyle, and the beautiful country. When Uncle Phil showed up, everything changed.

Uncle Phil had been as *un*successful in his life as his cousin, Hailey's dad, had been successful. Uncle Phil could never hold down a job for an extended period. He could not make friends or be part of a community, and he was mean and ornery. He drank to excess, and it was speculated, although not proved, that he did drugs. One day Hailey's dad received a call about Uncle Phil from Hailey's grandfather. Her grandfather said that Uncle Phil had hit rock bottom, had been in and out of jail for public intoxication and disturbing the peace, and needed help. He desperately pleaded with Hailey's father to take Uncle Phil in and try to straighten him out. Her father and mother were opposed to the idea, but her grandfather persisted. Her father reluctantly acquiesced, primarily because of his belief that that's what families were for, to take care of one another.

Their house was a nice four-bedroom, two bath home, nothing fancy. The fourth bedroom was used as a den, with a desk for Hailey's father. There was also a little cottage, not connected to the main house, a "mother-in-law" unit. It was self-contained, with its own bedroom, bathroom, and kitchen. The kitchen was small, really an alcove, but it had the basic appliances to allow the occupant to prepare meals.

Uncle Phil turned out to be morose and unappreciative of the efforts of Hailey's family to make him feel welcome. Hailey's father created a part-time janitorial position in the hardware store to keep Uncle Phil busy and to give him some spending money. The family invited Uncle Phil to join them for meals, but most of the time he declined. *Just as well,* thought Hailey's dad, because on those rare occasions he did join them, the atmosphere at the dinner table was strained. Never did Uncle Phil ever express gratitude for what the family was doing for him. On several occasions, Hailey's father considered sending Uncle Phil on his way, but rejected the idea, having promised her grandfather.

One day, Hailey came home from school and was in the house alone. Her mom and dad were working at the store, and her little brother was in pre-school. She was in her bedroom sitting on her bed when, without warning, Uncle Phil walked in. He sat next to her on the bed and put his hand on her shoulder. She tried to move away, but he moved his hand to her arm and kept her from moving. His breath smelled of alcohol. He said, "You are a very pretty girl, Hailey. Do you have any idea how pretty you are?"

She squirmed and redoubled her efforts to get away from him, but now he grabbed her forcefully, preventing her from moving. "I won't hurt you if you are good," he said, "but if you aren't good, I *will* hurt you, and your little brother too. Now don't try to make any noise."

Hailey was now crying but didn't try to move away.

Hailey was wearing gym shorts and a tee shirt. Uncle Phil said, "I want to see how pretty you are." With his other hand, he pushed her shorts and panties down to her knees. He looked at her but didn't touch her. "You are indeed a very pretty girl," he said, "I really like you."

Then he said, "I'm going to leave you now, but you must never tell anyone about this, do you understand?"

Hailey was now crying and shaking violently. She said nothing but she shook her head violently from side to side.

He said again, in a harsher and louder voice, "You must never tell anyone about this, do you understand?" She continued to shake and cry while nodding her head up and down. He continued, "Do you know what will happen if you tell anyone?" She again shook her head from side to side. "First of all," he said, "no one will believe you. You are a child, and no one will take the word of a child on something like this. And second, if you do say anything, your little brother will have a horrible accident, and he will be brain-dead. Do you understand?"

She nodded, and mercifully, he walked out the door and went to his cottage.

By the time her parents got home, her fear and anxiety diminished somewhat, but not before she vomited twice, and then after the nausea spasms diminished, she took a shower. She said nothing to her parents about Uncle Phil.

Uncle Phil's visits with Hailey continued for weeks, each visit becoming more extreme; more cruel, forceful and violent, causing physical pain and injury to the ten-year-old girl. For Hailey, even worse than the assaultive conduct itself was the awful fear that Uncle Phil had instilled in her. "No one must ever know about this," he repeated often. "You must never tell anyone; ever! If anyone ever finds out, horrible things will happen to your little brother. He will never be the same after. He will never grow up to be normal." For a long time, the ten-year-old complied, and told no one about Uncle Phil. But she began exhibiting changes in her demeanor that other people observed. Her natural childlike energy and enthusiasm for life diminished. She became quiet and sullen. She would awaken screaming during the night. These changes did not go unnoticed by her parents, who became more worried each day. They repeatedly asked her what was wrong, but received no meaningful response. They talked with the school nurse, who gave them the name of a child psychologist, who met with Hailey and her parents several times without progress. Hailey never mentioned Uncle Phil.

One day, while walking home from school with her best friend, Dolores Davis, Hailey let go, and blurted out everything. She simply couldn't keep it inside her any longer. Afterward, she was overwhelmed with fear, and pleaded with her friend, "Please, please promise me you won't tell anyone. Not even your mom and dad. He will hurt my little brother. And no one will believe me."

Dolores was beside herself. She had promised Hailey she would tell no one, but she knew she had to, and finally she did. Dolores and her family lived less than a block from the Madisons, and the families were close friends, often socializing and getting together for dinner. Dolores asked her parents not to tell anyone, fearing for the safety of Hailey and her little brother, and fearing that people wouldn't believe Hailey. After hearing the story, Dolores's parents, Mark and Jennifer Davis, had real qualms about what action to take. Their first thoughts were to immediately pass the information on to Hailey's parents, or to the police, or both. They too were concerned about the children's safety, and whether people would believe Hailey's story. They were also a little concerned about how Hailey's father might respond. He was a good guy, but with a temper.

After much thought, Mark Davis called David Solus, the Yreka Chief of Police, and set up a meeting with him. In the Chief's office, he repeated everything Dolores had told him, emphasizing the fear that no one would believe Hailey's story and Uncle Phil's threats to harm Hailey's little brother. "We have a protocol for these kinds of cases," Chief Solus said. "You'd be surprised at how many we get. We refer them to Child Protective Services. Their social workers have special training in investigating cases of child abuse, and they are very professional."

"What will they do?" asked Mark Davis.

"They will interview the appropriate people; probably starting with you folks and your daughter. And then with the Madisons, and their daughter. As you can imagine, investigations of this sort are very delicate, and that's what the CPS people specialize in. Police officers generally don't have that kind of training. Especially questioning child victims; that takes real skill and training. Children who are victims of abuse often have a difficult time opening up. They are afraid, or embarrassed; or, in some instances, particularly the young ones, don't have the ability to express themselves. When questioning a child, the social worker necessarily has to focus the child's attention on matters that the child is uncomfortable with, or doesn't know anything about, and about parts of the body the child is embarrassed to talk about. Leading questions are almost always required, but there is a real danger in that. If the questions are too leading and suggestive, a good criminal defense lawyer can later argue that the child's testimony is tainted; that the facts are simply the product of the child's imagination, fueled by the suggestive questioning of the investigator. The lawyer would call it a child abuse witch hunt. Do you remember the McMartin Preschool cases in the 1980's? In those cases, several teachers were charged with hundreds of counts of child sex abuse involving forty-eight children. No one was convicted."

"So, the CPS workers will interview Hailey and her parents?"

"I'm sure they will," said the Chief.

"That's a real problem. Our daughter, Dolores, promised Hailey she would never tell anyone. It's a betrayal of trust. Dolores pleaded with us not to tell anyone."

"Well, it will be difficult. These cases always are. Look at it this way, if the abuse is occurring, it has to stop. And stopping it won't be easy for anyone. But it has to be done. Nothing about this will be easy. It won't be easy at the beginning; and it won't be easy at the end, the criminal trial if there is one. And even then, assuming there's a trial and a conviction, that's not really the end. These cases take a tremendous toll on everyone, especially the child victims. Some victims never get over it."

Police Chief David Solus was right.

Later that day, two social workers from the Child Protective Services Division of Siskiyou County's Human Services Agency began their investigation. They went first to the Davis home and talked to Mark and Jennifer Davis, and to their daughter, Dolores, interviewing them together and individually. The process was difficult and upsetting for Dolores. She was emotional, but able to answer all their questions. By the time they had finished their interview the CPS workers got from Dolores everything she had been told by her friend Hailey. Several times throughout the process Dolores asked if it was necessary that they let Hailey know it was she that told them Hailey's story. She pleaded with them not to tell. The CPS workers were professional and sensitive to Dolores's discomfort, but they didn't want to deceive her. They said they would try to avoid letting Hailey know who their source of information was but couldn't guarantee it. The main thing, they explained, was to make Uncle Phil stop doing the bad things to Hailey. She agreed, and it made her feel better, despite that she had betrayed her friend's confidence.

As difficult as was the interview with Dolores, the social workers' interview with her friend Hailey was much worse. She was the only person with first-hand knowledge of the crimes Uncle Phil had committed, but they couldn't get her to open up. They spent a lot of time with her, in several sessions, but she consistently refused to tell them that Uncle Phil had ever done anything to her, or that he had ever entered her bedroom. It was painful for the CPS questioners, because they understood the distress they were inflicting on her, but they had to keep at it. They had no choice but to press on. It was important for her to personally tell the story. Dolores's testimony would be hearsay, and hearsay is not admissible in criminal trials, unless it falls within certain exceptions. The California Evidence Code has provisions allowing hearsay statements from child victims of sex crimes under certain circumstances, but admissibility can be problematical, and getting a conviction is far more difficult when the actual victim doesn't testify. The social workers had to weigh the adverse emotional consequences to the child of their persistent questioning versus the importance of getting a statement from her. Initially Hailey didn't waiver, and withheld the truth until later, after Uncle Phil was in custody. It was only then that she felt that her little brother was safe. As part of the investigation, Hailey was also subjected to a sexual abuse medical examination. Most sexually abused children manifest no abnormal physical findings, but, in Hailey's case, the physical findings corroborated that what Uncle Phil did to her was physically, as well as emotionally, egregious.

After bringing CPS into the case, but before he felt he had sufficient probable cause to make an arrest, Chief Solus devised a plan to stake out the Madisons' house, to keep an eye on Uncle Phil's activities when Hailey's parents weren't home. Since Hailey didn't disclose in her interviews that Uncle Phil committed a crime, he felt that an immediate arrest was premature. He wanted to investigate quietly, hoping that his officers' activities wouldn't alert Uncle Phil that he was under suspicion. He also wanted to continue as much as possible the normal routine of the Madison household. Hailey had told Dolores there was a pattern to Uncle Phil's visits. They would occur after she got home from school on days when he wasn't working at the hardware store, and when neither her parents nor brother were home. The plan was that when Hailey was home alone, an officer in plain clothes would position himself in a location where he could see the Madisons' back yard and observe if Uncle Phil walked from his cottage to the main house. This plan was initially met with resistance by Hailey's parents, especially her father, who simply wanted to kick Uncle Phil out. He reluctantly agreed to give it a try for a day or two, only after Chief Solus convinced him of the importance of building a case good enough to get Uncle Phil off the streets.

The stakeout immediately proved productive. The officer saw Uncle Phil heading for the house, and quickly texted the Chief and asked for back-up, no sirens or lights. The Chief himself and another officer pulled up in an unmarked car and parked about forty yards from the Madisons' house. The three proceeded to the house and entered without warning; the Chief going in the front door, and the other two in the back. Neither door was locked. Hailey was sitting on her bed, and Uncle Phil was standing in front of her with his penis exposed when he heard noises and realized someone was in the house. When the officers entered the room, they saw Hailey, crying, fully clothed, sitting on the bed, and Uncle Phil standing in front of her, also clothed, but possibly adjusting the zipper of his pants.

CHAPTER 2

Bob

My name is Bob. I'm a septuagenarian. I'm retired, and live in Yreka, a small rural gold rush town in northern California. I live with my dog, Bebe, a black Labrador Retriever. Bebe is also a septuagenarian, but in dog-years. Our town of 7,500 people is in Siskiyou County, just south of the Oregon border. Siskiyou County is very large in area, but small in population, with about 45,000 people. The county has a total area of 6,347 square miles. Compare that with Rhode Island, which covers an area of 1,214 square miles. You could fit a little over five Rhode Islands into Siskiyou County. What actually does fit into Siskiyou County are mountains, capped by Mount Shasta, forests, lakes, rivers, waterfalls, lava beds, and desert.

I was a thirty-year-old lawyer when my wife and I moved to town, fresh from a four-year tour as a JAG officer in the United States Air Force during the Vietnam war. After I had practiced law for eighteen years, I was elected to the Superior Court in a runoff after seven candidates competed for the job. Fortunately, no one ran against me after that, and I served twenty years unopposed. After retirement, I heard cases on an occasional basis for another five years. Before I was elected, most of my law practice experience had been in civil law, but I quickly discovered that much of my new job was criminal law. I often worked into the wee hours of the morning bringing myself up to speed.

Although child molestation cases occur with alarming frequency, there was one that stands out in my memory. The victim was the ten-year-old daughter of a prominent local family that owned one of the hardware stores in town. The alleged perpetrator was a cousin of the girl's dad. The family had taken him into their home to help him get on his feet. He was known as Uncle Phil to the family members. Although I was acquainted with the family, I didn't consider my relationship to be close enough to justify recusal. Apparently neither did anyone else. California law allows any party to a litigation a one-time right to disqualify the judge, without having to show a reason. Neither side did that.

The D.A. filed an information with the Superior Court charging Uncle Phil with numerous Penal Code violations involving child molestation. If convicted, Uncle Phil faced a possible sentence of life in prison.

Child molestation cases are difficult to try. Many settle before trial because of the toll such trials take on the child victim. The Confrontation Clause of the

Sixth Amendment provides that "in all criminal prosecutions, the accused shall enjoy the right ... to be confronted with the witnesses against him." This generally describes the right of an accused to face-to-face cross examination of witnesses testifying against him or her. This can be terribly traumatic for a child victim whose testimony must be taken to prove the case. At one time it required the child to testify in front of a horde of people, including attorneys, court personnel, jurors, and, worst of all, the very person who abused the child. However, most states, including California, now have laws that mitigate the horrible ordeal for the child witness by allowing the child's testimony to be given from a location away from the courtroom and out of the direct presence of the defendant via closed-circuit television. Although this helps, the process can still be brutal for the child, perhaps as horrible as the criminal acts themselves. Although rare, sometimes the process is traumatic for the accused as well as the child, and some offenders are genuinely remorseful and embarrassed.

This wasn't the case with Uncle Phil. The only remorse he demonstrated was that he had gotten caught. He was angry and was sure his constitutional rights had been violated when the police barged in on him in the girl's bedroom. He damn well would not give up his right to a jury trial, no matter how much additional trauma it might cause to his already traumatized victim.

The jury trial lasted two weeks. The first week was devoted to jury selection. It was complicated because the girl's mother, father, and entire family were well known in the community, and many prospective jurors were excused because they admitted they could not be fair and impartial. The selection process was further complicated because of the type of case it was. I presided over many child-molest trials in my career, and I was always surprised at how many potential jurors described molestation events in their own lives that permanently affected them or people close to them. Often the events were so significant that the memories hindered their ability to be fair and impartial jurors. The standard protocol for such cases is to summon an extra-large number of prospective jurors. Even having done so, we came close to exhausting the entire panel before finally swearing in twelve jurors and two alternates.

The second week of trial went relatively smoothly. The most dramatic and difficult part was during the victim's testimony, which was essential. Without it, the case would have hinged upon the testimony of the officers, who didn't see enough to prove the case. All they saw when they entered Hailey's room was the girl sitting on the bed with Uncle Phil standing in front of her, possibly with his hand on the zipper of his pants. This testimony was valuable to corroborate the girl's story, but, taken alone, wouldn't have been enough.

Although Hailey initially did not disclose what Uncle Phil had done, once he was in custody, she felt safe enough to tell the story.

Even though Hailey's testimony was taken using closed-circuit television, the girl was fragile and emotionally distraught while on the witness stand. Her testimony took the better part of a morning. She broke down three times, once while being questioned by the deputy district attorney, and twice when the defense attorney cross-examined her. She became so distraught that she burst into tears and simply couldn't go on. Overruling objections by the defense attorney, I declared a short recess on each occasion to give her a chance to compose herself. I was struggling to maintain my own composure and attitude of impartiality. I knew it would take this girl a long time to recover from the ordeal of testifying, if she ever did. And this was in addition to what she had already endured directly from Uncle Phil.

The defense counsel's role is a delicate one. While he has the ethical duty to his client to be probative and even harsh during cross-examination, he still has to demonstrate compassion, lest he alienate the jury. He did a good job for his client, but the girl valiantly did not waiver from her account of what Uncle Phil did, and presented a compelling case.

On the Friday morning of the second week of trial, the jurors began their deliberations. At about 3:00 PM that afternoon, the jury advised the bailiff they had reached a verdict. The bailiff passed that information on to me in my chambers, and I told him to advise all interested parties that we would resume court in one-half hour, and to tell the jury they could take a break during the interim.

At about 3:40 PM, after the jury had reassembled in the jury deliberation room, I called court back into session. The jury filed back into the jury box. I asked who the foreperson was, and juror number 3, a tall gentleman who looked to be about forty, raised his hand.

"Has the jury reached a verdict?" I asked.

"We have," was the answer.

"Does the verdict represent a unanimous vote of all jurors?"

"It does," he said.

"Please hand the verdict form to the bailiff." He did so, and the bailiff brought the form to me. I reviewed it to make sure it was properly filled out, and handed it to the clerk.

The clerk read the verdict verbatim, which took a while, due to the number of charges. The jury had inserted the word "Guilty" in the blank for each count.

Before the clerk finished reading, Uncle Phil, his face bright red, flailed his arms and bellowed, "This is bullshit! That lying little cunt got together with her little friend, and they concocted a story against me, because they don't like me! I'm not their kind, and they think they are better than me. This is bullshit! I'm going to appeal this joke of a trial and sue everyone in this room!" I warned him, but he kept on ranting, disrupting the proceedings, and I finally instructed the bailiffs to take him back to the jail. I thought at the time that Uncle Phil, besides all his other appalling qualities, was just plain stupid. He was acting out, profanely accusing a ten-year-old girl of lying about the horrible experience he had subjected her to, in the presence of the judge who would determine his fate.

After Uncle Phil was escorted out of the courtroom, I thanked and excused the jury. Following protocol, I scheduled a date for pronouncement of judgment and sentence approximately four weeks later and referred the matter to the Probation Department for preparation of a Pre-Sentence Report.

Four weeks later, when I reconvened court for judgment and sentence, the courtroom was jammed with people. Not a surprise, given that the case was high-profile for our small community, and that the victim's family had a lot of friends.

The Probation Department had submitted its report several days before the court proceeding, with copies provided to the defense attorney and D.A. The California sentencing law is complicated, and the amount of discretion that it gives to the trial judge varies, depending on the crime. Here, although for the record it was necessary to calculate sentences for each crime, the bottom line was a life term, which was the recommendation of the report. Probation was not an option.

I announced my tentative decision to follow the recommendation, and then heard statements from the attorneys, and also from family members of the victim. Uncle Phil declined to speak; probably, I thought, because of the wise and adamant advice of his attorney. After considering the statements, I was satisfied that the recommendation from the Probation Report was appropriate and imposed the life term. Upon hearing his sentence, Uncle Phil again acted out in the courtroom, screaming vile comments about his victim, and about me. He was out of control, and although shackled, tried to bolt. He was restrained by the court security people and escorted away. I could have held him in contempt for his conduct and sentenced him to up to six months in the county jail in addition to his life prison term, but that would have been a waste of time and resources, and anyway the county jail was full.

CHAPTER 3

Hailey and Rex

After her ordeal with Uncle Phil, Hailey's happy life fell apart. She became sullen and introverted, and the kids at school considered her to be antisocial. Her high school grades weren't good enough to get her into a four-year university, so she initially went to community college, the College of the Redwoods, in Eureka, California, a five-hour drive from her hometown. Getting away was good, and her emotional state improved at community college along with her grades, which were good enough to get her into nursing school.

She lived in a dorm at the College of the Redwoods and began to experience a somewhat normal college student social life. She began to feel comfortable being around other college students of both sexes. She became more relaxed and enjoyed going to parties, but in groups, not one-on-one dates. Not that she didn't get asked out by college boys. Her natural beauty was beginning to shine, and, initially, they were all over her. But she turned them down, and soon they stopped asking, speculating that she might be a lesbian, which wasn't the case. She was not sexually attracted to women. Even though still plagued with flashbacks of Uncle Phil's abuse, she had an active fantasy life, always involving men. The men in her fantasies were handsome and virile, but also gentle and considerate of her wishes, and never pushy or sexually aggressive. Other than in her fantasies, and disregarding what had happened to her as a child, she had never had sex. She feared men and feared letting them get close enough for sex to be an option. Another thing she feared was what a man would think of her if he knew what had happened to her when she was a child, as if she had been somehow tainted. She thought about these things a lot. She was aware of the irrationality of it, and aware that Uncle Phil was the source of her demons, not herself. She had undergone counselling and therapy for years after Uncle Phil had assaulted her. Intellectually she understood the problem, but when faced with a real-life encounter with a man that could lead to sex, she backed off. *I'm probably the world's oldest virgin,* she told herself with a laugh, but the laugh was hollow, and not funny. Technically, she wasn't a virgin, she couldn't help thinking, because of what Uncle Phil forcibly did to her when she was a child. Then she would shift her mind-set back to, *Sooner or later the right guy will appear. I just haven't found him yet.* This thought brightened her outlook a little, but not much.

She was still a virgin when she graduated from nursing school, partially because of her demons, and partially because school was demanding, leaving little time for socializing. She did worry because the right guy still hadn't appeared, and maybe her time was running out.

Hailey received notice that her job application to Fairchild Medical Center, Yreka's small but state-of-the-art critical access hospital, had been accepted even before her nursing school graduation ceremony. The acceptance was conditioned upon her actually graduating, but neither she nor the hospital had any concerns she would fail to graduate. The happiness she felt thinking about moving back to her hometown to start her nursing career surprised her. It hadn't been that long ago that she felt she never wanted to even visit her hometown ever again, let alone move back to it. Also, although not as often, she still had nightmares of Uncle Phil suddenly showing up in her bedroom. *What if he escaped from prison? Or what if he was mistakenly released because of some bureaucratic paperwork blunder?* But the fond memories of her childhood were overcoming the post-Uncle Phil demons. Buried, at least for the moment, was the lingering awareness of how small her hometown actually was. And how there were no secrets in such a small town.

Now, Hailey Madison's life was good, despite the demons that had plagued her for over seventeen years. Occasionally they resurfaced, but she was strong and had learned to focus on the good things. She kept her demons under control.

She was twenty-seven years old, and through hard work and perseverance had gotten herself to the place she wanted to be, back home. She purchased a modest house in the town in the northern California mountains where she was born. She was a Registered Nurse in the hospital's Intensive Care Unit. Her work was demanding, but she thrived on it. She was confident in her knowledge and skill, and took pleasure in knowing she was helping others.

The hours suited her. She worked "three-twelves," fairly standard in the medical field. This meant that she worked three twelve-hour shifts per week, with occasional adjustments so that over the long run she averaged forty-hour weeks. The twelve-hour shifts could be grueling, but the time zipped by when she was busy. She liked the schedule because it gave her ample time off to do the other things she loved. She was an outdoor person, and during the warm weather months the surrounding forests, mountains, and rivers beckoned. In winter, there were two ski parks with groomed trails within an hour's drive of her house, one to the south and one to the north, and many undesignated areas within the National Forest great for cross-country skiing.

Having been born and raised in Yreka, she knew many people, of course. Many remembered her as a sullen antisocial high school girl, but her personality had changed, and they gradually started warming up to her. She was included in the social milieu, such as it was. A popular place where people congregated was an establishment simply called the Wine Bar. Located downtown, it primarily catered to the folks getting off work. People would walk to the Wine Bar at quitting time from their jobs in the courthouse and the offices, businesses, and shops nearby. Even though the hospital was not within walking distance, and her three-twelve work schedule differed from the nine-to-five routine of the downtown folks, Hailey enjoyed showing up at the Wine Bar on Thursday or Friday nights around 6:00 PM. There was a good crowd and live music, and people were in TGIF cheerful spirits. She had enjoyed that routine for several months after moving back to town. Occasionally she would go out to dinner afterward, but with a group, not like a date. None of those encounters lead to long-term relationships, or to sex. *This has to stop. I need to get a life*, she thought.

One Friday evening a guy showed up at the Wine Bar she hadn't seen before. He came in alone, but as he made his way to the bar, it became clear to Hailey that he knew practically everyone in the room, or, at least, practically everyone in the room wanted to be known by him. She was sitting at a table about twenty feet from the bar with five other people. When the guy came in, Hailey was conversing with her friend Dolores Davis, whom she had known forever, and had confided in years before about what Uncle Phil was doing to her. While talking with Dolores she was watching the guy at the bar. He definitely stood out in the crowd. Probably forty-ish, six feet tall, physically fit, with black hair. A good-looking guy. But what stood out was how he was dressed, a very expensive cowboy look. Five-hundred-dollar Tony Lama boots, Wrangler jeans, a Filson vest covering a plaid long-sleeved shirt with snaps, and a Stetson fur felt hat. He wore an oval-shaped silver buckle at least two-and-a-half-by-four inches in size with a mountain scene and a gold figure of a pack-horse led by a cowboy. Cowboy boots and hats aren't unusual in Yreka. There are cattle ranches all around, and rodeos proliferate throughout the county during summer. But no local cowboy would dress like this guy. And any local cowboy would respectfully remove his hat when entering a room. Hailey thought the guy looked bizarre in his outfit, but at the same time she was attracted. Certainly, the other patrons of the Wine Bar clamored after him like he was a celebrity.

"Who is this guy?" Hailey asked Dolores, nodding toward him.

"You don't know who he is?" said Dolores, surprised. "He's Rex Ryder. Actually, his name is Rex Randall Ryder The Third. He bought about a zillion acres of land in the Scott Valley. It abuts up against National Forest Wilderness Area. He built a gigantic house with a million square feet and has a cattle ranch. He's the grandson of some famous cowboy movie actor from the forties or so, who went on to become a billionaire businessman. He owned an NFL football team, some restaurant franchises, and a famous country-western music joint in Scottsdale, Arizona. I think Rex is kind of a jerk, myself, but everyone I know thinks he's Mr. Wonderful. He *is* good for the county, spreads money around like it was water."

"Why do you think he's a jerk?"

"Oh, I don't know. Something about him just rubs me wrong."

"Did you ever go out with him?" asked Hailey.

"Oh, not really." Dolores was evasive and appeared uncomfortable, and didn't follow up on her ambiguous statement. Hailey wanted to ask for more detail, but backed off, sensing her friend's discomfort. She would ask her again later.

The five people and Hailey stayed at the table for another hour, consuming a couple more rounds of drinks, having a good time. Hailey couldn't help herself from occasionally glancing over at Rex Randall Ryder The Third. Twice, she caught him looking at her, and one time he winked.

The crowd thinned out, and Hailey's table was down to just two people, Hailey and Dolores. Pretty soon Rex Randall Ryder The Third moseyed over to their table, and said, "Hello Dolores. Don't think I've met your friend."

Dolores looked uncomfortable, but she said, "Hello Rex. This is Hailey Madison. We've known each other since pre-school. Hailey, this is Rex."

"Pleased to meetcha," said Rex Randall Ryder The Third. His voice had a hint of a western twang, maybe just a little phony. "You must be related to George and Evelyn. There is a resemblance. Good people. When buildin' my house, I spent a lot of time in their hardware store. And money. But I always got my money's worth. You must be okay if you're their daughter."

Hailey thought he made it sound like he and her parents were close friends, but she didn't remember them ever mentioning him. Truth was, she had never heard of him before. But then, she'd been out of the loop, being away at college and nursing school. Even though she had been back in town for a few months, she was preoccupied; starting a new career, and fixing up and furnishing her house.

The three of them, Hailey, Dolores, and Rex Randall Ryder The Third made small talk for a few minutes, Dolores looking increasingly uncomfortable. Finally, Dolores stood up. "I've got to go," she said. "Hailey, do you need a ride?"

"No thanks. I came straight here from the hospital. My car's just around the corner."

"Okay," said Dolores. "See you later." She went out the door, leaving Hailey and Rex as the only two occupants of the table.

The Wine Bar was winding down, still lively but quieter, and the musician was packing up his guitar. "Can I buy you dinner?" asked Rex. Hailey accepted, and together they walked to the Mexican restaurant three blocks away.

The restaurant had been there for about forty years. Juanita, the owner, greeted them both by name. "Nice to see you Hailey," she said. "It's been a long time." It *had* been a long time, but Juanita had known Hailey since she was a little girl, coming into the restaurant with her parents. She had observed her growing up. "And nice to see you too, Mr. Ryder," she said with a smile, although Hailey thought she detected a little edginess in her voice.

The dinner was good, and the conversation was okay. Although Rex did most of the talking, he asked Hailey to tell him about herself, and she did, although reticently. She talked about growing up in this small town, about going to College of the Redwoods and nursing school. She didn't tell him about being molested as a child, or about her psychological issues, or about the fact that she was a virgin.

Rex Randall Ryder The Third, on the other hand, talked about himself effusively. He talked about his famous grandfather, and the fact that he had inherited such a fortune from his famous grandfather that he could acquire and own "anything I want on this planet." He talked expansively about the magnificent house he had built in the Scott Valley. Walking out onto the street after dinner, he asked her if she had to work the next day. When she said no, he said, "Wonderful. I want you to come see my house tonight. It has a world-class view of the valley and the mountains surrounding it. There will be a great moon tonight. It will be beautiful! You've got to come see it. It's as beautiful as you are."

Hailey's mind was reeling. She wasn't sure if it was because of her demons or because of Rex's blatant aggressiveness. Or was there something else, something she couldn't quite put her finger on? This was too quick. She needed time to think! It would be at least an hour's drive to get to his remote place in the Scott Valley. Was he expecting her to stay the night?

"I'm sorry," she said. "Not tonight. Maybe some other time. I've got some things I really have to do early in the morning. Thanks for inviting me."

He was quiet as he walked her to her car; in Hailey's mind, almost sullen. When they got to her car, he asked, "Where do you live?"

She didn't know why, exactly, but she was reluctant to give him her address. "Just a few blocks from here, on Lane Street." Her reluctance to give him a specific address was stupid, she realized. Hell, in this small town, anybody can find anybody's address by just asking around.

Then he asked her phone number, and she gave him her cell number. "Thanks for dinner," she said.

"My pleasure," he said, then he put his hands on her shoulders, pulled her body against his, and kissed her. "I've got your number memorized. I'll call you. You'll really be sorry if you don't take me up on my offer."

CHAPTER 4

Rex and Melinda

Hailey had trouble sleeping that night. She couldn't get Rex Randall Ryder The Third out of her thoughts. She couldn't figure out why. The evening wasn't that unusual by a normal person's standards. But Hailey was abnormally vulnerable, and she knew it. She was, after all, a twenty-seven-year-old virgin. She feared men, or at least feared sex with men, even though she fantasized about it all the time. Rex Randall Ryder The Third was an anomaly. His brashness was both a turn-on and a turn-off. He seemed to believe he could have any woman he wanted, any time. She was attracted, but frightened. What did he mean by, "You'll really be sorry if you don't take me up on my offer."? Her fear was something deeper than just the fear of rejection, or of a bad relationship. It was more primal. Yet she was attracted. Like a moth to a flame.

Rex Randall Ryder The Third didn't waste any time. He called her the next day. "How about tonight?" he said, with no prefatory words. "The moon will be perfect, and I've got some tenderloins. Beef from my ranch. I can pick you up at six."

She had expected him to call, but not so soon. She hadn't yet formulated a strategy. She was caught off-guard. "Um," she said. "Okay, that sounds nice. Thank you. But I can drive myself to your place. I have a couple of errands in the Scott Valley that I can do on the way."

"It will be my pleasure," he insisted. "I can drive you to your errands."

She thought, and wasn't sure why, that she needed to dig in on this issue. The guy unnerved her. But still, she felt a strange attraction. Was it to him, or only a desire to break out of her self-imposed cocoon? She said, "No. I insist. I'll feel guilty if I let you do that, and it will ruin my evening. You would have to come all the way into town unnecessarily. Twice. What can I bring?"

"Well, if you insist. Just bring your pretty self, darlin'. Take the Shaughnessy Gulch Road off of the Scott River Road. My house is at the end of the road, easy to see. The gate combination is R-E-D-Y-R, my name spelled backwards."

The drive to the mansion of Rex Randall Ryder The Third took about an hour. Hailey brought a nice bottle of Pinot Grigio. This made it seem more like a dinner invitation among friends than a date. It made her more comfortable, but her mind continued racing throughout the drive. She remembered how Dolores had acted when discussing Ryder the evening before. There was something that Dolores hadn't told her. When Hailey arrived at the end of the road, she encountered a wall with an arch surrounding a wrought-iron gate that opened when she tapped the combination code onto the electronic touch-pad. As she drove along the lane leading to his house she was awe-struck. It wasn't just a house. It was like a small city. Besides the main house, there were three other buildings, all new. There was a mother-in-law cottage, but bigger than most people's homes. Actually, upon closer look, it was a guest-quarters. It probably could have housed ten people, or ten couples. A quarter of a mile away was a barn with a corral and stables, and another building that looked like a workshop, possibly with a tack room. She could count at least ten horses in an open field adjacent to the corral. Closer to the house was a swimming pool with its own cabana, and a tennis court with a retractable roof. But the house itself, *oh my god,* she thought. It was huge. It was a modern version of the American Craftsman Bungalow style of architecture popular in the early 1900's. But unlike the original American Craftsman Bungalow homes, this one had three stories, and must have contained at least 10,000 square feet, with decking in front and on two sides. Behind and near the house was a helipad. A helipad! Surrounding the house-garden-pool area were beautifully maintained grounds. *There must be an entire staff of gardeners,* she thought. She wondered what people actually do in a place like this.

In front of the house was a semi-circular driveway, with a new Dodge Ram 3500 Bighorn pickup parked in front. Hailey parked behind the truck and walked up the steps to the front door of the house, carrying the bottle of wine. She was greeted at the door by a strikingly beautiful woman with long jet-black hair. She was taller than Hailey, with fiery dark eyes. She was about Hailey's age. She was dressed western-style, similar to how Hailey remembered seeing Rex the day before, but without the boots, hat, and vest. She was barefoot. Her jeans were skin tight and the top few buttons of her Western shirt were unbuttoned, amply displaying cleavage. Hailey was sure there was no bra under the shirt. "Hailey, so nice to meet you," she oozed, in a voice tinged with a Western drawl. "Rex has told me *so* much about you. I'm Melinda. Please come in. We are *so* looking forward to seeing you."

Hailey was confused. *Who is this woman? Is she Rex's wife? Or girlfriend?* Had she misread the intent behind Rex's invitation? She reflected back on their conversations from the evening before, when he invited her to his house. He spoke only in the first person singular. It was always "I," not "we." "*I* want you to come see *my* house tonight." And then when he called her today, "*I've* got some tenderloins. Beef from *my* ranch." Now, Hailey's mind was racing.

Melinda took Hailey's hand and maneuvered her into the house. "Rex is in the kitchen," she said, and walked her into the entryway. "Follow me, let's get you a glass of wine." Hailey followed her through a sitting room and then through a door that led into the kitchen, where Rex was seasoning filets.

Rex immediately walked over and greeted her with a full-on hug, pressing his body tightly against hers for longer than a conventional greeting hug, but without the kiss he delivered the night before. He wasn't wearing Western wear. This time it was cargo shorts, a Malibu tee shirt, and sandals. He said, "We'll eat outside on the deck. The view is wonderful, and there should be a great sunset tonight. After the sun goes down, it will get a bit chilly, and we'll come inside and get to know each other better. You'll love Melinda, she's sensational." He topped off Hailey's wine glass, and said to Melinda, "Honey, give her a tour of our home; dinner will be ready in about half-an-hour. Be sure to show her the house's centerpiece. How do you like your steak, Hailey?"

Hailey said, "Rare," as Melinda took her hand again, directing her toward a large great room with huge windows and a spectacular view of the valley. On one wall was the largest flat-screen television screen Hailey had ever seen, almost like a movie-theater-screen. It was positioned so it could be comfortably watched from a large very plush couch. In front of the couch, between it and the television screen was a gorgeous mahogany coffee table. The great room and kitchen were actually one large space with the two areas separated by a bar with five stools. Melinda was prattling on cheerfully in her southern drawl as she escorted Hailey through the house. Melinda was in physical contact with Hailey throughout the entire house tour, holding her hand, putting her arm around her shoulder, or putting her hand on her hip, sometimes casually letting it slide around toward Hailey's butt. Hailey didn't hear a word she was saying. Her mind was racing again, impinged upon by a rapid succession of thoughts and questions in random order, sometimes repeating themselves, mostly about this unusual house and the unusual people occupying it. *The house is magnificent, opulent beyond belief ... Who the hell is Melinda? ... No one else seems to be in this house, except for the three of us ... The house has 10,000 square feet, shouldn't there be servants, housekeepers, cooks, or others taking care of it? ... Or family members? ... I'm feeling a little weird, maybe should slow down on the wine ... Why does Melinda have her hand on my ass?*

Melinda opened the door to another room, and declared, "And this is our centerpiece! Isn't it lovely?"

It was the most amazing bedroom Hailey had ever seen, even in movies. Not just a room, actually a suite, with an attached bathroom, or, in modern real estate jargon, an *ensuite*. Whoever designed the room must have been tasked with creating the most decadent bedroom on the planet. And succeeded. The room was designed for sex, pure and simple, complete with velvet curtains, chandelier, a Jacuzzi soaking tub, lots of mirrors, giant windows with an expansive view of the Scott Valley surrounded by mountains, and the biggest bed Hailey had ever seen.

"Kick your shoes off and stretch out on that bed," invited Melinda. Reluctantly but dutifully, Hailey did as she was told. She moved about five pillows from the head of the bed and stretched out on her back, hands behind her head, which was perched on a remaining pillow. Melinda sat on the side of the bed next to her, putting her hand on Melinda's belly. "Isn't this fabulous?" asked Melinda. "You can look forward to delicious feelings in this bed that you've never experienced before. Trust me. Aren't you excited? Rex and I will show you the ropes. You'll never be the same."

Hailey was now more numb than excited, although her mind was still racing. She was feeling the effects of the wine. Usually, wine did have the effect of turning her on, but not this time. It was just the opposite, and she felt like she was losing control of her faculties. She awkwardly sat up, scooted to the side of the bed, and stood up. She didn't know what to say, so she remained silent.

Without skipping a beat, Melinda took her hand again. Leading her out the bedroom door she said, cheerfully, "It's a lot to grasp all at once, but you just have to dive in. It's delicious. But first, let's get some dinner. Rex is *such* a great cook."

Rex was a great cook, Hailey had to admit. The food was sensational, the steak just right, and during dinner they were treated to a memorable sunset. If she ignored Melinda's *double entendres* and frequent placements of her hand on Melinda's thigh under the table, the dinner conversation was unremarkable. It was dominated by Rex Randall Ryder The Third, who expounded on many topics, highlighted by the magnificence of his ranch (not *our* ranch), the high quality of the beef it produced, and the many economic and other benefits *he* brought to Siskiyou County. Most of Melinda's contributions to the conversation were her giggling *double entendres*, and Hailey mostly nodded her head. Rex made sure Hailey's wine glass was never empty.

After the sun went down, the temperature dropped precipitously, not unusual in Siskiyou County that time of year. Melinda led her by the hand back into the great room, to the couch, and sat next to her, with her right arm around

Hailey's neck. Rex came in with the wine bottle, and placed it on the coffee table. He sat on the other side of her. They had her pinned between them, and Hailey was feeling like she was trapped. Melinda's right hand casually dropped down and her fingers gently squeezed Hailey's right nipple through the cloth of her shirt. At the same time Melinda touched Hailey's left ear with her tongue, and whispered, "Don't you think it's time to test-drive the centerpiece bed?"

Hailey squirmed, and said, "I've got to go home. I apologize, but I'm not feeling well." Feeling a little dizzy, she started to get up off the couch, but was restrained, gently, by Melinda's arm.

Softly, Melinda whispered in Hailey's ear, "You shouldn't go out in the dark if you're not feeling well. You must stay. Rex and I will make you feel better, I promise."

Hailey squirmed again, and she successfully rose from the couch and away from Melinda's arm. Her mind racing again, she frantically tried to remember where she left her purse with her car key, then spotted it on the bar. She lurched toward it. This time it was Rex that stopped her by grabbing her shoulder. He said, "You shouldn't go out in the dark after drinking so much wine." His voice wasn't oozing its usual charm; it was ... sinister. "You need us," he said. "We can help you. If you let us, we can cure your fears about sex. We can help you get rid of your demons."

"My ... demons?" Now, anger was taking over. "What do you know about my demons?"

"We know all about you," said Rex. "We have incredible resources. We know about Uncle Phil. We know about your therapy and counseling. We know about your sex life, or lack thereof. We know you are a virgin. We can help you, if you let us."

Hailey was now shaking, and shouting, "This is crazy! How can you know about my life? And what makes you think you can help me?"

"Like I said, we have resources you can't fathom. You must let us help you. And you can't get away from us. We will always know where you are. You can never hide. Now, calm down and relax. This will be good for you, and pleasurable, I assure you."

Hailey gathered all her strength and broke free, pushing Rex backward. She grabbed her purse and ran toward the front door. At the front door she was intercepted by Melinda, who tried to tackle her. Hailey, who was stronger and more fit than Melinda, broke the tackle and slammed her against the wall, hard, stunning her.

Hailey, without looking back, raced toward her car. She heard Rex's voice calling after her, "You're making a big mistake. You will regret it for the rest of your life, however short that might be." She climbed into the car, started it, backed it up, and jammed it forward around the pickup, tires screeching on the driveway pavement. As she headed toward the gate, she saw no one behind her. The gate was closed, of course, and she stopped. *Shit! What does it take to open it from the inside?* Agonizingly slowly, the gate opened, apparently activated by a sensor. When it opened just enough, she slammed through, having to zig-zag the car to do so. When she turned onto the Scott River Road toward Fort Jones, the adrenaline was dissipating, and she felt a little sleepy. By the time she got to Fort Jones she thought she would pass out any minute and was having trouble steering the car. In her haze she realized she couldn't make it home, another half-hour away. Everything was darkening. Struggling with every fiber to remain conscious, she turned onto a back road in Fort Jones, then into an alley. There was an old vacant structure with a dirt floor, what could at one time have been a garage. It had no door, so she pulled in and turned off the car, just in time. Everything went black...

CHAPTER 5

Bob and Hailey

About mid-day on a Sunday my cell phone performed Bob Seger's "Old Time Rock and Roll." It displayed a phone number, the first three digits of which I knew to be from a commonly used cell service in Yreka, but did not identify the caller. "Hello Judge, this is Hailey Madison," announced the caller. "You may not remember me, but you were the judge in my child-molestation case seventeen years ago."

"I remember. What can I do for you?"

"Can we get together and talk? Something happened that I think may be important that scares me. I don't know if it's a big deal, but I need to talk to someone." She did sound scared, almost frantic.

"Sure. When would you like to get together?"

"The sooner the better," she said. "I know you're busy."

"Hey, I'm retired. My calendar isn't exactly full. Any time."

"Can I come to your house?" she asked. "I can be there in fifteen minutes."

I said, "Okay. You know my old house burned down? I'm building a new one, but living in a rental in the meantime." I gave her the address.

She rang the doorbell about fifteen minutes later, and Bebe gave a perfunctory bark and got to the door before I did. Bebe knew no strangers. I opened the door to let her in, and Bebe was all over her, tail wagging furiously. Hailey responded joyfully, rubbing Bebe's head with both hands. Hailey obviously loved dogs, which gave her instant credibility with me.

There was some small talk. I asked her about her parents, and she said they were doing well. I offered her a cup of coffee, which she accepted, then we sat down in my small living room.

"How well do you know Rex Ryder?" she asked.

"A little, mainly from seeing him around town. We're not what you would call social friends."

She asked, "Can this conversation be confidential?"

"Sure, within reason. I don't know what you're going to tell me. If you tell me you are going to shoot someone, I probably will need to report it. But yes, I promise, confidential within reason."

"Okay," she said. "I didn't know who else to turn to." The fear in her eyes, which had temporarily disappeared during her happy interaction with Bebe, was returning.

"It started two nights ago. I was at a table at the Wine Bar after work with friends. Rex came in alone and sat at the bar. I had never seen him before and didn't know who he was. I was probably the only person in the whole county that didn't know who he was. I was sitting next to my friend Dolores, and she told me all about him. She said he was the wealthy grandson of a famous movie cowboy from the forties and owned a large ranch with a mansion." Hailey then gave me a detailed account of her encounters with Rex Randall Ryder The Third and the woman named Melinda, beginning with her first dinner with Ryder after leaving the Wine Bar, and ending with her frantic escape from the mansion. As Hailey was talking, Bebe, who normally would be snoozing on the carpet, was sitting on her haunches intently watching her. Was she tracking what Hailey was saying?

Hailey was distraught, and her anxiety level built to a climax when describing her getaway from the house and Ryder saying, "You're making a big mistake. You will regret it for the rest of your life, however short that might be."

Hailey continued, "I woke up this morning in my car, parked in an old beat-up garage in Fort Jones. The sun was already up. I had a terrible headache. I still have a headache, but now it's more manageable. I don't know if they tried to come after me. If they did, fortunately, they didn't find me. When I ran out of their house, I was really scared. Now, in the light of day, the whole thing doesn't seem so sinister. But I'm still scared. I really can't explain why. The logical explanation is that I was invited to some sort of a sex party, a three-some. That wasn't my cup of tea, so I left. But that's not the way it felt last night. I felt like they wanted to, like, capture me, keep me against my will. Make me a prisoner. That might be an irrational reaction, and that's one of the reasons I wanted to talk to you, Judge. You presided over my case when I was a child. You were very understanding and made me feel as comfortable as possible during the trial. Since then, I have had therapy, and now lead a relatively normal life, but still have occasional nightmares. My problem today is that I don't know if I am overreacting because of what happened to me as a child, or if I really do have something to be afraid of. I don't know how to express it, but there was something about Rex and Melinda, and about that big house, that felt like a horror movie. That huge empty house, and there was no one there except for the three of us." The fear in Hailey's eyes was continuing to escalate.

I asked, "Did you tell anyone else about this? Did you tell your parents?"

"I didn't tell anyone. Especially my parents. They would freak out and do something crazy. I'm not sure in my own mind if anything really bad happened. I don't know if they did anything illegal. That's why I came to you."

"Do you know why you passed out, and why you have a headache?" I asked.

"I've been thinking a lot about that. I don't think I had that much wine, but Rex kept filling my glass, so it's hard to tell. I'm a pretty responsible drinker. I had a bad experience once in college, but never again. They possibly may have drugged me, but I can't prove that."

I said, "If they did, that would constitute a crime. I don't know how long it would take to get something like that out of your system. It's been less than twenty-four hours. I'm no expert, but if it's a date-rape drug, I believe the ones commonly in use dissipate rapidly. I suppose you could be tested, maybe a urine drug screen."

"How can I do that?"

"I honestly don't know. As a nurse, you're probably more knowledgeable than I am. I suppose you could go to your personal physician, if you have one, or maybe go directly to the Emergency Room, and ask for a drug screen. The only other way I can think of would be to file a crime report with the sheriff. Maybe then they could have you tested as part of a criminal investigation. In any case, you would be referred to the hospital for the blood draw. Just thinking out loud now. Since you are a nurse at the hospital, do you know a lab technician or someone who would be willing to do it for you, privately?"

She thought for a minute, then said, "I don't think any of those options will work. I don't have a primary care doctor. I know I should, but I just haven't gotten around to it. I don't know any way to get a drug screen without having it get all over town, and that scares me. Also, I doubt any drug like that would still be in my system. I'm going to rule out the drug screen idea."

I said, "I'm at a bit of a loss about giving you advice. I think the proper advice is to file a report with the sheriff, to make a record of what happened, for future reference. But there is a downside to that. Without evidence that you were drugged, it's a little hard to determine if a crime has been committed. False imprisonment and criminal threats come to mind, but the evidence is weak, and proving either might be impossible. It would be your word against the two of them, and there's the fact that you drove to Ryder's place and then discovered he had a lady there. Well, I think you can anticipate how that might be perceived. If you filed a report, about all the Sheriff could do would be to send a couple of deputies to Ryder's place and ask some questions, which might make it more dangerous for you."

I could see in her eyes that her fear was genuine, and what I was telling her didn't help. "What should I do?" she asked.

"I have an idea," I said. "I know Sheriff Brad Davis quite well. We go back a long way, and I trust him. Let me talk to him informally about what happened to you. He may have some ideas about what to do and may have some useful information about Ryder and that big house of his. Maybe there have been complaints against him by others. I personally don't know much about Ryder, other than that he has provided an economic boost to the county. Also, he seems to have a lot of local community involvement. That's a bit unusual. Over the years we have had celebrities buy up ranches and other properties in Siskiyou County, but they have tended to be reclusive.

"In the meantime, I think you should just continue on as if nothing had happened, but be vigilant. I will also talk to the police chief. I trust him too, and maybe he can have his troops keep an eye on your place when you are home alone."

"Thank you," she said. She still looked worried, but somewhat relieved. And genuinely grateful.

Bebe stayed awake and seemed to have taken in the entire conversation. After Hailey left, she said, "I can sense things people can't. I sense evil, and believe that Hailey is in danger." I agreed.

CHAPTER 6

Bob and Sheriff Brad Davis

I called the sheriff's office that afternoon, and got Betty Ferrano, his administrative assistant. I was happy to hear her voice. Before I retired, and still gainfully employed, I was on a first-name-basis with most everyone in the law enforcement community. But I'd been retired for over ten years and was drifting out of the loop. People I knew and worked with for years retired or moved on, replaced with younger people I didn't know. Betty Ferrano was there a long time, having worked not only for Brad Davis but also for two sheriffs before him. So, I knew her well. She was a trusted employee and did her job well. "I'd like to come in and talk to Brad," I said. "Is he available today?"

"Today's your lucky day. He's around, and at least right now, doesn't have anyone with him."

"I will be there in five minutes." The distance from my rental house to the S.O. was about five blocks. I considered driving, as I wanted to get there before someone beat me to it, but I realized that I could make it quicker on foot.

The receptionist who greets you when you walk into the sheriff's office is behind a window that is probably bullet-proof. Conversation is via a microphone and speaker system. A slot below the window allows documents to be passed back and forth. It wasn't always like that, but times have changed. The first sheriff I had gotten to know well during my forty-seven years in this town was Charlie Byrd, a big guy, and legendary. He had been dead about sixteen years. He was the first elected black sheriff in the State of California, especially remarkable given that our county is rural, and pretty red-neck. According to legend, he didn't even carry a gun.

"I'll let the sheriff know you are here," said the receptionist. I didn't recognize her, but she apparently knew who I was. Betty Ferrano came out and escorted me back to Brad's office.

"It makes me nervous to see you in my office," he said. "The last time you were in here, people got killed and buildings burned down, including your house." He was referring to when Bebe and I stumbled onto a murder in progress while we were hiking along Cougar Creek a few years before. That incident and its aftermath probably brought more violent excitement to this town than it has seen since its rip-roaring gold mining days in the 1850's.

"I sure as hell hope it's nothing like that. I'm getting too old for that kind of stuff. But I do want to tell you about a disturbing thing that happened to Hailey Madison. And ask you some questions about Rex Ryder. You know who Hailey Madison is, right?"

"Sure," he said. "She's a very nice lady, who has had more than her share of troubles. She doesn't need more."

"I agree," I said. I then told him about Hailey's encounter with Rex Randall Ryder The Third and the mysterious Melinda, as Hailey had narrated it. "I'm not sure what she described constitutes a crime. Even *if* it does, it's pretty skinny to justify filing charges against someone as prominent as Ryder seems to be. But Hailey Madison is genuinely scared. What can you tell me about Ryder?"

Brad said, "I personally think he's a jerk. But I guess I'm the only one. Everyone else thinks he's God. He's certainly been good for the county. An advocate. Particularly when it comes to donating and raising money for local causes. He's very visible, a member of the Elks Lodge and Rotary Club. He always attends Rotary meetings if he's in town."

"Good for him," I said. Better him than me. In my younger days as a lawyer, I was an active member in the Kiwanis Club. It was pretty much mandatory to join a service club if you were a local business person. When my wife and I moved to town in 1972, I joined a firm with two other lawyers. One was in the Lions Club and the other in Rotary. It was preordained that I would join the Kiwanis Club, part of the job description. I duly did that, became an officer, and ultimately president. I benefited from and enjoyed the experience, but after I became a judge, attending the weekly noon meetings just didn't work for me, so I dropped out. Since then, particularly after I retired, I have become more reclusive. And I don't like too much structure. I would rather walk barefoot on shards of broken glass than be required to attend a meeting every Wednesday at noon for the rest of my life.

"Is he married?" I asked.

"No, and he's always hitting on the local ladies, even the married ones. I think it's just part of his persona, and I don't know if he ever scores, but that's one of the reasons I don't like him much. It's probably just me. I think it's kind of disgusting."

"Well, it does jive with Hailey's story," I said. "Who the hell is Melinda?"

"She's his sister. Very mysterious. She's as reclusive as he is out-going. She's rarely seen in public. The word is that she's a lesbian."

"That also jives with Hailey's story," I said. "The way she tells it, Rex didn't put any significant moves on her, only Melinda. It almost sounds like his job was to collect Hailey, and deliver her into the web of the Black Widow. Is that possible? Does Rex have any kind of a criminal record? Or Melinda?"

"I've actually checked that. As I said, there is something about Ryder that just rubs me wrong, so I checked. There is nothing, nada. Almost too clean. Most normal people have something, maybe nothing more than a traffic violation that slops over into misdemeanor status. Maybe an unpaid parking fine that ultimately goes to warrant, or at least a driver's license hold. But there is nothing. Same with Melinda."

"Who did the construction work on his property? The big house and all the other improvements?"

"I don't know," he said. "That's an anomaly. He dumps money into all kinds of local projects, but no local contractor, or laborer for that matter, had anything to do with those construction projects. I have no idea who the contractors were. I actually checked to see if he got all the required permits, and I couldn't find any discrepancies or problems. He didn't really need much in the way of permits. He didn't subdivide anything. Actually, just the opposite. He bought adjoining parcels and put them together. The property acquisitions took a while, about five years, I think. Then, when construction started, it was a whirlwind. Probably all done in six months or so. Incredible. And very secretive. No publicity, and the property's always been posted. He passed all the requisite inspections required by the county building department but used his own inspectors. I've always thought it to be weird that you can do that, but his inspectors all had the necessary credentials."

"Sounds like you've spent a lot of time checking up on this guy."

"I have," he said. "More than I probably should. But like I said, there is just something about him that rubs me wrong. Also, I'm always leery of strangers with lots of money who move into our county and try to take over. Sometimes they want to change how we live."

"I hear you. Do you think I gave Hailey the correct advice? Is there something else she should be doing?"

"I can't think of anything. I'll call Dave Solus, and ask him to keep an eye on her," he said.

"Thanks," I said. "Always nice to see you."

As I walked home, I let everything sink in that Brad had told me. The more I thought about it, the more sinister it seemed. Sort of like a Stephen King horror story.

CHAPTER 7

Hailey and Ben

A month after Hailey made her escape from Rex Randall Ryder The Third's mansion in the Scott Valley, her life was gradually becoming normal again; normal, that is, by her somewhat unusual standards. She was still a virgin, and it was looking like she might remain a virgin forever. She continued to be on edge from her experience with Rex and Melinda. Would they somehow come after her, maybe abduct her? That line of thought seemed paranoid, but they were strange people. Or was it just her, Hailey, who was strange? Was it normal nowadays for people to do things like Rex and Melinda did that night? Sex is a lot more casual these days, and Hailey presumed that threesomes probably weren't that unusual. But Melinda was Rex's sister. Wouldn't that be, like, incest? Or, maybe she wasn't really his sister?

The bottom line was that Hailey was extra alert and anxious after the incident, but wasn't sure exactly what it was that she feared. She half expected to get a phone call from Rex, but it never came. What would he say? Would he apologize? Would he say he was sorry if he and Melinda scared her? That they were out of line? Or would he take the opposite approach and be threatening, ominous? None of those things happened. She heard not one word from either Rex Randall Ryder The Third or Melinda. She was calming down a little.

One morning Hailey was working on her do-it-yourself home remodel project. Her garage door was open and she had set up in the driveway three saw-horses, to prepare for cutting a piece of drywall. There were some four-by-eight sheets of drywall leaning against the wall inside her garage. Drywall is unwieldy for a single person to maneuver, due to its weight and size, and Hailey was struggling to drag a piece toward the sawhorses when she heard a male voice from behind her. "Let me give you a hand," said the voice. She turned around and saw a tall, athletic-looking guy dressed in gym shorts and a San Francisco Giants tee shirt coming toward her. He reached down, picked up the other end of the drywall sheet, and together they carried it to the sawhorses. Hailey recognized him as a local guy but couldn't quite remember who he was. "You're Hailey, aren't you? I'm Ben," he said. "Ben Thompson. I'm home for a few days and I was jogging down your street, when I saw you with that sheetrock. You know that's a two-person job."

Hailey laughed. "Thanks for the help. This is the hard part. After I get it cut down to size, it'll be a lot easier to handle. I think your dad might be my dentist."

"Probably so," he said. "I think he's everybody's dentist. What are you working on?"

"I've had this house for several months. It's a fixer-upper, but a labor of love. I'm remodeling a bedroom. Want to see?" After she said it, she grasped the suggestiveness of her question, and got a little flustered. Continuing on quickly she said, "I've already redone a bathroom and the kitchen." Even after this short conversation, she felt drawn to this guy, and wanted to invite him in. He was nice to look at, and had a great smile.

"Sure," he said, and followed her inside the house.

As she was giving him the tour, she said, "I've never remodeled a house before, so it's a new experience. I'm trying to do it all myself, but there are some jobs that take at least two people. My parents own the hardware store, so I'm not a stranger to tools and construction. And I can do my own wiring and plumbing. My work schedule gives me quite a bit of free time to work on my house. It's very satisfying, and therapeutic." She wasn't sure why she added the "and therapeutic," and immediately regretted it. She always assumed everyone in town knew she had been molested as a child, and her comment probably refreshed that in his mind.

"What do you do?" he asked.

"I'm a nurse. I work three-twelves, so every weekend is a long weekend. The schedule is perfect for me. How about you?"

"I'm not gainfully employed, like you. I'm going to medical school. I spend most of my time at the UC Davis Med Center in Sacramento, but have a few rare days off, so I came home. I've lived here all my life, and this is where I like to be. I haven't totally decided, but I think when I finish medical school and my residency, I want to come back here to live and work. I've been warned that I can't make much money here, but lifestyle is more important than money. You must feel the same way, or you wouldn't be here."

"Pretty much," she said. "When I was going to school on the coast, my friends always asked me if I get cabin fever living in such a small town. They would ask, 'What is there to do?' But there's really a lot of stuff to do right here. And if you want art and culture, Ashland is just forty miles away."

As Hailey showed Ben through her house, their light banter continued, and Hailey was having feelings she never felt before. There was a warmth inside her she had not experienced. He was definitely good-looking, charming, and had a great smile. But it was more than that. He just seemed … genuine. Gentle but strong. Quiet but intelligent and articulate. *Is he too good to be true?* Undermining her warm feelings was a nagging dread. *There's got to be a catch. Maybe he's already attached. Or gay.* Hailey's life experiences, including her ordeals with Uncle Phil, and more recently with Rex and Melinda, taught her to be cautious. *Trust no one.*

Her house tour and their conversation lasted about an hour. Then he said, "Well, I guess I've taken enough of a break from my run, better get going."

"Yes, and my project isn't going to do itself," she said.

They walked together to the front door. He took a few steps into her front yard, then stopped and turned around. "Do you have any plans tonight?" he asked.

She simply shook her head, and he said, "How about having dinner with me? Have you been to the Denny Bar restaurant in Etna?"

She shook her head again.

"Can I pick you up at six?"

She nodded her head up and down, again wordlessly.

"I'll see you then," he said, as he jogged on down the street.

Wow! Did that just happen? Did he just ask me out? Unlike when Rex Randall Ryder The Third asked if he could pick her up, Hailey didn't bat an eye. The logistics were different, of course. Rex had wanted to drive her to his house, in the middle of nowhere. Ben's proposal was to take her nearly as far away, but to a restaurant in the town of Etna, where there would be other people. But that wasn't the real difference. *I would have accepted if he asked to drive me to Alaska,* she thought. *Without reservation.*

The rest of the day seemed to pass at glacial speed. She felt like a high school girl waiting to go out on her first date. Well, maybe she was entitled to feel that way, since she missed it the first time around. She made some progress on her remodel project, but her mind kept wandering. She scored a piece of drywall with a razor knife, turned it over and snapped off the piece she wanted, and carried it into the bedroom. She held it up against the studs, only to find she cut it about three-quarters of an inch too short. *Damn! What is the old adage? "Measure twice, cut once." I did measure twice, damn it! I measured it wrong both times.* She was definitely distracted. It felt good, but not entirely. Her emotions were mixed, mostly excited, but there was also some trepidation. *Just like a high school girl,* she thought. *But not quite the same. Most high school girls don't have the same baggage I have. I wonder if he knows about Uncle Phil. Surely, he must. Everybody in town must. Does he care? Does he maybe think because of Uncle Phil that I'm just an easy lay? But he seems so nice. And he has a great smile. But he was the most popular boy in high school, and he will be a doctor. He can have any girl he wants.*

Hailey did make some progress on her project, but not a lot. She took a shower, and took much more time than usual deciding what to wear. *Hell, this is Siskiyou County, and we're only going to Etna. Just a pair of jeans and a top.* But finding just the *right* jeans and top was time-consuming. And then there was the underwear. She realized she hadn't bought new underwear in a long time. She picked out the least-frumpy bra and panties she could find. *Tomorrow I'll order some things from Victoria's Secret. Well, we'll see how tonight goes.*

Six o'clock finally rolled around. Ben pulled up in front of her house at six o'clock on the dot. He drove a small Japanese or Korean car, probably ten years old. Hailey watched him through the window as he got out of his car and walked up to her door. His Khaki pants and button-down shirt didn't show off his muscular body like his gym shorts and tee shirt had earlier in the day, but her heart was pounding as she watched him.

"Hi. You look great. Here," he said, handing her a single red rose. "The first rose to bloom on my parents' rose bushes."

After she placed the rose in a skinny vase, he walked her to his car and opened the door for her. *Do men actually do this anymore?* She wondered.

It took approximately forty minutes to get to the small village of Etna, population about seven-hundred people. In verdant Scott Valley, and at an elevation of 3,500 feet, the town is surrounded by incredible natural beauty. There is a gas station, a grocery store, a bank, a hardware store, Corrigan's Bar, the Avery Theater, a public swimming pool, and seven churches. The Scott River runs nearby, and the town is nestled at the bases of the expansive Russian and Marble Mountain Wilderness Areas. In the summer, Etna is a haven for weary hikers seeking a respite from their trek along the Pacific Crest Trail, and for backpackers coming out of the Wilderness Areas.

A relatively new addition to the town is the Denny Bar Distillery. It is in an historic brick building originally built in 1880, it was originally a mercantile business that sold goods and merchandise to the miners and settlers. The business became part of the first chain of retail stores in all of California, boasting nine stores throughout Northern California. It operated its own pack train and contracted for mail and freight to be transported over the mountains to the large gold mines in the area. The old brick building still houses an operational large walk-in safe originally used to safeguard gold purchased from the miners until it was transported by Wells Fargo to the nearest banks in

Sacramento. The company traded goods and services for over a million dollars when gold was less than thirty-dollars an ounce.

The place is more than a distillery. A shop sells its own crafted vodkas, gins, clear whiskeys, and bourbons, and Denny Bar merchandise. And there is the bar and restaurant, serving pizzas and dinner entrees, including locally raised beef.

This is where Hailey Madison and Ben Thompson went on their first date. When they were settled in at their table, Hailey said, "Would you believe it? I've never been here. I've heard a lot about this place, but this is the first time. I've been in this building before, when it was a pharmacy and gift shop. It was pretty cool then, but this is great."

"Yeah," he said. "I've been here a couple of times since it opened. The food's always been really good."

They found it easy to talk to each other. The drinks didn't hurt. She ordered a "Self-Starter," which, according to the menu, was "Our rendition of a 1930s cocktail: DBC Barrell Aged Gin with a touch of peach liqueur and a splash of Lillet Blanc. Let the sipping begin!" He ordered a shot of "Stiller's Cut Un-Aged Whiskey" over ice. The menu said, "You may know it as – Moonshine, White Lightening, Clear Whiskey, White Dog, or White Whiskey."

Their conversation was getting-to-know-each-other comfortable, and likely would have been so even without the help of the cocktails. Neither dominated the conversation. *Not like Rex Randall Ryder The Third,* she thought.

Ben told her about himself. He was a year younger than Hailey, born in the old Siskiyou General Hospital in Yreka on Main street, before Fairchild Medical Center, Yreka's new state-of-the-art hospital, was built. His parents were native Siskiyou County folks from ranch families. They got married right after his father graduated from dental school and bought a house in town. So, Ben grew up in Yreka, attending elementary, middle, and high school. He liked school, got good grades, and enjoyed sports. He was the quarterback of the Yreka High School football team his junior and senior years and played on the tennis team in the spring. His parents encouraged him to go to college somewhere away from home, and he chose the University of Arizona in Tucson. Being raised among the mountains and forests, he wondered what the desert would be like, and he was interested in their tennis team, "the Saguaro Soldiers." Playing college-level tennis was great, and he felt good about his college tennis career, but it made him realize that he didn't have the talent to go to the next level. He loved tennis and was glad he went as far as he did, knowing it was something he could enjoy recreationally for the rest of his life. When he was a junior he started thinking about medical school, and ultimately was accepted to the UC Davis School of Medicine.

"And that's about it," he said.

Hailey's history wasn't so great, and she was initially reticent about disclosing too much. Maybe sipping the "Self-Starter," with its "DBC Barrell Aged Gin with a touch of peach liqueur and a splash of Lillet Blanc" did help start her. She finally decided, *What the hell? I might as well tell him the whole story now and get it out of the way. If it will have a bad outcome, I'd rather find out now than later. I will survive if this turns out to be our first and last date. But I don't know if I can survive if we start a relationship and I get dumped later.* She first tested the water by asking him, "Do you know what happened to me when I was a little girl?" When he nodded, she began her story, sparing no details, including her ordeals of testifying in the court proceeding, the emotional trauma she suffered, and the years of counseling and therapy. She did stop short of telling him she was still a virgin.

They pulled up in front of her house a little before eleven o'clock, and he walked her to her front door. He said, "I really enjoyed this," put his hands on her shoulders, and kissed her lightly on the lips. Once again, it was like a first date in high school.

She said, hesitantly, "Would you like to come in?" It was hard for her to muster the courage to ask that.

"Not tonight, but thanks," he said. "I've been working on a paper that I need to have finished when I get back to school. I'm going to try to get it done tonight."

"Okay, she said," disappointed. "I really had a good time tonight." And she watched him walk toward his car.

As he got almost to the car, he turned and faced her. "I'm heading back to Sacramento day after tomorrow, so I have one more day here. Do you want to get together tomorrow night?"

She nodded, without a word, much like her response had been that morning. "Is there anything special you'd like to do?" he asked. When she shook her head, he said, "Well, I'm sure we'll think of something. Is six o'clock okay?"

She managed to say, "Sure," as he waved, smiled his killer smile, got into his car, and drove off. Her heart was beating furiously as she watched him.

Hailey had the next day off, and her agenda was to do some more work on her house. She was up at six o'clock, and although preoccupied, made good progress. This time she measured three times before making each cut, and all her cut pieces of drywall turned out just fine. At around two o'clock, she realized she hadn't had anything to eat, so she took a break. She walked the few blocks to *Zephyr Books and Coffee* on Miner Street and ordered a homemade scone and a cappuccino. While eating the scone, she chit-chatted with a couple of people she knew, and browsed through the rows of books. Her glance fell upon an opened newspaper on a table. It was a current edition of the *Siskiyou Daily News*, with a headline: "Sheriff Continues Investigation of Cold Cases – Disappearances of Young Women in the Marble Mountains." For some reason she connected that with her ordeal with Rex and Melinda Ryder, and she shuddered.

When she got home, she sat down in her living room, and realized her house was cluttered. She picked things up, thinking *why am I doing this, my house always looks like this. It looked like this yesterday when he was here.* She continued anyway, working her way into the bedroom she slept in, not the one being remodeled. There were clothes lying around, some she hung up in the closet, and some she threw into the clothes hamper. Then, without thinking, she stripped the sheets off of her bed, replaced them with clean ones, and made up the bed neatly. By then, she was fantasizing images that made her blush, even though there was no one else present. When she was satisfied as to the condition of her house, and particularly her bed, she opened her laptop computer and Googled *Victoria's Secret.* She passed over the more bizarre items. *Do women actually wear this stuff?* she wondered, and then ordered some nice understated (by *Victoria's Secret* standards) but sexy bikini bras and panties. It would take a few days before they were delivered. *Better late than never.*

Waiting for six o'clock to roll around, she felt like a kid on Christmas Eve, like time was standing still. Around five o'clock she searched her closet for jeans and a shirt that were actually clean, rummaged through her dresser drawer for the least-frumpy underwear she could find, and took a shower.

Again, right on the dot, Ben pulled up at six. This time when she opened the door, he kissed her on the lips, a light kiss that nevertheless made her tingle. "Once again, you look great," he said. "Any ideas what you'd like to do tonight?"

Again, she was speechless, and just shook her head. Most of the time, she was generally outspoken, and this wasn't normal for her. She wondered what was happening.

"How about we start with dinner?" he said. "This time somewhere local, somewhere we can walk to. How about *Strings?*"

"Sounds good to me." *Strings* was a nice Italian place next door to *Zephyr,* where she had been earlier that day.

They were in *Strings* for almost two hours, although it seemed much shorter. As speechless as she had been when he came to her door, Hailey was surprised at how easy Ben was to talk to. Ben felt the same way, and their conversation flowed naturally. They lost track of time. Finally, Ben said, "It's a nice evening, let's go to Greenhorn and take a walk around the lake." It was the time of year when the days were long, and longer yet, due to Daylight Savings Time. In years past the Greenhorn dam and reservoir south of town was the city's main water supply, but since then the city maintained the reservoir as a backup water supply and developed it into a lovely recreational area and park.

After they walked around the lake, Hailey built up her courage and said to Ben, "I've got some vanilla gelato and some apple pie we can heat up. Want some dessert?"

At her house, Ben sat on Hailey's couch while she opened a bottle of Zinfandel she had purchased months before from Costco. It was a fifteen-dollar bottle, which she considered appropriate only for special occasions. She poured a glass for each and set about to prepare the pie and gelato. She handed him a dish and sat down next to him. They were quiet while eating, until he said, "I enjoy coming home, and needed a break from the grind of medical school. It's been nice, but the best part has been the time with you."

She was back into her speechless mode and didn't know what to say. He put his dish down on the coffee table and put his hand on her cheek, drawing her face toward him. When he kissed her gently, she opened her lips and moaned softly. His kiss became more aggressive and she responded in kind, their mouths open and tongues exploring each other. "I've never met anyone like you," he said. "And I've only known you for two days." Their hands were now all over each other, and he unbuttoned her shirt and unsnapped her bra. When he kissed her on the nipple she moaned again. She had never experienced such a feeling. As for Ben, it wasn't the first time he had put his mouth and tongue on a woman's bare breast. He had been the quarterback of the football team, after all, and girls were attracted to him. But this was different. He had never experienced such pleasure. After only two days, he was sure this was the woman he wanted.

Hailey said, "Come with me." She took his hand, and led him into the bedroom, where they undressed each other. When they were both naked, she pulled down the sheets, lay back on the bed and pulled him down with her. As she pressed him close, she whispered, "Please be gentle with me."

Hailey didn't wake until eight o'clock the next morning, late for her. She went to her front door, opened it, and inhaled the lovely morning. She had never been so happy. Ben had left her house around one o'clock. She invited him to stay, but he said, "I really want to, but I'm staying at my parents' house, and they are kinda old fashioned. I can do whatever I want when I'm at my own apartment, of course, but when I'm in their home, I respect their feelings. I hope you understand. There will be many more nights."

Such a sweet man, she thought, as she stood at her front door, enjoying the sunshine. *My life has definitely changed.*

CHAPTER 8

Hailey and Ben – Two years later

Hailey's birthday occurred during a weekend in September after Labor Day, and she and Ben looked forward to it with great anticipation. She actually had four consecutive days off, and Ben had three, a rarity for a fourth-year medical student. Months in advance, they planned a road trip to Sonoma County's wine country.

That Thursday, she spent her morning at home, catching up on things she had been putting off. She did her laundry and did some house cleaning. She changed the sheets on her bed, and cleaned out her refrigerator, discovering long forgotten unidentifiable objects inside that looked like science experiments gone wrong. At about noon, she packed a medium-sized suitcase. That her tasks were menial didn't bother her, as her mind was full-speed fantasizing and picturing the pleasures of the weekend ahead. Absence definitely makes the heart grow fonder. A little after 1:00 PM she loaded her suitcase into her car and began her drive to Sacramento, all the more exciting because it was her first journey in the brand new car she had purchased days before.

Ben had an apartment in Sacramento within walking distance of the medical school. It was small, but nicely furnished, and comfortable. Hailey arrived at his place around 6:00 PM and let herself in with her own key. She didn't expect him for another hour, so she selected a bottle of Decoy Sonoma Cabernet Sauvignon from a kitchen cabinet, and made herself comfortable, unpacking a few items from her suitcase while sipping the wine. Ben walked in a little after seven, and she greeted him with a kiss that took on a life of its own. In the nick of time, he said, "I need to take a shower. I reserved a table down the street for eight o'clock." While he was in the shower, she poured another glass of wine and took it into the bathroom and handed it to Ben. For a moment they considered skipping dinner, but then, again in the nick of time, decided there would be plenty of time after.

Friday morning, they set off in Hailey's new car for the historic but touristy town of Sonoma. Not a long distance, but they took their time. Her new car was a "velocity blue" Mustang convertible with a 6-speed transmission. Great for exploring Highway 12 and the other roads through the vineyards and hills of Sonoma County; top down, of course. It was the first new car she had ever owned. Driving was a pleasure, and they took turns. It was a beautiful sunny day, and half the automobiles on the highways were convertibles.

They had booked two nights in a room with a balcony overlooking the Sonoma Plaza, at the small, elegant Ledson Hotel. Their stay coincided with the annual Valley of the Moon Vintage Festival. The hotel was steps away from the non-stop activities of the festival, including live music, wine tastings, and art exhibits. The weekend exceeded their expectations and included a very nice mix of enjoying the festival activities in the plaza, and quality time in the king-size bed of their elegant room.

On Sunday morning, they both participated in the 10K run at 8:00 AM. They ran together the entire race, until they were about 50 yards from the finish line, when it suddenly got competitive. Hailey sprinted first, leaving Ben a few steps behind. He turned on the after-burner and passed her. They laughed all the way to the finish line, their positions alternating back and forth. When they crossed the line the scorekeeper gave the nod to Ben by a millisecond. Hailey vigorously disputed this call and told Ben they needed to get back to the king-size bed to "arm-wrestle" who really won.

That afternoon they checked out of the Ledson Hotel and kicked back at the festival as it was gradually winding down, enjoying the last of the music, art, and wine-tasting, going easy on the wine. Hailey had to get back home, as her twelve-hour shift began at six Monday morning. Ben also had to be at the med center early, but they both wanted to stretch their weekend as much as possible.

They left Sonoma around 5:00 PM for Ben's apartment, arriving a couple of hours later. It was sunset, but still light. Hailey had a four-hour drive ahead of her, and hoped to be on the road by seven, but by the time they finished saying their good-byes it was closer to eight. The good news was that most of her journey was northbound on Interstate 5, an easy drive, and the traffic would be light.

Ben had expected her to call him when she got home, probably around midnight, so he stayed up, doing some last-minute preparation for the next day at medical school. At 12:15 AM he was a little worried when she didn't call but didn't try to call her. She was a big girl. At 12:30 he was more than a little worried and clicked on her name in his cell phone. He got a message: "The wireless customer you are calling is not available." He sent a text, which seemed to go through normally. He knew she would have to stop for gas somewhere within 100 miles of his house, but that wouldn't take over five or ten minutes. He kicked himself for letting her leave on a nearly empty tank. He waited ten minutes. By now he was frightened, feeling a churning in his gut. There was no response to his text, so he tried to call again. Same distressing message. The fear and helplessness were building up.

He called Hailey's parents' home number. He had a good relationship with her parents, and they knew where she was spending her weekend. After three rings, a sleepy-sounding female voice answered, Hailey's mother. He said, "Evelyn, I don't want to alarm you, but Hailey should have been home by now. She promised to call but hasn't. I've tried her a couple of times and gotten a 'customer not available' message. She should have been home at least by twelve-thirty."

The voice on the line no longer sounded sleepy. "Let me try from here," she said, "I'll call you back." She called Hailey's cell and got the same result. She woke up her husband. "George," she said, "Ben is on the line. He says Hailey should have been home at least by twelve-thirty. He tried to call but didn't reach her. I tried just now and didn't get her either."

Hailey's father was now also wide awake. He said, "Let's go over to her place."

Evelyn called Ben and told him what they would do. "You just stay put. She's probably sound asleep in her bed. I'll call you immediately when we find out."

It was ten blocks from Evelyn and George Madison's home to Hailey's. They threw on some clothes and got there within ten minutes. The garage door was closed, so they couldn't tell if her car was there. They could see some light through the windows, but they knew that Hailey always left a low-wattage light on in her kitchen. They could see no activity.

After ringing the doorbell, George unlocked and slowly opened the front door, saying, "Hailey? Are you home?" She wasn't.

Her living room and kitchen looked just like she would have left it if she were going to be gone a few days. The bedroom was tidy and the bed made. There was no car in the garage. Evelyn and George felt a rising level of anxiety. George withdrew his phone from his pocket and tried Hailey's number again. Same result. He called Ben, who answered with a weak "Hello."

"She's not here," said George. "I tried her phone again with no response. Enough time has passed that we need to get some help. I'm going to call the police, and maybe you should too, at your end."

"Okay."

"If she shows up, we can call them off, but it's been too long, and we have to do something. I don't know what else to do," said George. "Keep your phone close by and let us know immediately if you hear anything. We'll do the same."

George called 911, and gave a brief account to the dispatcher, a woman. She told him she would have police officers at Hailey's house within five minutes. It's a small town, and her house was a few blocks from the police station.

A few minutes later two young police officers arrived at Hailey's house. The officers and Hailey's parents together walked around and inspected the house and yard, finding nothing out of place or unusual. While they walked,

Hailey's parents told the officers what they knew of her weekend plans and who she went to see. The officers tried, unsuccessfully, to ease their fears by offering possible explanations as to how she reasonably could have been delayed. "She could have been sleepy and stopped to get coffee." Or, "She might have had to call Triple A to fix a flat tire." None of those explanations helped. She would have called. And calls to her phone resulted in the "not available" message. The officers told them they would broadcast a "missing persons" report and make sure that law enforcement agencies from there to Sacramento, including the California Highway Patrol, would be on the lookout. The officers meant well, but George and Evelyn were now overcome with dread.

At his end, Ben called the Sacramento Police Department, who sent two officers to his house, although it took an hour and a half before they arrived. His conversation with them was similar to the one George and Evelyn had earlier, although the attitude of his officers was more skeptical. Ben perceived an almost accusatory edge to it. It was getting close to morning. He was a mess and decided not go to med school that day. Besides the fear, he was gripped with mounting guilt. *What was I thinking, letting her drive alone for four hours, knowing she wouldn't get home till after midnight?* he asked himself. And then, *She's a twenty-nine-year-old adult*, but that didn't help his mental state. As night passed into morning, he realized not going in to the med center was a mistake. There wasn't anything he could do. The fear, helplessness, and guilt were horrible. He finally decided to join the search, and set off in his car, following the route he knew she'd take. He couldn't think of anything else to do. He drove north all the way to Yreka looking for her car, or any sign of her, to no avail.

CHAPTER 9

Bob and Bebe, David and Lillian

Fall is a great time of year in Siskiyou County. Or at least it used to be, before northern California wildfires became prevalent. Over the last few years our air quality in September and October has often been poor, due to smoky conditions from fires from as far away as several hundred miles.

This fall was different. The weather has been great, with enough occasional rain to dampen down the lightning-caused fires that did occur. The temperatures in the fall are perfect, with highs in the 70's and the lows near freezing. The crisp night air feels good. And the fall colors in the forest are breathtaking. Bebe and I decided to take a day-hike. We don't do that as often as we used to, as neither of us is getting any younger. That seems to affect me more than Bebe, because she still has the energy level of a puppy. I'm fairly fit for a geezer, but don't move as well as I once did.

We picked the Shackleford Creek Trail for our hike. The trailhead isn't too far from town, and the trail itself, at least as far as Campbell Lake, our chosen destination, is easy. For the more adventurous, the trail keeps on going beyond Campbell Lake, farther into the Marble Mountains Wilderness, and gets much steeper. It's a beautiful hike through the forest, and a beautiful time to be there. We were on the trail about halfway to Campbell Lake and still in cell phone range, when Bob Seger sang "Old Time Rock and Roll" on my phone. The caller was David Thompson. David is a retired dentist. I have known him and Lillian for years. When my wife was still alive, it was common for the four of us to have dinner together on Friday evenings, either at someone's home or at a restaurant. We watched their kids grow up, and I was close to their son Ben. I also knew Hailey, who was now Ben's girlfriend, from the trial all those years ago, and from our more recent conversation about Rex Randall Ryder The Third. I remembered what happened to her as a child and was horrified to learn that she was now a missing person as an adult.

"We need to talk to you," said David. "It's about Ben. They are going to charge him with murder."

"What?"

"Even though Hailey hasn't been found, they are treating it as a homicide," he said.

"Who is?"

David replied, "Some district attorney in Pineland. He is very aggressive and seems unreasonable. I'm thinking he has an agenda. Can you come over tonight and talk to us?"

"Sure, but I'm not sure I can do anything. Especially if it's in Pineland."

"Maybe you can at least point us in the right direction. We're scared. Come over around six. We'll grill something for dinner."

"Okay."

We concluded the conversation.

Bebe and I kept walking toward Campbell Lake, but I had lost my enthusiasm, a fact not lost on Bebe. After a while, she said, "There's no way."

"No way what?" I asked.

"No way Ben could have committed murder."

"How do you know?" I asked.

"Dogs can sense things that people can't. Remember when Ben was going to be a veterinarian, before he decided to become a people doctor? When his family came over for dinner, he spent a lot of time with me in the yard. I trained him to throw the tennis ball. I know Ben very well. He could never kill anybody."

"Are you sure?" I asked.

"Positive."

Bebe and I continued our journey to Campbell Lake and back. It was a pleasant hike on a lovely fall day, but David's phone call dampened our pleasure. I did catch a fish, a nice Brook Trout, which heightened my spirits somewhat. When I was playing the fish, Bebe was so excited she wanted to jump in after it. I learned from experience that attempting to fish from the shore with Bebe is next to impossible. With every cast of the lure she can hardly contain herself, wanting to go in after it. Most of the time she holds back, knowing that otherwise her boss would be unhappy with her. After landing the fish, I released it, and Bebe and I watched it slowly swim away, ending our brief period of euphoria.

Bebe and I have gone on many day-hikes together, exploring the nooks and crannies of vast, mysterious, and beautiful Siskiyou County. We have been rained on and snowed on; and we have gotten lost. But regardless of some occasional bad weather, and a few mishaps, they have all been worthwhile and enjoyable experiences, save for one, which Bebe reminded me of as we walked out of the Wilderness Area. "I have a bad feeling about this," she mused. "I sense evil, and I am afraid for Ben, and for Hailey. This reminds me of our Cougar Creek hike. Dogs can sense things that humans can't," she told me for the thousandth time, and I was counting. She was referring to a hike more than four years before, along Cougar Creek, in an entirely different drainage, miles from where we were. That day we came upon a mysterious old mining cabin which we felt compelled to explore. As we approached the cabin, we witnessed a crime in progress, the vicious, sadistic murder of a naked young woman. This accidental encounter led to two years of terrible consequences for me and people I cared for. We had exposed a powerful and brutal human trafficking organization that kidnapped women, and the organization came after us. I was shot and hospitalized, and my daughter was brutalized. My house was torched. Other people were victims of violent assaults, some fatal. As the series of events played out, it became apparent that the crime we happened onto during our innocent day-hike was only a small part of a large and vicious international human trafficking ring that reached into and corrupted the highest levels of government. When it was over, we believed we had done major damage to the organization, and brought its mastermind to justice, but the aftermath continues to have an impact. I am still subjected to FBI interviews, court appearances, and media intrusions, which probably won't go away. The memories never will. And questions linger. Did we eradicate the beast? Did we bring down the right people? Walking along the trail, independent of Bebe's expression of concern, I also experienced a sense of dread of what lay ahead.

We walked awhile in silence, but Bebe must have continued to dwell on the horrors of our Cougar Creek experience because suddenly, out of nowhere, she said, "One good thing came out of Cougar Creek. That was how you and I met Brenda."

She was right about that. She was talking about Brenda LeHane, the young federal government official from Washington, DC, who came into, or rather was swept into, our lives four years before; the young woman who, the first time I saw her, I dubbed the "BBL," which stood for "Beautiful Black Lady." The thought of Brenda brought a smile to my face, as well as other stirrings that may be unusual for a septuagenarian man. I was happily reminded that she had a business trip coming up in Sacramento, and I had a lunch date scheduled with her.

We got back to our house about five o'clock, which gave me time to feed Bebe and take a shower before heading over to the Thompsons' house.

I took a bottle of wine. David had marinated chicken breasts and fired up his grill. Lillian was assembling a Caesar salad. It all looked like a typical weekend barbeque in the good old days. But there was an edge. There was no joy in the banter.

After we sat down at the table, I asked, "So, what is going on?"

David said, "We don't know very much. The Pineland authorities ask us a lot of questions, but don't give us much information. So, most of what we know is scuttlebutt, or what we have learned from Ben." David is a well-educated man. When speaking, he always expresses himself in a well-reasoned and thoughtful manner. That evening, however, not so much. His conversation was more disjointed and random than usual. He was clearly worried. "There was blood in the car. They did a DNA analysis and determined that there was DNA from a man and a woman. They also found a necklace on the ground near the car and did a DNA analysis on that too. There was DNA from the same man and woman on the necklace."

"Could they match the DNA with anyone?" I asked.

"Not at first," he said. "Apparently there is a central depositary, a database, where they can send the DNA samples to see if there is a match. Initially there was no match. The police asked Ben if he would voluntarily provide a DNA specimen, and of course he agreed. His DNA matched the samples taken from the blood and from the necklace. They still do not have a match for the woman's DNA. They didn't have a sample from Hailey in the database. Generally, at least in California, they take swabs for the database from people who have been convicted of crimes. Hailey has never been convicted of a crime, of course. Apparently, there is no DNA from what she went through as a child. I don't know why. Either they didn't do DNA analyses back then, or the evidence is lost. Or maybe it is somehow protected because she was a minor. In any event, they don't have a match."

"Can Ben explain why they found his DNA?"

"He can't. His fingerprints were in the car, too. But that makes sense. They spent the weekend together in Sonoma and drove her car. They took turns driving. But he has no idea about the blood. My theory was that maybe the DNA was actually from the car itself, not the blood, but the police don't agree. They are sure it's from the blood. Ben is sure that nothing happened in the car that would cause him to bleed."

"And the necklace?" I asked.

"He gave it to her a year ago. So, he did touch it, but he can't remember recently. You'd think that over a year the DNA would wear off, but I don't know that much about DNA. Also, he may have touched it and not remembered, possibly during some period of intimacy. Ben doesn't know if his fingerprints were also on the necklace."

I said, "It seems premature to charge him with murder, especially since they have never found a body."

This time Lillian entered the discussion. "It's that Pineland district attorney!" she said, agitated. "His name is Murphy or something like that. I think he's crazy, or just wants headlines. He is loud and obnoxious and gives press releases to the media all the time, claiming the evidence is substantial."

"That's a slippery slope," I said. "If the evidence is substantial, why haven't they arrested Ben? If he is a killer, he should be off the street."

David said, "I don't know. The whole thing is very strange. It seems Murphy is feeding the media and enjoying the constant publicity but doesn't have the balls to file a criminal complaint. What is lacking is a motive. Ben loves her and is devastated at what happened. Plus, anyone who knows Ben would know he would never do anything like that. But no one knows him in Pineland. Can't we get the venue changed to here?"

"The proper venue is the county where the crime was committed, although it seems to me that there might be a question as to whether the crime was committed in Pineland, which is Morrow County, or Sacramento County. Whatever the crime might have been, murder or kidnapping, it certainly wasn't committed here in Siskiyou County. The location issue does add another weakness in the prosecutor's case. There is no dead body, no motive, and the difficulty in proving where the crime occurred. To me all that reeks of reasonable doubt. I think a prosecutor would be crazy, and unethical, to proceed under those facts. Maybe he is crazy, as Lillian suggests. Or maybe there is something more out there that we don't know about."

"In the meantime," said Lillian, "this is taking a horrible toll on Ben. He is a mess. He's having a terrible time with the fact that she's missing. He loves her. All he could talk about for weeks before that weekend was how much he was looking forward to it. And the threat of prosecution is almost too much. He's barely getting by on his studies, and would have asked for a leave of absence, except he thinks he's better off keeping occupied. Now he's worried that people will think he's guilty because he is continuing to work. If he is prosecuted, regardless of the outcome, it will ruin him. He will never get his M.D."

"Is he in good standing with the school?" I asked. "Has there ever been any doubt about his making it through?"

"None whatsoever!" said Lillian. "He has always been at the top of his class. Can you help him?"

"I'll do what I can. But you know I'm retired. As a retired judge I have no credentials to do anything official. I pay dues every year to be an 'inactive' member of the state bar, but that doesn't buy me anything either, except the right to reinstate and take a boatload of continuing-ed courses in the event I want to practice law again. At age seventy-seven, I'm not likely to do that. Hell, I never liked practicing law in the first place, and never thought I was very good at it. I did like being a judge. A lot. And I thought I was pretty good at that. It was the best career choice I ever made. Does Ben have a lawyer?"

"No," David and Lillian said simultaneously.

David said, with a frown, "Does he need one? I wouldn't have any idea who to hire. We've had the good fortune of needing a lawyer only on rare occasions, and none that we know does criminal law. Do you have any suggestions?"

"Let me see who I can come up with. There are important reasons why he needs a lawyer. One is the attorney-client privilege. He needs someone he can talk to confidentially. Anything he says can be used against him in court. What he says to you, what he says to me, what he says to the police or to Murphy, none of that is confidential. As a matter of fact, you should tell him to not give any more statements to anyone, not even you. The easiest way for him to do that is just to say that he is in the process of hiring a lawyer and doesn't want to speak until he has done so. I do have someone in mind for Ben to retain, but he would be somewhat of an unusual choice, and I want to talk to him first. I'll do that and get back to you right away."

David said, "So, I guess you can't go and talk to Ben, because of the 'no confidential relationship' thing?"

"That's right, at least for now. If we get him a lawyer, maybe I can somehow shoehorn my way in as part of the defense team, and then the privilege should apply. I plan to go to Sacramento day after tomorrow. I have a 'date' with a very special person. I will meet with Ben when I'm there. Tell him I'm coming and will meet with him, but we'll just discuss logistics of his defense, nothing about actual events. In the meantime, I'll call the lawyer I have in mind and see if he will take Ben's case."

Before I left their house Lillian and David understandably wanted more information about the lawyer I had in mind. I told them who he was, why it would be an unusual choice, and why I thought it was a good idea. They agreed that I should talk to him. I had no idea if he would accept the case.

CHAPTER 10

Bob, John Dickenson, and Brenda LeHane

Most people, other than those litigious-minded jerks who seem to be over-populating the country, would rather have a root canal than retain a lawyer. The process is difficult. It is hard to find someone with the qualities that the potential client needs and wants. Someone understanding and kind yet will bluntly tell the client the bad news he or she needs but doesn't want to hear. Someone who can fiercely advocate for the client without being an asshole. When I started practicing law, ethical rules prevented lawyers from advertising. That was changed and now you see advertisements for lawyers everywhere. On television there are the class-action hucksters soliciting clients who have contracted cancer from you-name-it. In the yellow pages (those that still exist) half the pages contain enlarged glossy photos of lawyers who will get you paid. And then there are the giant billboards along the interstates: "Are you an accident victim? No charge for initial consultation!" The advertising doesn't help in the lawyer selection process. Trust me. For most people, word-of-mouth may still be the most reliable method of evaluating who to retain.

When it comes to evaluating lawyers, judges are in a uniquely good position. Judges are neither clients nor adversaries. They can assess everything from a neutral standpoint: competency, ethics, preparedness, reasonableness, trustworthiness, courtroom skills, and all the other qualities lawyers should possess.

John Dickenson was the lawyer I had in mind to represent Ben. To the best of my knowledge, he hadn't done a criminal case in at least twenty years, which made my choice unusual. He was extraordinarily successful in the civil litigation field and won some remarkable verdicts. He had the talent, skill, and ethics to succeed in any area of law. I had observed him in my courtroom on several occasions, including criminal cases he took early in his career. And, even though he was now nationally recognized, he lived right here in our rural backwoods county. Over the years I sometimes thought about who I would hire if I needed representation in a criminal case (fortunately I never have, at least so far). I concluded I would hire two lawyers, one being John Dickenson, and the other my friend and former law partner Jerry Thatcher who died fifteen years ago.

I called John later that evening, hoping he would be at home. He was, and I made an appointment to see him the next morning in his office. His office is in an old abandoned schoolhouse out in the country about a 50-minute drive from town. I took Bebe because I knew she would insist on being in the loop, and because she loved being out in the country. When I pulled up to his place, I just let Bebe run free. His schoolhouse/office was surrounded by fields, and Bebe was always on good terms with horses, cows, and all the other critters normally found on ranch land.

I spent a couple of hours talking to John that morning. It took that long to convince him to take Ben's case. He was reluctant for a lot of reasons. He hadn't done a criminal case in years. He didn't have time. He had his own specialized practice and was already swamped. One thing he didn't mention was the money. The fee for taking a case such as Ben's would be insignificant compared with the typical income from his regular practice, and the time spent on Ben's case would take him away from that practice. But he didn't mention that.

In the end, I prevailed. John knew Ben's parents, although he didn't know Ben. He knew they were good people and he wanted to help them. I told him of my plan to meet with Ben the next day, and that I would have Ben and his parents contact him to formalize the attorney-client relationship. I thanked him and collected Bebe, who was having such a good time she didn't want to go home. Once we were on our way, she asked, "How did it go?"

"He's going to take the case."

"That makes me feel a lot better," she said. Then she snoozed the rest of the way home.

I left for Sacramento early the next morning. A four-hour drive, it gave me time to reflect, my mind travelling to and from several subjects, mostly centered on Brenda and Ben.

I had a lunch date with Brenda, which had been planned for some time. Brenda LeHane is a very special friend. She is less than half my age. She lives and works in Washington, D.C., for the Department of Interior. I met her four years ago under some strange circumstances, which I will explain. It started when Bebe and I took a day-hike along Cougar Creek in the Klamath National Forest. After walking deep into the forest, we heard the sounds of a girl screaming, coming from the direction of what looked like an abandoned miner's cabin. We moved closer and observed the mutilated but still alive body of a naked young woman, about twenty years old, suspended by her wrists and bleeding profusely. Before I could do anything to help her, a man appeared out of nowhere and shot me in the chest. Before losing consciousness, I sensed that I recognized him, but couldn't remember who he was or why I recognized him. Later, after I recovered from the gunshot, I was running errands in the courthouse and observed a meeting in progress in the county Board of Supervisors' chambers. The room was full of people, so I squeezed in to see what was going on. Some high-level folks from the United States Department of the Interior had travelled from Washington, D.C., and were giving a presentation to the Board. I watched as the spokesman from the delegation addressed the Board of Supervisors and when I got a good look at him, I immediately realized that he was the guy. This was the asshole that tortured and killed the girl and shot me! He was accompanied by two others, whom I didn't recognize, but I tried to make mental notes of what they looked like and gave them names. One was a woman, who even in her government-prescribed business attire, was something else. She was about five feet four, beautiful, and black. She looked thirty-ish. I dubbed her The Beautiful Black Lady, or, for short, the "BBL."

After satisfying myself that she was not complicit in the murderous activities that the asshole had committed, I followed her to the Wine Bar in downtown Yreka and introduced myself. I told her that I had seen her associate commit a brutal murder.

It was dark when I walked her back to her hotel. As we were talking outside her door, a large car suddenly roared up, almost hitting us. Two people with guns, a man and a woman, jumped out and attempted to force us into the car. The man had positioned me on one side of the car, trying to push me in, and the woman was doing the same thing to the BBL on the other side. I jammed my sharp septuagenarian elbow into his throat with as much power as I could muster, with a satisfactory result; he went down, losing control of his gun. I looked across the car in time to see the BBL in action. It was breathtaking! I saw her grab the woman's wrist with one hand, and her elbow with the other. She jerked the woman's arm down while at the same time bringing her knee up. There was a sickening crunch of splintered bones and a scream, and the woman was on the parking-lot asphalt, writhing.

And that was the beginning of my relationship with the BBL, Brenda LeHane.

CHAPTER 11

Bob, Brenda and Ben

I called Brenda that morning before I left Yreka and told her I wanted to have a third person join us for lunch, if it was okay with her, which it was. I then called Ben and asked him to meet us. I wasn't sure where our conversation would go, but I wanted Brenda's assessment of Ben's credibility. I had known Ben since he was a child, and his parents were good friends. I didn't believe it was possible for him to commit a murder. Brenda didn't know him at all. In the relatively short time I had known Brenda, we experienced an epoch of dangerous life-threatening adventures together, and I knew she had a knack for evaluating people's character. I wanted to pick her brain later.

We met for lunch at Frank Fat's in downtown Sacramento. Located near the State Capitol, it is more than a restaurant. Serving Chinese food since 1939, it is an institution whose patrons have been movers and shakers of California politics since it first opened. It's fair to say that a significant number of California's laws were created out of deals struck over meals at Frank Fat's (including two or three Mai Tais). Although very popular and busy, it's possible to have a private and confidential conversation.

When I met Ben and Brenda at around one o'clock, I was immediately struck by two impressions: how good Brenda looked and how utterly terrible Ben looked. It had been a while since I had seen either of them. All other things being equal, both are naturally exceptionally good-looking people. Four years before, Brenda had been kidnapped and held captive by a criminal organization. During her captivity she had been raped and physically brutalized to where she had to undergo multiple surgeries, including plastic surgery. Besides the obvious physical injuries, her mental state was broken. At the time, she lamented, "I will never be the same." It had been a long haul, but it certainly appeared she was well on her way to being back to "the same" again.

Ben, on the other hand, was a mess. In better days he could have been a television model for physical fitness programs. He was over six feet tall with Robert Redford blond hair and blue eyes, and a muscular frame, more like a tennis player than a football player. But this day his shoulders slumped, and his facial expressions and body language projected despair. His hair was showing signs of gray.

I introduced Ben and Brenda to each other, and we talked as we ordered lunch. I moved the conversation toward Ben's predicament and told him John Dickenson had agreed to take his case, and why I thought it was a good idea.

Then, casting aside good judgment and the correct warning about not discussing the facts of the case, I went right at it, and asked him to detail the whole story, not only to me, but to the BBL, a total stranger! I wanted to help him, but to do that I needed to hear his story. Also, Hailey Madison was either dead or had been kidnapped, and Brenda's personal experience gave her a unique perspective on kidnap victims. It would be useful for her to hear what he had to say, and I trusted her as much as I have ever trusted anyone.

"We had a great weekend," Ben said. "The best time of my life, and I think hers, too. We had planned it for weeks, and everything came together as planned, better even. It was like a honeymoon. We stayed at a really cool hotel in Sonoma, right where all the festival activities were going on. Even the drive getting there and back was good. Slow, with lots of traffic; but she had just taken delivery of a new car, a convertible. And we had the top down the whole time."

"They found DNA from your blood in the car," I said. "How did that happen?"

"I don't know. There is no way that could have happened. I lie awake at night trying to figure that out. I was in that car a lot over the weekend, so my fingerprints and DNA should have been all over it. But not blood."

I said, "When I first became a judge, around 1989, the DNA technology was still primitive, and was just beginning to be accepted by the courts. If I remember correctly, there was only one place in the country, in Maryland I think, that processed and prepared forensic reports on DNA samples. And the turnaround time was, like, weeks or months. Now the technology is routine, the turnaround time is immediate, and all United States courts accept the results. And the accuracy is incredible. For Caucasians, the odds of an incorrect identification are something like 1 in 1.2 quintillion. We had an interesting case in Yreka when I first started judging, where DNA analysis was critical. A young woman was brutally murdered in a partially burned home in a subdivision. There was evidence that the likely killer was a guy named Donald Bowcutt. I handled the preliminary hearing in his case and ruled that there was sufficient evidence to hold him to answer for trial on the murder charge. But there was insufficient credible DNA evidence to be used at trial because of the primitive technology at the time, so the District Attorney elected not to proceed, fearing that the case couldn't meet the reasonable doubt standard without it. Bowcutt was released from our jail, but had 'holds' from other jurisdictions for other crimes he had committed, so he wasn't going to be out on the streets. Years passed, and in the meantime, DNA became routine in criminal trials. The sheriff's office still had a usable amount of DNA in their evidence locker, and Bowcutt was still in custody somewhere, so his case was refiled. Bowcutt was brought back to Siskiyou County, tried and convicted, and was sentenced to life without the possibility of parole."

"Couldn't there be a mistake somewhere else in the process, not in the technology?" Ben asked. "I know my DNA was on surfaces in the car; couldn't the swab have picked that up, instead of from the blood? Or, couldn't DNA from some surface come in contact with and transfer to Hailey's blood?"

"I'm not an expert on DNA, so I don't know," I said. From what little I know of the prosecution's case, it seems weak. The DNA is important. Without it, I can't see how any ethical prosecutor would proceed. But with the DNA, there's a case. It's a problem."

We talked for another hour. I asked questions. Brenda asked a few. Most of the talking came from Ben. The conversation largely focused on the Sonoma weekend, but also spanned his relationship with, and courtship of, Hailey. It was the happiest time of his life, and he was sure she felt the same way. A romance made in heaven. They were talking about a wedding after he finished medical school and his residency. Then they would settle down in the town where they had lived all their lives. He wanted to be a small-town family practitioner and was even willing to deliver babies, knowing that babies generally made their appearances in this world at three o'clock in the morning. It was perfect. I wondered, *maybe too perfect?*

I did ask him one question, which kind of just came out. "Was she pregnant?"

That question jarred him. "No!" he answered, agitated. "She is a nurse, and I am almost a doctor. We know all about planned parenting."

Tempting as it was, we all declined dessert, and Ben excused himself, saying he needed to get back.

After he left, I asked Brenda, "What do you think?"

"Maybe I'm a sucker for handsome white guys," she said. "But I believe him. The blood's a problem, but I don't think he could have killed her."

CHAPTER 12

Bob and James H. Murphy

Brenda needed to be at the Sacramento International Airport (SMF) to catch a flight back to Washington, D.C., and I gave her a ride. As we were driving, I asked her if she had any further plans to come to the west coast. "Nothing specific," she said. "I probably will need to come back to Sacramento for meetings in the next few months, but they're not on the calendar yet. I've accumulated some vacation time. I'd like to take some time in the spring and hike the mountains in Siskiyou County, particularly in the Marble Mountains Wilderness." Then, she laughed and added, "Preferably under more enjoyable circumstances than the last time I was in your mountains. And I really want to see what Medicine Lake looks like in the daytime." I laughed too, but four years before, our experiences together in the mountains and at Medicine Lake were far from funny. They were horrific, and people died. We were fortunate to have survived.

"Don't forget to text me, a week from Thursday," I said. Without fail, every other Thursday before midnight eastern time, she sends me a short text message that ends with "Love, Brenda," or "Love, B." The actual content of the message is irrelevant. What matters is that the message is transmitted on time, and that it closes with "Love, Brenda," or "Love, B." Today we continue to do this little ritual primarily because it feels good and keeps us connected. It's become a tradition. But when we started it four years ago, it was a matter of survival. Brenda was in a very dangerous circumstance and the emails were code messages that she was all right. We agreed that if a message wasn't sent on time, or if it was sent with the wrong closing, it was her signal she was in trouble and needed help. Had we not had that ritual in place, she wouldn't be alive today. The human trafficking organization that abducted her back then is now apparently out of business. At least there have been no recent threats. But what's the harm in continuing our little custom? And, it feels good.

When I dropped her off in front of the terminal, she assured me she would send me the text. And then she kissed me. A nice kiss. I may be a septuagenarian, but I'm not too old to appreciate a kiss like that.

I got back onto I-5 and continued driving north. According to Google Maps, the address of the Morrow County District Attorney is on Second Street, near where it intersects with Dead Cat Alley, in Pineland. I had Googled the Morrow County District Attorney's website and learned that James H. Murphy was a new District Attorney, having been elected just a few months before. The D.A.

he succeeded had been in office for years and was well-respected. The website was sketchy about the background and qualifications of the new guy. I thought I might get in to see him before quitting time. I arrived at the office a little before 5:00 PM and asked the receptionist if I could see Mr. Murphy. "Do you have an appointment?" she asked.

"No," I answered. "I don't live here. I actually live in Yreka. I was passing through town and hoped to talk to Mr. Murphy about the Hailey Madison murder case. I'm a retired judge and personally acquainted with Ben Thompson, who apparently is a suspect."

"Mr. Murphy isn't in at the moment," she said. "We have a policy here that if you wish to talk to the District Attorney, there is a form to submit. I can give you the form, and you will be notified of an appointment date and time. Usually, the appointments are about three days out."

I wasn't used to that. The D.A. in my home county is generally accessible, unless he is in trial. But maybe that is because at home I still have a little recognition as a retired judge. Or maybe because of the relative number of constituents. Morrow County has a population of about 220,000 people. Siskiyou County is more like 45,000. I accepted the form, filled it out, and returned it to the receptionist. "I think I'll spend the night here in Pineland," I said. "Will he be in tomorrow morning?"

"I think so. But he's very busy. If you stay here overnight just to see him, you will probably be disappointed."

"I'll take my chances," I said. "Office hours are from eight o'clock, right?"

She nodded in affirmation. I thanked her and went out the door. There wasn't any particular reason I needed to get home that night. That's one benefit of being a retired septuagenarian. I called my grandson and asked him to feed Bebe, and I set out for the Fairfield Inn to see if they had a room. Pineland is about a three-and-a-half-hour drive from Yreka, and I'm fairly familiar with the town. I fly quite a lot out of SMF. It is convenient for me to drive to Pineland the night before a flight and spend the night at a park-and-fly hotel like the Fairfield Inn. I can leave my car and catch the hotel shuttle to the airport the next morning. From experience, I knew of a nice Mexican restaurant in Pineland called Maria's Cantina, and Mexican food was sounding good.

The overnight in Pineland was pleasant. I had excellent chile verde at Maria's Cantina, went to bed early and slept well, then enjoyed the "complimentary" breakfast at the hotel. I arrived back at the D.A.'s office promptly at 8:00 AM. When I walked into the office, the same receptionist from the night before simply said, "He's not here yet."

"Do you know what time he'll be coming in?"

"Should be any time. But, as I told you yesterday, he has a very full schedule and probably won't be able to see you," she said crisply.

"I'll wait," I said, sitting down in a waiting-room chair. There was a door with a frosted glass window behind the receptionist's desk that I assumed led to the D.A.'s office. A light was on from behind the door, but I couldn't see or hear anything indicating if the office was occupied. I wondered if he had to come through the waiting-room area to get into his office, or if there was access from some other direction. I took out my Kindle and read. I was one hundred pages into a mystery-thriller by C. J. Box, one of my favorite authors. *I can be quite comfortable here all day, if necessary,* I thought, as I settled in.

An hour went by. No one came in or out of the office, and the receptionist and I didn't exchange a word, but she looked like I was making her nervous.

About half-way through the second hour, a man came through the hallway door dressed in a navy blazer, blue shirt, striped tie, and khaki slacks. He went straight toward the door behind the receptionist's desk without saying "good morning" or anything. He entered his office, followed by the receptionist, who didn't close the door behind her. I heard her say, "This gentleman is here to see you, Mr. Murphy."

"Does he have an appointment? I'm really busy."

"No sir, but he's been here all morning. He wants to talk to you about the Hailey Madison murder case. He says he's a judge from Yreka."

"Oh hell. Tell him he can come in but I've only got a few minutes."

The receptionist came back out, delivered her message, and motioned me in. Murphy extended his hand. "What can I do for you?" he asked.

After I shook his hand, we both sat down, and I said, "First, I need to clarify. I'm not a judge. I'm retired, but I was on the bench in Siskiyou County for more than twenty years. I only need a few minutes of your time. I want to talk to you about the Hailey Madison case. As you know, Yreka is a small town. Everybody knows everybody. I am acquainted with Hailey Madison, but not close. I do know Ben Thompson pretty well, and the rumor is that he's about to be charged with murder. The reason that I'm here is to tell you that people that know Ben, including myself, don't believe he's capable of committing such a crime. And we don't think there is a motive." I then gave him the background information I had, and the reason I was interested. I treated everything that Ben had directly told me as confidential, even though technically it probably wasn't, and didn't disclose Ben's statements. "I'm not a percipient witness, and don't have direct knowledge of the events surrounding Hailey's disappearance," I said. "But I do know Ben. I guess I'm more of a character witness. I thought it might be important for you to hear what I have to say, and factor that into your decision as to whether to charge Ben with a crime. If he is charged, it will all but ruin his future medical career, regardless of whether he is convicted."

I was not prepared for the reaction I got from District Attorney James H. Murphy.

"Are you telling me not to prosecute Ben Thompson?" he asked, with a hard edge to his voice.

"I don't think that's my place, to tell you who you should prosecute. You're the D.A."

"You're goddamn right it's not your place!" he almost shouted, ramping up the stridency. "This is my county. Who the hell are you to come into my county and tell me who I should or shouldn't prosecute?"

"It wasn't my intent to tell you who you should or shouldn't prosecute. I came to see you because I thought my information would be useful in making your decision. I've known Ben Thompson and his family for a long time. I just don't think it's in his DNA to commit a murder. I also know Hailey Madison and her family. Hailey and Ben and their families are solid people. The dynamics of the relationship between Ben and Hailey aren't likely to trigger a murder. Plus, there is no motive. I thought you should have this information. The D.A.'s job is not just to seek convictions, but to seek justice." I realized immediately after that last sentence that it was a mistake. But it was too late. I couldn't unsay it.

"Go back to your Podunk county where you belong! Get the hell out of my office! You force your way into my office without an appointment because you are a judge, and now you are telling me how to do my job! You are totally out of line. I'm going to file a complaint with the Commission on Judicial Performance!"

Go for it, I thought, but didn't say it. I'm just a septuagenarian retired guy who happens to once have been a judge. The Commission on Judicial Performance doesn't have jurisdiction over me and could not care less. What I did say was, "Sorry to have ruined your day," as I walked out the door. I saw no point in prolonging the conversation. He wasn't receptive to anything I had to say. Our short encounter reinforced Lillian Thompson's previous observation that the guy might be crazy. Also, he was an asshole.

I got in my car and headed for home. After about two hours of driving north on I-5, I received a phone call from John Dickenson. He had just heard from Ben, the proverbial "one phone call," telling him he had been arrested, booked, and was in custody. I wondered about the timing. The arrest couldn't have been provoked by my visit with the Pineland D.A. Could it?

"Good luck with the Pineland D.A.," I said. I described my brief conversation with James H. Murphy. "I think Lillian Thompson might be right, he's crazy. Either that or he has a higher agenda."

CHAPTER 13

John Dickenson and Ben Thompson

The next day, John Dickenson drove to Pineland to talk to his new client. The drive took four hours. The first forty-five minutes was mainly along the Gazelle Callahan Road, a two-lane county road through farms and ranches with little traffic, except for the occasional hay-truck that he had to pass. The rest of the trip, until he got to the town of Pineland, was along Interstate 5.

John was having second thoughts about agreeing to represent Ben. It was keeping him from working on projects which had deadlines, and he reminded himself that he hadn't done a criminal case in many years.

The day before, after he discovered that Ben had been arrested, he called the Morrow County District Attorney's office and told them he had been retained to represent Ben Thompson, that he would be driving to Pineland the next day, and could he pick up the discovery? The law requires that the prosecution "discover" to the defense all the evidence it has against the defendant, including anything that might be exculpatory. This means the prosecution must provide to the defense such things as witness statements, lab reports, police reports, crime scene photos, and video and audio tapes, by a certain deadline and continuously thereafter as such material is acquired. The defense has a similar obligation to provide discovery to the prosecution, but to a somewhat lesser extent, due to defendants' Fifth Amendment rights. The objective of the discovery requirements is to achieve a just result: to assure that trials are not won or lost by surprise or ambush, but by a fair and unbiased process of arriving at the truth. The vast majority of attorneys, both on the prosecution side and on the defense side, are honorable and ethical, and freely comply with their discovery obligations. But human nature being what it is, some don't. Judges hate to referee discovery disputes, because they often disintegrate into personal "he said, she said" attacks between attorneys. They add unnecessary acrimony to trials and can be time-consuming. Also, trials can be reversed on appeal or habeas corpus for "prosecutorial misconduct" when a prosecutor withholds information favorable to the defense which should have been disclosed. No judge wants to preside over a trial that is reversed on appeal, even if, or maybe especially if, it wasn't the judge's fault.

Upon first arriving in Pineland, Dickenson went to the D.A.'s office and asked an assistant if his discovery packet was ready. It wasn't. The assistant said, "I'm sorry sir. We've been exceptionally busy, and just haven't been able to make the copies."

Dickenson was pissed, but didn't make a big deal out of it, realizing that the assistant was just the messenger. He said, "I'm going to spend some time with my client today, I'll stop by later. I've driven down here from Siskiyou County, a four-hour drive for me."

He then went to the Morrow Detention Center, the main jail for Morrow County. The correctional officers who processed him treated him courteously, but warily. He was new to them. He knew from experience that how such officers treat attorneys depends on how the attorneys treat the officers, and how professional they are. Generally, the men and women working in county jails have a good handle on how competent and ethical the lawyers are that regularly come to the jail to visit clients. To a lesser extent, an officer's courtesy toward the attorney will also depend on the officer's attitude toward the client. But a good lawyer who is not a jerk to the jail staff will have their respect and be treated well, even if the client is a slime ball. Here, they didn't know John Dickenson, but they had come to know Ben Thompson, and thought he was okay.

Dickenson spent several hours with his client. They had never met before, and neither knew much about the other, so the first hour was mainly getting acquainted, learning about each other's background and personality. Ben looked and sounded terrible, obviously scared. Being incarcerated is tough for anyone, but for someone like Ben, a middle-class adult with hardly a traffic infraction on his record, it is dreadfully frightening. Even so, he was practical in his conversation, and answered John's questions in a straightforward manner, without embellishment or undue elaboration. John began by asking him to tell the story of what happened, in narrative form, beginning with when Ben first met Hailey Madison. John listened intently without interruption. Once Ben's story was finished, John went back and grilled him on specific areas, much like a police interrogator would.

John focused hard on Ben's blood having been found in the car. This was pivotal. Without an explanation as to how the blood got there, Ben had every right to be scared. "Believe me," Ben said, "I have gone over in my mind every minute of my trip with Hailey. Many times. I can't remember even a slight nick of my skin. And I've been told that there was a fair amount of blood. Not a huge amount, but more than just, say, a finger cut."

"Well, if it didn't come directly from you when you were in the car, it must have been planted. The question is, if someone had planted it, where did they get the blood? Have you ever had a blood draw?"

"Sure," said Ben, "But it's been a while. I try to get an annual physical, but you know how that is. I've always been in good health. It's probably been two or three years."

"No emergencies, where you might have ended up in ER or ICU, or something like that? Or maybe you simply donated blood?"

Ben shook his head.

"What about in connection with medical school? Doing blood draws seems pretty basic. Something you have to learn how to do. Do medical students, like, practice on each other?"

"Yes, but most of that is done in first year. We practiced a lot of things on each other." Then, he laughed, and said, "We drew the line at prostate exams. Also, because we work in a hospital setting, we get our blood drawn to check for communicable infections, such as Hepatitis B or C, but that's also first year."

"Is there any reason why that blood would be retained somewhere? And how long does it keep?"

"The answer is no, not from that. And it wouldn't keep. A couple of years ago I did participate in a clinical trial, and consented to PG."

"PG?"

"Pharmacogenetics, the study of how people respond differently to drug therapy based on their genetic makeup. Research subjects are asked to consent to an extra tube of blood that is set aside and stored in a minus 80-degree centigrade freezer. Minus 80 centigrade is minus 112 Fahrenheit, colder than the average temperature of Mars. It is so cold that it is handled with insulated gloves, like oven mitts. The samples are shipped in dry ice. During shipment, continuous digital temperature monitors are used to make sure that when the blood gets to its destination there have been no significant temperature excursions."

"So, your blood may still be in storage somewhere? Where might that be?"

"Probably yes, but I don't know where."

"Can you find out?"

"I think so, but it's kind of hard when I'm locked up."

Dickenson said, "Sure, I understand that. I can do the leg work. Can you give me the information to get me started?"

Ben gave him the name of the doctor at the Medical Center in charge of the project. "Talk to Doctor Pendleton. Roberta Pendleton. She should be able to give you all the information you need."

After the interview with his client, Dickenson went back to the D.A.'s office to see if the discovery packet was available. "Sorry," said the assistant, with no apparent remorse. "It's just been chaotic around here."

He was now more than a little ticked, but didn't display it. It wasn't a big deal, at least yet. "I understand that my client's arraignment is tomorrow afternoon, I can get it then. Can you verify that for me, and let me know what time it's scheduled?"

"All arraignments are posted in the courthouse bulletin the morning of the arraignment, on the first floor. You can check there in the morning. Also, you can check online."

"Can you just tell me?"

She gave an audible sigh, picked up a clipboard right in front of her, and said, "Yes, tomorrow, courtroom number three, three-thirty PM."

"Thanks for your trouble," he said as he walked away.

It didn't make sense to drive all the way home, just to return the next day for the arraignment, so he found a Holiday Inn Express, and checked in. It was late afternoon, still during business hours, and he remembered that he knew an acquaintance in Pineland: Fred Erbe, a law school classmate. It had been years since they had communicated, but he vaguely recalled that Erbe had a law practice in Pineland. In his hotel room he googled the name "Fred Erbe," and found a listing for "Law Offices of Frederick J. Erbe, Attorney at Law," with a Pineland address and phone number. He called the number.

Erbe was in his office, and was genuinely pleased to talk to John, a feeling that was mutual. After they talked a few minutes, Erbe said, "I'm on my own tonight. My wife's got a ladies' dinner thing. Do you want to have dinner?"

"Sure," said John, and they agreed to meet at 6:30 at a Thai restaurant downtown. The dinner was enjoyable for both. Each had war stories to share from their Santa Clara University Law School days, and they brought each other up to date on the status of mutual acquaintances.

John filled him in on the reason he was in Pineland. Erbe said, "Yeah, the case is in the local news big time. Based on the media coverage, Ben Thompson sounds like a bad dude. But I don't put much stock in media coverage. I don't do criminal law, but I am active in the local bar association, so I'm in the loop to some extent with all the lawyers in the county, including the criminal folks."

"Why do you think Ben Thompson might be a bad dude?"

"I didn't mean to say I think that. That's the picture the local media paints."

"Why is that?"

"The D.A. issues press releases almost daily, and the press gobbles it up. Like I say, I don't do criminal law, but the constant publicity seems counterproductive. When the case gets to trial, I think jury selection might be a problem. A likely case for a motion to change venue out of the county. But then, I'm not the D.A."

"Is that the D.A.'s normal practice?"

"I can't really say for sure. He's a relatively new guy, not from here. So, I really don't know him. And we don't get cases as juicy as this very often. Occasional murders, yes, but not involving upper middle-class people, medical

65

student, nurse, and all that. And certainly not many cases where the victim simply disappears."

"What do you know about the D.A.?"

"I don't know him very well. The scuttlebutt from my friends that do criminal law is that he's an asshole. My secretary knows some of the gals that work in his office, and she says they don't like him either. They're unhappy in their jobs."

"How did he get to be the D.A.? Especially if he's not from around here. It's an elected position."

"I don't know. He ran unopposed. Our previous D.A. retired after a long career. He was well thought of. Normally there would be an heir-apparent for the job, maybe a deputy in the office. But, strangely, no one tossed their hat in the ring except Murphy. He did it early on, even before the old D.A. formally announced his retirement, although it was pretty much an open secret that he intended to retire. Murphy seemed to have lots of financial backing and got in ahead of the curve. By the time anyone else gave much thought to running for the position, Murphy already had gotten endorsements from a lot of the town's movers and shakers. It was a done deal before it started."

"What was the incentive for an outsider like Murphy to just show up and aggressively go after the job?"

"You got me. I wouldn't want it. There is nothing remarkable about the county's crime rate. Violent crime is, if anything, below average. Narcotics crimes are up, despite the decriminalization of marijuana, especially cocaine. We are a relatively poor, agriculture-based community. Methamphetamine has always been a scourge, but until recently, not much cocaine. Cocaine's more of a rich man's addiction. But the last few years have brought more cocaine."

"I'm just thinking out loud," said Dickenson. "If you were a cocaine distributor, having a D.A. in your pocket would be highly beneficial. The D.A. could aggressively prosecute meth, and keep the constituents happy, but back off on the coke. Hell, he could even tip the coke distributors of any upcoming raids. The D.A. would be a valuable asset."

"He sure would," agreed Erbe. "But the scuttlebutt that I get is that he's just an asshole. Nothing about being corrupt or being involved in drug trafficking. I don't think there's any evidence of that."

"Right," agreed Dickenson. "As I said, I'm just thinking out loud. But can you think of a reason why he's making such a big deal about going after Ben Thompson? Ben's a genuinely good guy, not a hardened criminal or a scumbag."

"No reason that I can think of," said Erbe. "Unless he's in somebody's pocket."

The two men left the restaurant about 9:00 PM, each genuinely telling the other how much he enjoyed the evening and promising to get together again soon.

The next morning, Dickenson returned to the D.A.'s office. Although he expected the worst, a discovery packet was ready for him. He took it back to his hotel room and studied it until the twelve-noon checkout time. Mostly, it contained nothing significant that Dickenson wasn't already aware of. Conspicuously missing, of course, was mention of a dead body. Nothing new there. But he was surprised at the overall lack of evidence of motive. The word "motive" was not mentioned anywhere. One entry, however, caught his eye and concerned him. In one police report an officer named "Reynolds" had written, "CI#2, an acquaintance of suspect Thompson, who lived in the same apartment complex, reported that Thompson had told CI#2 that Hailey Madison was pregnant, and that Thompson was 'really pissed' about it, and 'didn't know what he was going to do.' I asked CI#2 if he/she was romantically involved with Thompson, which CI#2 denied." The initials "CI" indicate "confidential informant" in cop-speak. Nothing in the discovery materials indicated the identity of CI#2. Dickenson made a mental note to find out who CI#2 was.

After he checked out of his hotel room, John picked up a cheeseburger and an order of fries at an In-N-Out Burger drive-thru and found a picnic table in a small public park near the courthouse. While eating lunch, he googled the UC Davis Medical Center in Sacramento, and called its main number. After about five minutes of recorded messages, he was finally connected with a live person able to direct his call to Dr. Roberta Pendleton, the doctor in charge of the pharmacogenetics project.

She was a pleasant lady. John introduced himself as Ben Thompson's lawyer, and explained why he was calling her. With genuine concern in her voice, she said, "This whole thing is horrible. There is no way Ben could be a murderer. I'm sure everyone at the med center who knows him would be happy to be a character witness, if that would help. I know I would be. And if he needs money for his defense, I'm sure we could raise some."

"That won't be necessary, at least for now," said Dickenson. Then he explained the importance of Ben's blood having been found in the car and asked about the sample Ben had given for the PG study. He told her the information could be crucial to Ben's defense.

She said, "I can check our records. Off the top of my head, I don't know where the blood is stored. We used to ship frozen blood samples off-campus to a facility in the Midwest, but more recently UC Davis has developed its own storage facility. It's quite specialized. The blood has to be stored at a crazy temperature, and there are very few places that do that. It will take me a little while to find out where it is. But it shouldn't be a problem. And we keep very detailed and specific records, including chain-of-custody. Can I call you back?"

"Sure. And thank you."

John arrived at courtroom number three a half-hour before the time scheduled for Ben's arraignment. He walked around a little bit, just wanting to get the feel of that part of the courthouse, and then went in and sat down in the back of the courtroom itself, for the same reason. Also, he had hoped to observe the judge in action. When he went in, however, no proceedings were in progress. So, he just waited. He knew the arraignment would be pro forma. The primary activities that would take place would be the formal entry of Ben's not guilty plea and setting a date for the preliminary examination. It was also the first opportunity for John to see the criminal complaint filed against his client. The complaint is the formal charging document that expressly sets forth the specific crimes and special allegations. He wanted to find out if the D.A. was charging special circumstances that could make the case a death penalty case under California law. Also, he would make a pitch for Ben to be released on bail but knew that realistically it wouldn't be granted.

At 3:30 the judge took the bench, and the day's arraignments began. There were ten criminal defendants on the list, eight male and two female, all in orange jumpsuits with their hands and feet shackled. They were all brought into the courtroom together and seated in the jury box. Ben looked miserable, even worse than the day before, if that was possible. The cases were individually called, and Ben was third on the list. When a defendant's case was called, his or her attorney would stand in front of the rail, close enough to be able to talk to the client, but with little privacy. When his case was called, Ben stood up, and John went over to him. The bailiff handed the complaint to John, who looked it over, and said to the court, "We will waive formal arraignment, and enter pleas of not guilty to all charges and deny all special allegations. We request a preliminary examination be set within the statutory time."

The judge set a date and time for the preliminary examination, one week away. "Can I have just a word with my client, your honor?" asked Dickenson.

"Sure," said the judge,

John whispered to Ben, "I will come see you the day before the prelim." Then he went on, in an even quieter tone, "I finally got the discovery, and went through it this morning. There is a police report from an officer that said he talked to someone who lives in your apartment complex. The identity of the person wasn't disclosed, and it didn't say whether the person was male or female. Anyway, the person reported that you said Hailey was pregnant. Did you tell anyone that?"

That got Ben's attention, and he started to blurt out an answer, when John shushed him. "Just whisper to me."

"I didn't, and she wasn't," he said, in a low tone, "and I'm sure she would have told me if she was."

"The person was listed as a 'confidential informant.' Do you have any idea who that person might be?"

Ben looked genuinely puzzled and thought for a couple of minutes. Then he said, "I really don't have any idea."

The judge said, in a kindly manner, "Mr. Dickenson, I'm afraid we have to move on with today's cases."

"I'm sorry, your honor. Thank you. We're done." Then to Ben, "I'll see you soon."

Dickenson was in his car headed home, when his cell phone rang. It was Roberta Pendleton, the doctor in charge of the Davis Med Center PG project. She sounded upset. "This is very strange. I cannot find any record of Ben Thompson's blood sample. Nothing. So, I don't have any evidence that a blood sample exists, either here on the campus, or elsewhere."

"What about the actual blood draw?"

"No. Not even that. There is nothing."

"Nothing to prove that he actually gave the blood?" asked John.

"Nothing recorded. I could testify to it."

"From personal knowledge?"

"Yes. Normally, I wouldn't have anything to do with that. A technician would do it. A phlebotomist. But this time was different. I had gotten to know Ben pretty well. He was very interested in the project, so we talked about it. I was actually there with him when he gave the blood. I saw it happen. I keep a personal diary, just jot down a few notes each day. I was able to find the entry, so I know the exact date. That helped me when I searched the records. Usually all you need is the name, and the date of birth helps, too. When I found nothing under his name, I checked chronological records. I even checked a few dates before and after the date I had in my diary, in case I recorded it wrong. There is nothing."

"Would you be willing to testify as to your personal observation, if necessary?"

"Of course. But I also intend to find out what happened; why there is no record."

This worried Dickenson. He had already come to believe there was something more going on than a routine homicide, a crime of passion. He was becoming a conspiracy theorist, and that wasn't his style. He asked, "Is it possible that the records could have been intentionally obliterated?"

"I don't see how. Entries for a specific blood sample are made at various times and places, by different people. I guess it might be theoretically possible, but it would take a lot of planning. And would have to involve someone from the inside. One of our own people. I don't know anyone who would do that. And why would they do that?"

"Someone who doesn't like Ben Thompson. Are you absolutely sure you personally saw Ben give the blood?"

"Yes. Absolutely."

"I don't want to scare you, but maybe you shouldn't tell anybody about this, at least until I can learn a little more. Your testimony could be the key to an acquittal for Ben, and you could be in danger. Have you told anyone else about what you have found?"

"No, not really. I initially asked one person in the records department to locate and copy the records relating to the blood sample. When she called me back and said she could find nothing, I went and searched for myself. My conversation with her was just that. 'Can you look up and copy the records?' And she responded with, 'They're aren't any.' Nothing more specific."

John was concerned. His own anxiety level was rising, and he was fearful for Dr. Pendleton's safety, but he didn't know what to tell her. It was premature to ask her to be placed under police protection. To ask her to hide seemed extreme, at least for now. "I don't know what to tell you," he said. "This is all really speculative at this point. Ben's girlfriend Hailey Madison's body has never been found. There are three possibilities. One, she just took off somewhere, of her own volition, and didn't tell anyone. That is not likely. Two, she was kidnapped, and is being held captive. Or three, she is dead. If she has been kidnapped or murdered, that means there is someone out there who didn't like her and wants Ben Thompson to be convicted, someone who is a very evil criminal. If that person knows about you and what you can testify to you might be in danger. I honestly don't know what you should do, but I will do whatever I can to protect you."

"I'm a big girl," she said. "I don't want you to do anything."

"Are you sure?"

"Yes, I'll be cautious. Don't worry."

"Thank you," he said. "We'll keep in touch."

CHAPTER 14

Arturo and Floyd

Arturo and Floyd were in good spirits. Floyd, who was driving the ten-year-old nondescript full-size sedan, said to his partner, "Hey Turo. This is a sweet deal, no?"

"Don't count your fucking chickens, man," said Arturo. "And don't let her out of sight."

"I'm on it, man, but hey, seventy-five grand. Fifty for you and twenty-five for me, and only three days of work."

"A lot to do in the three days, and it's risky. Don't lose her, damn it!" said Arturo.

Following specific instructions they had received from their unknown employer, Arturo and Floyd arrived at Ben Thompson's apartment complex in Sacramento at 6:40 PM. The street fronting it was quiet, and they found a parking spot on the street a half-block away that gave them a good view of the complex and the driveway to the tenant parking area in back. The driveway's chain-link gate was activated by a card-key inserted into a slot. Their car faced the driveway and was parked on the opposite side from the direction a car would most likely come if it had exited the I-5 freeway, and the direction it would most likely go if headed back to the freeway from the apartment. Arturo and Floyd had no idea who their car belonged to, or who the license plates were registered to. Their employer had given them meticulously detailed instructions describing the task they must accomplish to earn their $75,000, but zero information about anything else, so they knew nothing of the big picture. They had done odd jobs for the employer before, so this was typical. They had no idea who the employer was. Not even whether it was a man or a woman, although they thought it was a woman. Following a pattern they had used before, Arturo received a text message on his cell phone asking him to call his Aunt Rosa. The text message did not specify a phone number, but Arturo had previously been mailed a postcard advertisement for an auto repair shop in Phoenix, Arizona. Receiving the postcard and text message prompted him to buy a burner phone at Walmart with pre-paid minutes and call the number on the postcard. He made the call and had a short one-way conversation with an electronically-garbled voice which sounded female. The voice gave him specific instructions, the first of which was to pick up the car they were now driving. It was in a downtown Sacramento parking garage; the key was behind the visor.

Around 7:00 PM, they observed a blue Mustang convertible drive toward them and turn into the driveway. It was occupied by a man and a woman, and the top was down. Floyd said, "Fucking beautiful car, man. Brand new. It still has the dealer name in the license plate holder. It's a shame to destroy it. Let's just take it."

"Don't be an idiot," said Arturo. "Don't you want your $25,000?"

"Well, we can at least take it for a ride."

"Shut the fuck up," said Arturo.

They waited with increasing impatience for another hour, and it was getting dark. Then the convertible emerged from the driveway. This time the top was up, but they could see, even in the dark, that it was occupied by only one person, the woman. The car turned out of the driveway, heading away from them, toward I-5. They followed, as far back as possible without losing sight of her. The woman drove the surface streets and then entered an I-5 onramp, heading north. About forty minutes later, she left the freeway, entered a Pilot Flying J Travel Center, and pulled up to a gas pump. She began fueling the Mustang and walked inside the travel center building. Floyd parked their sedan at a pump two lanes over and also began fueling. While Floyd was working the pump, Arturo quickly walked over to the convertible. He removed the valve cap from the right rear tire and with a small tool gave the valve stem a slight twist. He did not replace the valve cap. He walked back to the sedan and got in. Floyd was still outside the car fiddling with the fuel nozzle even though the fueling had stopped. He watched the woman return to the convertible and replace the nozzle. As she climbed into her car, Floyd also replaced the nozzle of the sedan and got into the driver's seat. When she was pulling away from the pump, Floyd, gesturing toward the woman, said, "Hey, Turo, that's pretty nice stuff. We can have some fun tonight."

"Fuck you!" said Arturo, "Don't you want your twenty-five grand? Our employer says the merchandise must be undamaged."

"We can have some fun with no damage."

"Fuck you," Arturo said again.

Back on the freeway Arturo and Floyd remained some distance behind the woman but kept her in view. After about fifteen minutes the woman took an offramp onto a narrow gravel road that seemed to lead to nowhere and pulled over. She got out and was examining her right rear tire when Arturo and Floyd pulled up behind her. It was very dark, and there were no lights from any houses or other buildings in sight. There were no other cars on the road. Both men put on latex gloves. Arturo had rehearsed in his mind every scenario he could think of about how to accomplish their mission, but this time they were lucky. This was a no-brainer, and he just went straight at it. With a semiautomatic handgun in his right hand, he grabbed the woman around her neck with his left arm. He pushed the gun into her side and said, "I will kill you if you make noise or resist." Floyd opened the rear passenger door of the sedan, and Arturo pushed her onto the back seat and climbed in behind her. Floyd removed from a container a towel soaked with something that smelled terrible, entered the back seat through the rear driver door and pressed the towel into her face. The woman struggled for a few minutes but was held securely by the two men, and she soon went limp. Working quickly, the two men duct-taped her feet together and then duct-taped her hands together behind her back. With a length of duct-tape, they connected her wrists to her ankles, effectively hog-tying her. They pushed a washcloth into her mouth and wrapped it with duct-tape around the back of her head and neck. Arturo popped open the trunk. Inside was a small ice chest, which he placed on the front passenger seat of the sedan. The men carried the woman's limp body around to the back of the sedan and dropped it into the trunk. They removed a necklace from around her neck. Arturo went back to the ice chest and removed a sealed plastic bag containing a very large hypodermic syringe. With some difficulty, he extracted blood from a vein on the inside crook of the woman's arm, filling the syringe. He returned to the ice chest, this time removing an odd-looking container. Inside the container was another syringe, this one full of a dark colored thick liquid. Meanwhile, Floyd removed every item from the convertible, including the woman's suitcase and purse, and tossed them into the sedan's trunk, on top of the woman. Arturo sprayed the contents of both syringes inside the convertible, onto the front seats, steering wheel, and dash, and removed the key from the ignition. He then tossed the necklace into the dirt off the side of the road a few feet from the car. No car had come along during the relatively short time it took the two men to accomplish their mission, although they had an explanation ready if one did. The two men quickly but systematically bashed the exterior and windows of the woman's car with large heavy crowbars, ripped the convertible top, and removed the valve stems from all four tires. As the last step, Arturo picked up a twig from the side of the road and used it to obliterate footprints.

Both men visually scanned the area around the Mustang and, satisfied, they drove off.

CHAPTER 15

Hailey

Hailey was on Interstate 5 headed north. It was about 8:00 PM and getting dark. She knew she had to buy fuel to make it all the way to Yreka. *Damn it, why didn't Ben and I get fuel before we got to his house? It's already eight o'clock. It'll probably add twenty minutes to stop for gas and will be midnight by the time I get home. I've got to start my shift tomorrow morning. What was I thinking?* But she didn't have a choice. She turned into a Pilot Flying J Travel Center, pulled up to a pump, and began fueling her new car. While the pump was running, she went inside to use the restroom and buy a bottle of water. As she walked back out, she thought she saw some guy looking at her car but wasn't sure. He was gone when she reached it. *It's a beautiful car,* she thought. *Not a surprise that people want to gawk.* On the Sonoma road trip, the car attracted several comments from strangers.

She replaced the nozzle, climbed in, and drove back onto I-5. After ten minutes on the interstate, the low tire pressure warning light was activated on the instrument panel. *Shit! I'll keep on going. It's probably a defective sensor. But I'll pull off at the next gas station and look at the tire.* She drove five more minutes on the interstate in the middle of nowhere and didn't see a gas station. Now the car was noticeably pulling to the right. *I'd better look,* she thought. She pulled off at the next offramp, not paying attention to the name or number of the exit. It was barely a road at all, and she drove for a hundred yards before finding a wide enough space where she felt comfortable enough to stop. Leaving the engine running, she climbed out and walked around the back of the car toward the right rear tire. She observed a pair of headlights coming from the freeway in her direction. This caused an immediate adrenaline rush, but she thought, *maybe it's someone that can help me.* "Shit, shit, shit!" she muttered aloud when she looked at her right rear tire. It was flat; too flat to drive. *My new car came with an emergency tire inflation and sealant kit. I'll have to figure out how to use it.* As she was examining the tire, she heard the oncoming car come up to a screeching stop behind her. She turned to see two male figures jerk the doors open, climb out of their car, and lunge toward her. She instinctively turned to run, but they were on her in an instant. One of them grabbed her around the neck, pressed something into her side, and said, "I will kill you if you make noise or resist!" He swiveled her around, and pushed her toward their car, as the other guy moved back to their car and opened the rear passenger door. He slammed her onto the back seat and climbed in on top of her. She was vaguely aware of the other guy entering the car from the other side, pressing a foul-smelling towel or cloth into her face. For a few seconds she struggled and gasped for breath, then everything went black.

As she was coming to, Hailey's first sensory awareness was that it was a struggle to breathe. She couldn't inhale through her mouth and had to take long deep breaths through her nose to get enough air into her lungs. It was terrifying. She thought she would suffocate. For several minutes she concentrated solely on breathing. When she satisfied herself that she was getting enough oxygen to sustain her, she focused on other things. Her back was hurting her. She was bent backwards, with her wrists connected to her ankles. The reason she couldn't breathe through her mouth was that her mouth was stuffed full of something soft, like cloth, that was apparently held in place by tape wrapped around her neck and back of her heard. She could see nothing and concluded that the tape was also wrapped around her eyes. She was lying on her left side on something soft, a mattress. She tried to scoot her body, first one direction, then another, and discovered that she could only move a couple of inches in any direction. Something was restraining her motion. After giving up on trying to move, she listened. This wasn't easy because of the noise that came from her attempts to breathe through her nose. She took a deep breath and held it as long as she could and listened until she was forced to exhale and breathe again. After she did this several times, she thought, but wasn't sure, that she heard men's voices from a distance, perhaps from another room. Just low murmurs. No way to tell what they were actually saying.

Hailey couldn't move; she couldn't see; and what she could hear was meaningless. She remembered being grabbed by two men and forced into a car, and a foul-smelling rag being pressed over her face. She didn't know how long it had been between that and when she regained consciousness.

More time passed. It could have been an hour, or six hours, she didn't know. She did know that her discomfort was increasing, both physically and mentally. Her body ached, particularly her back. The need to pee was becoming increasingly unrelenting. The mental part was worse. The terror was constant, even though she tried to head it off by talking to herself, asking questions of herself. *Who are these people? What do they want with me? They haven't tried to rape me. Do they want a ransom? Are they going to let me go if they get money? My parents have money.*

More time passed. Her physical condition deteriorated to the point of becoming unbearable. She gave up on resisting her need to urinate. She just let it go. It felt wet and horrible, and she could smell it. All the joints of her body ached. She tried to sleep, but there was no way. The pain was bad enough to prevent sleep, but the real discomfort was her struggle just to breathe. And she was thirsty. Hungry, too, but the thirst was paramount; her mouth was dry and raspy. Her mental state was also going downhill. She continued talking to herself, but her conversations were becoming more desperate, more morbid. *Am I going to die here? Does anyone even know that I'm here?* She had convinced herself that the men's voices she thought she heard were just her imagination. *Why me? Haven't I been through enough after what Uncle Phil did? Please, somebody help me.*

CHAPTER 16

Floyd

Floyd and Arturo were impatiently killing time in the kitchen of a small farmhouse a few miles east of the tiny agricultural town of Arbuckle, California. The house was surrounded by fields, and there were no other houses in sight. Their car was parked, out of sight, in the garage attached to the house. It had taken them about an hour to get there after trashing the Mustang. They had never been to the house before and had no idea who owned it. As they had done before for their employer, they simply followed instructions. This time the instructions were in the form of a map in the glove compartment of their car. The glove compartment also contained a garage door opener and a key. One of the two bedrooms was occupied by their houseguest, a woman who was securely hogtied and gagged, and who was resting not-so-comfortably on the double bed.

Floyd asked, not for the first time, "When are they going to come and get her?"

"Sometime between twenty-four and forty-eight hours of when we got her. Will you fuckin' stop asking me? You know our instructions as well as I do," barked Arturo. "The twenty-four-hour window hasn't even started yet. We got her at nine-thirty last night, so the earliest they will get here will be nine-thirty tonight."

"Turo, that means the soonest they will get here is at least two fuckin' hours. And they might not even get here until nine-thirty tomorrow night. This is fuckin' bullshit. I don't want to just sit around here watchin' the fuckin' TV."

"Yeah, like you have something more important to do, asshole? And look at it this way. You are getting paid twenty-five grand for three days of work. That is like thirty-five-hundred dollars an hour. And, we also get room and board. There's food in the refrigerator."

"But no booze. I've searched the whole fuckin' place, not a single god-damn beer. And it's fuckin' boring. We could make the time go faster with the *puta* in the bedroom."

"Will you shut the fuck up. You know the instructions," said Arturo.

"What instruction says we can't have some fun while we're waiting?"

Arturo, exasperated, said, "The instructions say, and I am quoting, 'the merchandise must be undamaged.' Don't you want to fucking collect your twenty-five grand? Now will you just shut up? You're beginning to piss me off. I want my share of the money, and I don't want you to fuck it up. Keep your dick in your pants. With your share of the money, you will be able to buy whatever the fuck you want. And these people that are paying us, our employers, they don't screw around. You remember what happened to Jaime when he fucked up a job. Do you want to be food for the fish?"

"Who's talking about damaging the merchandise? Man, we could have some fun with no fuckin' damage."

"Damage or not, if we do something to her that we ain't getting paid to do, the bitch will talk about it when she arrives at her final destination," said Arturo. "Our employers will find out. Just shut the fuck up. Tell you what. Our instructions don't say we can't help pass the time with a little booze. I'll drive back to that stupid little hick town and see if there's a place to buy some. I'll be back well before the twenty-four-hour window starts. I want to be here when they come get her. But don't you fucking touch her while I'm gone. And call me immediately if any weird shit happens."

Floyd heard the garage door open and close, and then went to the window and watched Arturo drive off in the sedan. He sat in front of the TV and watched for a while, but his mind was wandering. He reached his hand down and rubbed his crotch from outside his pants. After five minutes of that, he walked into the bedroom where the woman was, turned on the light, and sat down in a chair. She was awake, struggling to breathe through her nose. Even though her eyes were taped, she instantly knew the light was on and that a man was present in the room. She went rigid and tried to hold her breath, but could only do so for an instant before again desperately sucking air through her nose.

"Hey *puta,* you smell like piss," said Floyd, with a laugh. "That's disgusting. And your breathing is really fucked up. You want me to remove all that shit that's in your mouth?"

Hailey couldn't respond, but her body shook as much as her restraints permitted. Breathing became even more difficult, and her panic was overwhelming from the fear of this man and the even greater fear of suffocating.

"You want me to take the shit out of your mouth?" he repeated. "If I do that, I'll want something in return from you. Are you okay with that? If you're okay with that, nod your head."

Hailey now actually was suffocating. Because of her panic, she was slowly losing the battle to inhale enough oxygen through her nose to sustain her. A downward spiral, more panic, less oxygen.

"Come on *puta*, do you want me to let you breathe or not? Our employers say we shouldn't damage the merchandise. I don't want to do any damage. If you do a good job on me, I won't hurt you, and afterward I'll fix it so you can breathe better. I promise. Okay, *puta*?"

Hailey nodded her head as best as she could, still sucking oxygen through her nose. Floyd released the restraints that had kept her from moving in any direction on the bed. Then he grabbed her around the midsection and roughly pulled her off the bed onto the floor, still hogtied. He pulled her up by her hair until she was in a kneeling position, her wrists and ankles still bound behind her, with the back of her head pressed against the top of the bed. He reached down, grabbed her shirt with both hands, and pulled it open, exposing her bra. Floyd was now in an uncontrollable frenzy, and he yanked the bra downward, allowing her breasts to pop out. He ripped the tape away from her mouth and with his fingers pulled out the cloth. Her mouth was exposed and vulnerable, but her eyes still covered with the tape. He said, "Now let's see what you can do, *puta*. Open wide!" After he unzipped his fly and started to force his penis into her mouth, several things happened quickly. As he pushed into her mouth, he heard the garage door open and at the same time felt an excruciating stabbing pain. He fell backward and observed blood spurting from his penis. Frightened and enraged, he wildly swung his fist and slammed it into the side of Hailey's head, and then kicked at her. He thought he would pass out, but made it to the bathroom, grabbed a towel, and compressed it onto his crotch. When Arturo came into the room, he saw Hailey with her breasts exposed. She was lying on her side on the floor next to the bed, moaning. He saw Floyd doubled over, clutching a towel to his crotch. He was gasping for breath, crying and retching simultaneously. Arturo shouted, "Fuck! Fuck! Fuck! Floyd, you stupid bastard! What the fuck have you done!"

CHAPTER 17

Hailey

Before the man came into the bedroom, Hailey had convinced herself that she was not going to survive. She didn't know what the men wanted. Probably a ransom. If true, that gave them a reason to keep her alive, at least until they got their money. But her more immediate fear was of suffocation. And no one was paying attention. Her breathing had become increasingly difficult, and the panic that came from not being able to breathe was profound. She had always had a fear of drowning, but then, doesn't everybody? She remembered one time when she was a kid, swimming in a lake. She and other kids were playing with a large rubber inner-tube, riding it and jumping off of it. She had pulled herself up onto the inner-tube, slipped, and her head went down through the center hole and into the water. For a few seconds she was stuck, trapped with her legs up in the air and her head under water. She soon squirmed freed, but those few seconds of panic were so intense that the memory had stayed with her ever since. What she was experiencing now was far worse. It was continuous and unrelenting. Every breath took all her energy, and she wasn't sure if she could muster another.

Then the man came in. She could hear the light switch and sense the light come on in the room, even though she couldn't see it. What was he saying? Something about taking the stuff out of her mouth, so she could breathe better. But she would have to do something for him. She had a good idea of what he wanted her to do, but she was so desperate she would do anything; anything to help her breathe. Then he said something about damaging the "merchandise." What did that mean? Was she the "merchandise?" What did they intend to do with her? Were they going to sell her? He asked again if she wanted him to help her breathe, and she desperately tried to indicate yes. She couldn't tell exactly what he was doing, but thought he was loosening her bonds somehow. Then he grabbed her, threw her onto the floor, then pulled her up against the bed. She felt and heard him tearing at her shirt and pulling the tape off her mouth. He pulled the cloth out of her mouth, and she heard him say, "Open wide!" *Why is this happening? Why do I deserve this? First Uncle Phil, and now this. I have always tried to be a good person.* She could smell him as he pushed into her mouth. It was horrible. *I'm going to die anyway. I won't let him do this!* Then she bit down on him, as hard as she could! He fell backward with a scream. She was struck with a sharp blow to the left side of her head, causing her ear to ring, almost knocking her unconscious. Then another blow, this time to her abdomen.

She thought, but wasn't sure, that something was broken or torn inside her. Then mercifully she blacked out...

When she awoke, she could tell she was back on the bed again, immobilized much the same as before. She could feel that her breasts were covered by her bra, but that the lapels of her shirt were still open. The cloth was back in her mouth, which was again covered with tape. Thankfully, her breathing was much easier, but there was pain in her belly. She could hear no one in the room, and she sensed that the light was off.

Again, time passed slowly.

Hailey heard a strange sound. It sounded at first like it was off in the distance, but grew louder. An approaching helicopter? Soon the sound was almost deafening, and Hailey was sure. A helicopter had landed right next to the house! Men came into her room, talking excitedly in Spanish. She couldn't understand what they were saying, but it was clear they were arguing, and very angry. They removed the bonds securing her to the bed and the bond connecting her wrists to her ankles. They roughly pulled her off the bed and stood her on the floor, hurting her. She had been hogtied for so long that her muscles and tendons were sore, and she felt a sharp pain in her stomach. They adjusted her ankle bonds to allow a distance of about twelve inches between her feet. Then they shoved her, shuffling unceremoniously, out of the bedroom, through the rest of the house, then outside, and finally up into the helicopter. They strapped her into a seat. As she felt and heard the helicopter lifting off the ground, many anxious thoughts raced through her mind. *Where are they taking me? Why me? What did I do? Are they taking me to Mexico? Are they going to sell me to a cartel?*

CHAPTER 18

Arturo and Floyd

Among the men in the helicopter, the only non-Hispanic was the pilot. He was a tall, fit-looking black guy, late thirties, dressed in shorts, a tee shirt, and a Golden State Warriors baseball cap. While the others were loading the "merchandise" into the helicopter, he approached Arturo with a folded piece of paper in his hand. Before handing Arturo the paper, he asked, "What the fuck happened?"

"Floyd is a stupid fucking asshole," said Arturo. "He really fucked up. I stressed to him many times that our specific instructions were 'no damage.' He knew the rules, but he fucked up. Out of my control. I was away from the house no more than a half an hour to go get provisions, and he got fucking crazy. While I was gone, he tried to get a blow-job, and the bitch bit him. She practically bit his fucking dick off. It would actually be funny if it didn't violate our instructions. But I didn't have anything to do with it, I swear. He did it on his own. I wasn't here."

"Yeah, but he's your guy, right? You brought him in on the job."

"Yeah, but how the fuck was I to know he would do that? He's worked with me before, always followed instructions. How was I to know that he'd go fucking crazy this time. It's not my fault."

The pilot said, "Well, I don't think our employers will be happy. They don't tolerate screw-ups like this. You'll be lucky to get your money."

"It wasn't my fault. Nothing I could do about it. It's Floyd that shouldn't get his fucking money, not me."

"Hey, it's not up to me," said the pilot. "I'm just the messenger. And, by the way, here's the message." He handed Arturo the piece of paper. "Here are your instructions. What to do with the car, and how to get paid. Good luck. Time to go." Arturo didn't read the paper until after he watched the pilot enter the helicopter.

After reading the instructions, Arturo yelled to Floyd, "Let's go, motherfucker. Our instructions are just to get the hell out of here, someone will come later and clean the place up. We need to deliver the car in Sacramento and get our money. How are you doing?"

Floyd was zipping up his pants, but his face was white. "I think I need fuckin' stitches, but I'm pretty sure I got the bleeding stopped." He looked like he was about to cry. He took a full five minutes to maneuver himself into the passenger seat of the sedan. His primary duty in this operation was to be the driver, a duty he now could not carry out.

The instructions were to deliver the car to a certain public pay parking lot in a seedy part of Sacramento, then leave the car and walk to a boarded-up building a couple of blocks away in an even seedier part of town to collect their money. Floyd objected to this. "Turo, I can't fuckin' walk two blocks," he said. "It'll start bleeding again. I'll fuckin' bleed to death."

"It's your own damn fault, motherfucker. You're lucky they are going to pay you at all. I'll drop you off at the building and deliver the car to the lot. Then I'll walk back and meet you."

As they drove toward the building described in the instructions, both had misgivings. The word "seedy" gave the neighborhood the benefit of the doubt. There was litter strewn about the sidewalks and street and homeless people were sleeping in doorways. On one street corner, three mean-looking Hispanic guys with tattoos were hanging out, smoking joints. When Arturo stopped the car in front of the building, Floyd said, "This is shit, I don't like it. I'm not gettin' out."

"Don't you want your money?"

"Sure, I want my money, but this is shit. I'll get out but give me the gun."

"Fuck you," said Arturo. "Get the fuck out of the car, or do you want to walk the two blocks?"

Floyd opened the car door, and gingerly edged off the seat. He took a couple of minutes to get out of the car.

Arturo took about twenty minutes to locate the parking lot, park, and walk back to the boarded-up building. As he arrived, everything looked the same, except that Floyd was huddled along the side of the building opposite from the three guys at the street corner. The three guys were still there, still smoking, still looking mean; and the homeless people were still sleeping in the doorways. Arturo said, "Come on motherfucker, let's see how to get into the building." The building looked like no one had been inside for twenty years. The two of them moved toward what looked like the front door, but it was boarded up tight. Arturo had just said, "I have a bad feeling about this," when a black Mercedes-Benz pulled up behind them. They both turned around as two large white guys with baseball caps pulled low over their faces got out of the back seat of the Mercedes and approached them. Arturo began to ask a question of the two men, "Do you have our mo...." He never finished the question. White guy number one quickly put two bullets into Arturo, one into his head and the other into his chest, and white guy number two did exactly the same to Floyd. Then they switched, with white guy number two putting two bullets into Arturo's head and chest, and white guy number one doing the same to Floyd.

The two men quickly got back into the back seat of the Mercedes. As the car drove off, the homeless people were still asleep in the doorways, and the three Hispanic guys were still at the street corner, smoking joints and looking mean.

CHAPTER 19

Bob and Mountain Mongo

A couple of days after my less-than-productive conversation with the Pineland D. A., I was sitting at the kitchen table in my little rental house, looking over the plans for the new house that Bebe and I would be moving into, hopefully soon. Bebe was comfortably snoozing on the carpet next to my feet, when we heard a knock on the front door. Bebe popped her head up, alert, but made no noise.

We both went to the front door. Bebe was still strangely silent. Normally when someone is at our front door, she makes some noise, usually a restrained bark, enough to let me know that she is performing her watchdog job, but in a mature and thoughtful manner. When I opened the door and saw what, or who, was towering on the porch, I almost jumped out of my skin. Bebe should have gone berserk but didn't. She went up to the creature, tail wagging. He looked more like Bigfoot than a human. Two things struck me simultaneously: his size, possibly seven feet tall, and the odor emanating from his body. My brain slowly processed what I saw standing on our porch. It was Christopher Ray, known to most people as "Mountain Mongo," or, simply, "Mongo."

"Mongo, what are you doing here?"

"Judge," he said. "I've got intel for ya." The word "intel" seemed incongruous coming from this creature, but it was apparent he liked using it. Bebe went up to him, and he reached down and patted her on the head. Best of friends.

"Mongo!" I said loudly, and repeated, "What are you doing here? Are you okay?"

"Doing just fine," he said. "The new Forest Supervisor ain't a fuckin' asshole. She minds her own business and lets me mind mine. It's been at least two god-damn years since I been busted."

Mountain Mongo was a legendary inhabitant of the Klamath National Forest. A true mountain man, Mongo occupied (when he wasn't in jail) a small, dilapidated mining cabin deep in the woods within the National Forest boundary. The cabin had no utilities or running water and was of no use to anyone except to Mongo. But, according to Forest Service regulations it was protected, and Mongo was a trespasser. From the viewpoint of Forest Service law enforcement personnel, he was a criminal. His trespasser status was made all the more egregious by the fact that he cultivated and consumed marijuana. Like the man himself, the quantity of marijuana he could consume was also legendary. Eye witnesses claimed that he just ate marijuana, no processing required. It had been reported that he consumed other controlled substances, but he had never been arrested or charged with that.

With two exceptions, all of my contact with Mongo had been in the courtroom, when he was a criminal defendant charged with various crimes relating to his unlawful occupation of the cabin and his unlawful possession, use, and cultivation of marijuana. Most of the crimes were misdemeanors, but there were some felonies as well. To my knowledge he never committed a crime of violence or resist arrest, no matter how under the influence he was. He was despised by the Forest Service law enforcement personnel, and I could understand why, sort of. He was a thorn in their sides, and he was, after all, violating the law. But I had a soft spot for him. *Why can't everyone just get along?* I wondered. *He never hurts anyone, and never bothers anybody. Why can't he just be left alone?* When he was in court, he always refused appointment of a public defender, choosing to represent himself. He negotiated his own dispositions, pleading guilty to charges that were irrefutably true. He never asked for a jury trial. I sentenced him numerous times to county jail time. And once to state prison. With a heavy heart I ordered the prison commitment, but it was for a probation violation, and I felt I had no choice.

In today's world in California, state prison would not be an option for Mongo. The state's laws have changed significantly, and generally you don't go to state prison, unless you commit a crime of violence or a sex crime. You go to county jail, if you go anywhere. A few years ago, the U.S. Supreme Court determined that the California state prison system violated the Eighth Amendment's prohibition against cruel and unusual punishment. The court described a litany of horrible conditions, foremost of which was that the prisons were operating near 200% of design capacity. The court ordered the California Department of Corrections and Rehabilitation (CDCR) to reduce the state prison population to 137.5% of the designed prison capacity within two years. This required CDCR to release 40,000 inmates from its prison population of 150,000. The California State Legislature and Governor Jerry Brown "solved" the prison overcrowding problem by passing the "2011 Public Safety Realignment Initiative" (AB 109). AB 109 significantly changed the sentencing and supervision of persons convicted of felony offenses. It changed the place where people convicted of certain crimes were to serve their terms from the state prison system to the local county jails. The legislation shifted hundreds of crimes, mostly low-level felony offences, from state prison commitments to county jail sentences. This was a win-win for the State of California because state prisons and prisoners are an expense to the state. But the county jails and the prisoners they house are mostly paid for by the counties, not the state. Thus, the state government was relieved of the expense of housing 40,000 inmates, who became the financial responsibility of the counties, who were already broke. This freed up the state government to do other important stuff, like continuing to let its highways rot away, and passing environmental regulations making it impossible to accomplish anything worthwhile.

Also, recreational use of marijuana is now legal.

My two previous interactions with Mongo when he wasn't a criminal defendant in my court were interesting and amusing.

One of them was a criminal proceeding for theft. Mongo wasn't the defendant. He was the primary prosecution witness, doing his civic duty! About once a month Mongo would drive his old wreck of a truck into town to pick up his social security check, buy groceries, find someplace where he could take a shower, and do his laundry. While in the coin-operated laundromat, he witnessed a guy breaking into the change machine, attempting to steal the money inside. He tackled the guy, making a citizen's arrest of sorts, and asked a bystander to call the cops. It turned out that the theft from coin-op change machines throughout the county had become a significant problem, and this guy had committed thefts over time that amounted to thousands of dollars. Mongo not only caught the guy, but again doing his civic duty, showed up in court to testify against him.

My other interaction with Mongo occurred in the county jail. I had gone to the jail to sign some paperwork. There is a day-room inside the jail, where prisoners are occasionally permitted to lounge, giving them a chance to get out of their cells and relax. The interior of the jail, including the day-room, is continually monitored by closed circuit video cameras, and watched by a deputy seated in front of a bank of screens. Inside the jail, I was escorted to a small room with a desk and chair, which was connected to the day-room. The jail staff had apparently forgotten that they had permitted Mongo to be at-large in the day-room. Mongo saw me and headed in my direction. I looked up and saw him coming but had nowhere to go, so I just sat there, but there was definitely an adrenaline rush. The deputy monitoring the bank of video screens saw it too, and two deputies showed up to rescue me, but not before Mongo was actually in the room with me. He never threatened me or touched me. He only wanted to talk. He was actually crying, and probably was coming down off of a high. Before he was escorted away by the two deputies, he let me know how sorry he was to have to be in my courtroom so much, and how he wished that the Forest Service officers would just leave him alone, he never meant to hurt anyone.

I invited Mongo into my small living room and asked him to have a seat. When he sat down on a kitchen chair, he looked like he was sitting in a child's chair. I was afraid it would collapse under him. "Do you have some information?" I asked.

"I sure do. I move around the National Forest a lot, and know every god-damn inch of it."

"I'm sure you do."

"I usually don't get close to the fuckin' National Forest boundary, but some guys I know told me about some weird shit going on in that mansion owned by the grandson of that western movie guy. So, I made it my mission to go and gather intel."

He obviously likes to say, "gather intel," I thought.

"His property is at the edge of the valley, right up against federal land, which is pretty fuckin' steep right there. There is an overlook where you can look down and see his whole god-damn operation, in fact, the whole valley. So, I'd go there doin' recon."

I thought, *he likes using the word "recon."*

"I've been doin' recon there for several god-damn weeks. Not all the time, but I'd get over there whenever I had time."

He's a busy guy.

Mongo continued, "I've seen two things that might be of interest to law enforcement, but the asshole cops in town don't like me. That's why I came to you.

"First day I started my recon operation, I seen a helicopter land. There's a helicopter pad on the property, you know. The helicopter pad is pretty close to the house. If I could afford a house like that, I wouldn't want it so god-damn close, but now I think I know why they want it that way. There is a covered walkway from the house to the pad, so I couldn't see under the walkway roof, but the roof stops at the edge of the pad, so you can see guys gettin' in and out of the damn chopper, just for a short time. They was offloading some kind of boxes from the helicopter. Big boxes. It took four guys to carry each box.

"I didn't think much about that, the first day. Maybe the motherfuckers was bringin' in furniture and shit for the house, which is fuckin' huge. The whole deal with the helicopter pad and covered walkway was weird, but shit, they probably commute back and forth from Hollywood or wherever. They'd want the house to be comfortable. I guess they're rich enough to do whatever the fuck they want.

"So, I kept goin' up there, see? I was fuckin' curious. A few days later I stayed all day. The helicopter came again. Same thing, big fuckin' boxes unloaded. Later a truck came to the helipad and backed up to the covered walkway. The driveway that goes around to the back of the house connects to the helicopter pad. I couldn't see what they was doin' very well, because the truck backed up underneath the walkway roof. But I'm pretty damn sure they was loadin' boxes into the truck from the house, smaller boxes. I think they was usin' dollies. You know, the kind you would move a god-damn refrigerator with."

"What kind of a truck was it?" I asked.

"Just a regular truck. I don't know what kind. Looked fairly new. Not real big. Not a semi-truck or nuthin' like that. A single unit, like one of them brown delivery trucks."

"You mean, like a UPS truck? Could you get a license plate number?"

He said, "Yeah, like a damn UPS truck, but it wasn't a UPS truck. It was white. Maybe not as big. I couldn't get a license number. It's too friggin' far. Maybe with binoculars. It's pretty far from where I was watchin'.

"I saw this happen several times. I think maybe the chopper twice a week and the truck twice a week.

"That's all fuckin' weird, but last night I saw somethin' really fucked up. It was getting dark, so, hard to see, but I'm fuckin' positive I saw a female."

"A female?" I asked.

"Damn right," he said. "A female. A lady. She was, like, shackled. Like an inmate. I know all about that shit, thanks to you, asshole. So dark it was hard to see, but I'm god-damn sure. She had cuffs on her wrists in front of her belly, and her ankles was shackled. Two guys kind of pushed her off the chopper, and then to the walkway. She looked like she was hurtin'. She was havin' trouble walkin'."

"Can you describe her?"

"No. Too friggin' dark," he said. "But she looked kinda small. If the two dudes was normal size, say six feet, she was almost a foot shorter."

"Did you recognize any of them? Or is there anything about any of them that stood out?"

"No. Like I say, it was pretty damn dark. They was normal lookin' people, not fat or skinny. The female had a limp, couldn't walk worth shit. She may have been blindfolded; I couldn't tell for sure. I think the two dudes was brown, like Mexican, but I'm not sure about that either."

I asked, "What time did you see this?"

"Around eight o'clock. The helicopter took off right away after they got off."

"Do you know a lady named Hailey Madison? Lives in Yreka."

"Fuck, no," he said. "I don't know nobody in Yreka, 'cept you and some asshole forest rangers. I know some of the jail deputies. Actually, they treated me pretty fuckin' good, considerin'. The food in the jail was pretty good, better'n what I usually eat, 'cept maybe for the weed. I don't think I could recognize them if I saw 'em again."

"Would you be willing to sign a sworn statement? And, if necessary, testify in court?" I asked.

"Fuck yes! It's my civic duty. And those two dudes looked like they liked pushin' the lady around. They was fuckin' enjoyin' it. Anyone who pushes a lady around is a fuckin' scumbag asshole in my book. I should have gone down there last night and kicked their asses, but I didn't think I could get inside. The place looks like a god-damn fortress."

I asked, "How can I get in touch with you. Do you have a cell phone?"

"Me? A cell phone?" he laughed. "What would I do with a fuckin' cell phone? Besides, most places where I hang out ain't got service."

"How can I get in touch with you?"

"Just go to the Salmon/Scott River Ranger Station. They'll know where to find me. I'm sorry about what I said about asshole forest rangers. I'm gettin' along pretty fuckin' good with them guys right now. They finally understand we can help each other. I'm even gettin' along now with the fuckin' game wardens. I've helped those dudes track down poachers. Just ask at the Ranger Station. They can find me."

He got up out of his tiny chair. He'd talked about as much as he was capable of in any given day, and started for the door. Bebe had been lying down comfortably on the carpet during my conversation with Mongo, but was awake and seemed to pay attention. She got up and went over to him. He reached down on his way out and gave her a pat on the head.

After Mongo was gone, I asked Bebe, "What do you think?"

"I think that big house is an evil place. I think Hailey is in there and we've got to get her out."

I agreed.

CHAPTER 20

Bob and Sheriff Brad Davis

After Mongo left my house, I immediately walked over to the Sheriff's Office, without calling ahead. I walked into the reception area, and this time there was a different lady behind the bullet-proof glass. She didn't recognize me, and I didn't recognize her either. "Can I help you?" she asked.

"Is Sheriff Davis in? I need to talk to him."

"Is he expecting you?"

"No, he isn't. I didn't call ahead."

"Can I get your name, and can you tell me what it's about?"

Although being retired is great, there is a downside. As the years pass, you slowly drift out of the loop. The people you knew and worked with before gradually disappear by attrition. They retire or move on, and you deal with people who haven't a clue. I gave her my name and said, "Tell him it's about Mongo."

"About what?"

"Just tell him," I said. "He'll know."

When I finally reached his office, he stood up at his desk and said, "Surprisingly, nothing catastrophic happened last time you came to see me. I thought I was on a roll, but here you are again. Now I'm getting scared!"

"Maybe with good reason," I said. Then I told him what Mongo told me, in full detail, which took a while. He asked me questions as I gave my narrative. Finally, I asked, "Can you search the house?"

"I don't know if I can get the D.A. to ask the court for a warrant. The probable cause is pretty skinny."

"You've got an eye-witness who saw a shackled female being forced into the house. That seems pretty compelling to me. That coupled with the fact that Hailey Madison is missing, and you know what happened to her before at that same house. And what the sister, Melinda, said to her at the time. Something like, 'You'll regret it for the rest of your life, however short that might be.'"

"Here's the problem," he said. "Actually, several problems.

"First, the incident with Hailey Madison at that house was two years ago. If they, or maybe just Melinda, really wanted to do something bad, surely it would have been done by now. And Hailey didn't file a complaint about the incident. There was never a police report. And in any event, they've already arrested someone for Hailey's murder.

"Second, I hate to say this, but Mountain Mongo isn't exactly the most credible witness. You and I both know his criminal background. He's a convicted felon. And even if you don't consider his background, his story is sketchy. It was dark. What he saw was from a distance, and only a quick glimpse, just the time it took for them to get from the chopper to the covered walk.

"I told you before, two years ago, I didn't like Ryder, and I like him even less now. He and his unlimited wealth are taking over the county, and it scares me. I would like nothing more than to get a warrant and search his place, but I don't think it's in the cards."

"What about you and your deputies searching the house without a warrant? Exigent circumstances?"

"No way!" he said, with rising angst. "It's just too damn risky. If we go in there based on Mongo's story, and don't find anything, the shit will hit the fan big time. Ryder has become too prominent in the community. Hell, he seems to own just about everybody who has influence. And if we don't find anything, he's sure to sue us. Neither I nor my department would survive."

"Okay, I get it," I said, "at least for now. But if Hailey really is in there, what's she going through? What's happening to her?

"Let me ask you this," I continued, changing the subject slightly. "Taking Mongo's story at face value about the packages being delivered to and from the house, what do you make of that? Big packages going in, smaller packages going out."

"Beats the shit out of me. But here's a theory. Cocaine. We have experienced a rise in cocaine usage and sales the last few years. Marijuana has always been prevalent here, of course. Hell, it grows great here. Some say better than the Emerald Triangle counties. The hard drug of choice has always been meth. It's easy to cook, and cheap, and there are plenty of great hidden places here in the county to set up a lab. But cocaine has never taken hold here, until recently. It's always been too expensive. It's processed in the countries where the coca plants grow: Bolivia, Peru, and Columbia. Then shipped to the US, where it is then distributed by a network of players, who usually cut it along the way. Because we are a poverty-level county, and because coke is usually expensive, the distributors didn't find it worthwhile to conduct operations here. But that seems to be changing. Maybe the distributors found an untapped market."

"Do you really think Ryder might be involved in a cocaine distribution system?" I was incredulous. "Do you have evidence?"

"It's crossed my mind for some time," he said. "But no, I don't have any evidence."

"Well, there's always Mongo," I said, as I was getting up to leave.

He laughed, but without conviction. "I'm worried about it, and tracking it, and will do the same about the possibility the Madison girl is there at that house. But it's premature to do a search at this time. I think it would be a big mistake. We're just not there yet."

As I was walking back to my house, I thought, *Maybe Bebe's right. That big house is an evil place. Hailey's in there and we've got to get her out. Maybe Bebe can sense things that humans can't.*

CHAPTER 21

Bob, David, and Lillian

I invited David and Lillian Thompson to come over to my house for dinner that evening, to see how they were doing. We have a great meat market in town, and I splurged and picked up some beef tenderloins. I went to Raley's and bought greens for a Caesar salad and some vanilla bean gelato for dessert.

Even though it had only been a few days since Ben was arrested, they both looked like they had aged five years. They were haggard and unkempt, and had a downtrodden appearance, much worse than when I had been at their house. These were not the people I had known for many years. The Thompsons I knew were always suntanned, physically fit, and well-dressed. Both were active in our community's social scene and government. David had been on the City Council, serving two terms as mayor, and then served a term on the county Board of Supervisors. Lillian was on governing boards of several major organizations in our community, including the hospital and the YMCA. Both had become reclusive since Ben was arrested.

I didn't try to make our dinner party upbeat. The situation didn't call for it. My main objective was to let them know that I and others were supportive, and that we didn't believe Ben had done what he was accused of.

The food turned out great, if I say so myself. The filets were grilled perfectly, each topped with a dollop of my specialty blue-cheese-butter-and-thyme sauce. The Caesar salad was from a recipe I have used for forty-five years. The original recipe called for adding a raw egg with the final toss of the salad, but the raw egg ingredient was abandoned years ago due to salmonella fears. The result was still excellent, but maybe a percentage point less so.

The conversation drifted to Rex Randall Ryder The Third and his compound in the Scott Valley. As the conversation developed, I realized that the Thompsons might not know about Hailey Madison's encounter with Ryder and the mysterious Melinda a couple of years before. When Hailey originally talked about it, I told her I would maintain the conversation's confidentiality, and had done so. Even so, there are no secrets in our small community, and rumors spread like wildfire. Hailey's incident was the sort of story that usually makes the rounds in a big way, but for some reason hers didn't. Hailey probably didn't tell anyone, and Rex Randall Ryder The Third, as boisterous as he is, probably wasn't likely to share. Apparently, Ben hadn't told his parents, because they were unaware of it when I told them the story.

The subject of Rex Randall Ryder The Third got their attention, and they became more animated than I had seen them since before Ben's arrest. They weren't fans. "Ryder's an asshole," said David, bluntly. "Everyone around here treats him like God, and I'm not sure why. He's an asshole. I guess I do know why people treat him like they do. He either buys them or bullies them. Apparently, his wealth is unlimited, so he can buy or do whatever the hell he wants. I got crosswise with him when I was on the Board of Supervisors. When he was building his castle-fortress he needed permits from the county. Most of what he wanted to do wasn't controversial and was handled by the planning commission. But there were a couple of applications that were denied by the planning commission, which he appealed to the Board. The one that got the most attention was his request to approve water wells he intended to drill on his property. It seemed like he wanted to suck up practically all the water in all the aquafers in the valley. This didn't set well with some of the neighboring owners of agricultural property, who challenged the application. It turned out to be contested, and there were several public hearings, with the Board chamber jammed with angry people. Surface waters, including streams, rivers, and lakes, have been highly regulated for a hundred years. But regulation of water wells is something new in California. It used to be that the only limit on where or how deep you could drill your well was based on what you could afford. You had to get a permit from the county, but it was pretty much rubber-stamped. But now the county is required to scrutinize well drilling permit applications much more vigorously. This is partially because of a law passed by the California Legislature requiring groundwater to be managed more aggressively. You have to watch out for things like groundwater-level declines, water quality degradation, land subsidence, surface water depletions, and seawater intrusions; that sort of stuff, although seawater intrusion isn't something we worry too much about here. The law is called SGMA. The Sustainable Groundwater Management Act, or something like that.

"This can be frustrating and expensive for some poor soul not in the city limits who simply wants to drill a well for his home and garden, but I guess it makes sense. Water underground probably shouldn't be treated any differently than water above ground. It's just a little harder to figure out where it is. And water is scarce. You know how it is out here in the country. Next to sex, the most common motive for murder is water."

"What happened with his application?" I asked.

"There were several hearings, with people hanging from the rafters in the Board chamber. Finally, it came to a vote. It was four-to-one for approval, and I was the only dissenting vote. I was surprised at the time, and am still surprised, that my former colleagues on the Board voted to approve the application. In private discussions with them, I know that all four were opposed, at least philosophically. I still wonder why they voted as they did. I worry that somehow Ryder got to them.

"The bottom line is that he won a four-to-one vote. Ryder has never spoken to me since. I suspect, but have no way of proving, that he sent me messages indicating that he didn't like my vote. For example, do you remember our dog Lucy?"

"Yeah, I do." I said. "I noticed she hasn't been around for quite a while. One time I considered asking you about Lucy, but I was reluctant to do so. Since then, I just forgot to mention it."

"Well, she just mysteriously died. I believe she was poisoned, but there was no evidence. Everybody loved Lucy. Her loss was devastating to the family."

"She was a great dog," I said. "Bebe liked her too, but sometimes complained that she was just 'too nice.'"

"But that wasn't the only thing that happened," he continued. "We had just bought a brand-new SUV, a silver-colored Subaru. It was parked in my office parking lot when someone spray-painted it in broad daylight. Again, there were no clues as to the perpetrator, and it was done in the middle of the day! I have always linked these events to Ryder. But, of course, I have no way to prove it. I don't scare very easily, but Ryder scares me. Being in public life, you are called upon to vote on issues that make people unhappy. It's sometimes hard, but it comes with the territory. I've made a few people mad over the years, but usually they get over it. There are a few people that won't talk to me anymore. But I've never been actually threatened or had anyone kill my dog or vandalize my car. Like I said, Ryder scares me. I think he's a sociopath."

"He scares me too," I said. I thought about telling David and Lillian about what I learned from Mongo but decided against it. The fewer people that knew about it, the better. Although I was sure Mongo could take care of himself, his safety was a concern. But, more than that, I considered the wisdom of putting out on the street the information that Mongo had given me and ruled it out. It might be better, at least for now, for Rex Ryder and Melinda not to know they were under observation.

After the Thompsons left, I sat down in my Lazy Boy recliner, with Bebe sprawled on the carpet next to me. I sorted out my thoughts and jotted notes in my diary. It wasn't actually a diary, but a spiral steno pad, a habit I got into after I retired. When I get up every morning, the first thing I do is weigh myself. Then I get dressed, pour a cup of coffee, sit down in the lazy boy, and jot notes on the steno pad. I enter the current date and my weight, and then outline my goals for the day. Then, throughout the day I enter whatever thoughts come to mind, including events that have occurred. Thus, the steno pad is like a diary. I have now accumulated probably twenty-five, which I store in chronological order. Sometimes they come in handy when I want to refresh my recollection of what I did or who I talked to at some particular time.

The main point I took away from my meeting with the Thompsons was that David Thompson was on Ryder's shit list, something that I didn't know before. It added to whatever motives Ryder might have to harm Hailey Madison. If Ryder harmed Hailey Madison, he also harmed Ben, and therefore, Ben's father. I mentioned this observation to Bebe, and she agreed. She said, "Ryder is an evil person. I can sense it."

CHAPTER 22

Rex Randall Ryder The Third and Melinda

It was about 9:30 in the evening, and the big house was quiet. Rex Randall Ryder The Third and Melinda were sitting on the couch in the great room and had turned on the giant Samsung Q900 Series 98-inch 4320p television which Rex had purchased for the bargain price of $59,999.99. They had finished an excellent dinner that Rex had prepared: fresh crab flown in from the coast that day. For most of the day, the house had been bustling, a busy place. There were domestic servants whose duties were to keep the house immaculate. This was no easy task, given the house's size, and its huge collection of furnishings, paintings, sculptures, and *objets d'art*. Then there had been the comings-and-goings of business associates and ranch hands. There had been three shipments that day, two incoming, via helicopter, and one outgoing, via delivery truck. This involved many people, including the laborers unloading, unpacking, processing, repackaging, and reloading the product. There were the auditors and bookkeepers meticulously monitoring its quantity and quality. And then the bodyguards. As to the ranch side of the business, there was the day-to-day business of a working cattle operation. Rex often thought, *Siskiyou County is lucky to have us here, because of how many people we employ.* He conveniently overlooked the fact that, due to the sensitive nature of their operation, almost none of the employees were local.

But now there was no one else in the house. At least no one that could have been observed by a casual visitor. The house was quiet.

"Shall we check to see how your project is coming along." Asked Rex. "How long has it been now? A week?"

Melinda said, "It's been exactly one-hundred-and-sixty-two hours since she arrived. Let's see how she's doing."

"You're keeping track of every hour? You must be excited," said Rex Randall Ryder The Third, with a sly grin on his face.

Melinda fiddled with the TV remote until the huge screen showed a video image of what appeared to be a bedroom. The room looked dark, but the image was enhanced by the camera's technical capabilities. A blonde-haired woman could be seen sitting on the bed with her feet dangling over one side. She was naked. She had a collar around her neck. It was attached to a chain which came down from above. Also, it looked like her wrists were bound behind her. She was obviously crying, and speaking, although what she was saying could not be understood. It was more of a low moaning sound. She stood up, took a few steps toward the right of the screen, turned around, and sat down again on the bed. She repeated that activity one more time and then screamed. Her mostly unintelligible screams were interspersed with repeated pleas of, "why are you doing this to me?" She stood up again, took a few more steps toward the right of the screen until she was out of the picture. Although not visible, her screams and pleas continued to be heard, along with the distinguishable words, "Oh God! Somebody please help me!" She reemerged from the right of the screen and climbed back onto the bed with some difficulty due to her wrists being restricted behind her back. The chain from above connected to her neck collar had sufficient slack to allow her mobility within the room.

Melinda pressed the TV remote several times, allowing the room to be viewed sequentially from several angles. There were four video cameras in all that together showed the entire room. The room was sparse, like a prison cell, although the bed looked a little more comfortable than a typical prison bunk. There was a stainless-steel toilet and a washbasin, both attached to a wall. The single door was constructed of metal bars. There was an opening along the bottom which would allow a tray of food to be passed into the room. And there was a tray on the floor in front of the opening containing a plate with half-eaten food and a bowl partially filled with a liquid.

Melinda cycled through the camera angles for about 20 minutes, observing the woman in several stages of distress. As she did so, Melinda scooted her body until it was in close contact with Rex. While operating the TV remote with her left hand, she placed her right hand on his knee, gradually moving it along his inner thigh toward his crotch.

"What do you think, Melinda?" asked Rex. "Is she ready?"

"Pretty close, dear big brother," replied Melinda. "Tomorrow, I'll go down below and get to know her better. Life is good." After saying that, Melinda got off the couch and onto her knees in front of her "dear big brother," and worked on the fly of the cargo shorts Rex was wearing.

Rex put his head back and said softly, "Life is good, indeed."

CHAPTER 23

Bob and Brenda

The morning after I had the Thompsons over, my phone played the familiar Bob Seger song, followed by a mechanical voice that said "Brenda." While reaching for the phone, in my excitement I almost dropped it. During the last year or so, except for the every-other-Thursday text messages that ended with "Love, Brenda," or "Love, B," we communicated little. Things had died down substantially after the Cougar Creek fiasco four years before, and there wasn't a lot of reason to communicate. Most of our conversations were initiated by me. A few times a year I visited my son in Atlanta, and I would usually combine those with a side trip to Washington, D.C., and have lunch with Brenda. I would call her to see if she could meet me. A call *from* her was unusual.

"Hey, what's up?"

"Are you going to be around the next few days?" she asked.

"I plan to."

"Would you mind if I come out? I've wanted to come back to Siskiyou County, do some hiking, maybe see some of the places where you and I were four years ago, but under more relaxed circumstances. A big project I was working on came to an abrupt end, and I've got some time. I thought fall might be a good time. I checked the forecast, and it looks like you are going to have good weather for the next couple of weeks."

"I'd love it if you came out," I said. "But I don't know how relaxed it will be. You remember Ben Thompson, the guy we had lunch with in Sacramento? He's now in custody, and there is some strange stuff going on. I don't want to talk about it on the phone."

"Maybe I can help you with it," she said.

"The last time you tried to do that, you ended up in hospitals for months. I don't want that to happen again. But I'd love to see you. So would Bebe."

"Can I come tomorrow? I've looked at flights. I can do a red-eye and get to Medford tomorrow morning at 9:10 AM. Is that too soon?"

"I'll pick you up," I said, with enthusiasm.

"Okay. Looking forward to it. I'll see you then. I'll email you my flight information."

Wow! I thought. *It will be great to see her.* But I was worried about her timing. What Mongo told me about the woman he saw at Ryder's helipad had been constantly on my mind. I understood the sheriff's reluctance to apply for a search warrant based upon Mongo's statement, but I believed Mongo was telling the truth, and believed that Hailey Madison was in that house, a captive. Why was she there? And what was happening to her? Mongo didn't think she was there voluntarily. David Thompson said he thought Ryder was a sociopath. I would agree, but I would use the term psychopath instead of sociopath. I'm not a psychologist or psychiatrist, but I think there are subtle differences between the two terms. According to *The Fifth Edition of the Diagnostic and Statistical Manual of Mental Disorders* (DSM-5), both share the same diagnosis – antisocial personality disorder. Traits indicating such a diagnosis include regularly breaking or flouting the law, constantly lying and deceiving others, having little regard for the safety of others, and not feeling remorse or guilt. But psychology researchers believe that psychopaths are "born" – likely a genetic predisposition – while sociopaths tend to be "made" by their environment. Based on Hailey's story, both Ryder and his sister Melinda, if she really was his sister, could be psychopaths. Psychopaths are usually deemed more dangerous than sociopaths because they show no remorse for their actions due to their lack of empathy.

Brenda showed herself to be a very brave and resourceful woman four years before during the Cougar Creek incident, and could be of great help in rescuing Hailey Madison, if Hailey was in that house. But the Cougar Creek incident left Brenda with physical and emotional scars she will probably never recover from, and it was my fault she became involved. Much as I hated to do it, I would set the Hailey Madison matter aside for now, and make sure Brenda stayed out of it.

The next morning, I took Bebe with me to the Medford airport, about an hour drive. We waited at the cell phone parking area until I received a text message that Brenda had landed and collected her suitcase. When I arrived at the terminal area, Bebe saw Brenda through the window, clambered over me, and jumped out when I opened the driver side door. I'm not sure which one was more excited when they came together. After they finished their greeting, I got a nice kiss from Brenda, but less exuberant than the interaction between dog and human.

On the way to Yreka, we stopped at Callahan's Mountain Lodge and Restaurant for breakfast. Bebe knew she couldn't go in, and said it would be okay if she stayed in the car if we rolled the windows down. Callahan's is located just below the Pacific Crest Trail, the Mount Ashland Ski Resort, and the summit of the Siskiyou Mountains, the highest point on Interstate 5.

At Callahan's, over a good breakfast, we caught up on each other's goings-on, although our recent lunch at Frank Fat's with Ben Thompson wasn't that long ago. I filled her in on my bizarre meeting with James H. Murphy, the Pineland district attorney. I had intended to steer clear of the Ben Thompson/Hailey Madison topic, and kept trying to move the conversation in other directions but Brenda was interested and kept pressing. She should have been a police interrogator, because she extracted from me all the information I had. I even described my conversation with Mongo, something I promised myself I wouldn't talk about. Then she said, "I came here because I wanted to do some hiking in your mountains. Can we hike up there to where Mongo was, and look down onto Ryder's mansion?"

"I guess. I might have to do some research to find the trail, and I have no idea how difficult it is."

"Could we get Mongo to be our guide? He sounds like someone I'd like to meet."

"Look. I've already told you too much. The last thing I wanted to do was to get you hooked up with this thing."

"Oh, come on," she said. "What's the harm? I came here to hike. It'll feel good to get out. Just taking a look can't do any harm. And I'm really curious to see this mansion you're talking about. And curious about Mongo."

I pulled my cell phone out of my pocket and googled the Salmon/Scott River Ranger District Office. I clicked on the phone number link and got a dial tone. A male voice answered, "Salmon/Scott River District, this is Jackson."

"Uh, hello Jackson." I gave him my name, and said, "This may sound like a strange request, but can you tell me how I can get hold of Christopher Ray?"

"Who?" he asked.

"Christopher Ray. Um, Mountain Mongo."

"Oh, Mongo," he said. "Why didn't you say that before? Are you the judge?"

"Well, uh, yes. Retired."

"Mongo said you might want to talk to him. I don't know where he is right now, but one of us here can usually track him down."

"Is he staying out of trouble?" I asked.

"Yes. He's been a good boy. Can we give him a message?"

"I'd just like to be able to meet and talk to him, as soon as possible."

"Okay. Probably the best place for you to meet would be right here at the District Office. Do you know where we are? And how long it will take you to get here?"

"I know where it is. I'm at Callahan's Restaurant right now. Siskiyou summit. So, it'll take a while to get there. I'm headed toward Yreka."

"Okay. It'll take us a while to find him. Give me your cell number. Soon as we make contact, we can give you a time and place to meet him."

"Okay. Great. Thanks," I said, and gave him my cell number.

We pulled up to the California Agricultural Inspection Station around twelve-thirty, which meant we were about fifteen minutes from town. I asked

Brenda where she wanted to stay. "We can get you a room at the Miner's Inn, or you can stay at my place, your choice," I said.

"Your place, if it's okay," she said. I could sense Bebe in the back seat wagging her tail enthusiastically.

Just as we pulled up in front of my little house, my iPhone did it's Bob Seger *Old Time Rock and Roll* thing, and I answered. The voice in the phone said, "This is Jackson, Salmon/Scott River District. We got in touch with Mongo. He can meet you this afternoon at three, here at the office. Can you do that?"

"Sure, we'll be there. Thanks."

I retrieved Brenda's suitcase from the pickup, and wheeled it into my spare bedroom. "I'm going to take a nap," I said. "You know how it is with us septuagenarians. Make yourself at home. We should probably leave here around two-thirty to meet Mongo at three."

CHAPTER 24

Bob, Brenda, and Mongo

We arrived at the District Office on time. The Salmon/Scott River Ranger District covers approximately 585,000 acres and has three wilderness areas within its boundaries: The Trinity Alps, and the Russian and Marble Mountain Wilderness Areas. The country is beautiful, mountainous, and rural. The District Office is in Fort Jones, a community of seven-hundred people, about twenty miles from Yreka. Jackson, who introduced himself as George Jackson, said, "Mongo's in the conference room," and led us there.

"Hey Mongo," I said. "Thanks for meeting us." He was as big and smelly as ever. He looked curiously at Brenda, then looked at me. "This is Brenda LeHane, a real good friend of mine. She's here from Washington, D. C. She likes to hike in the mountains and wants to go where we can look down at Rex Ryder's place."

Mongo looked back at Brenda, and said, "Pleased to meetcha, ma'am. Are you with the FBI?"

Brenda gave him a warm smile, and said, "No way. I'm just a tourist." She didn't say she worked for the Department of the Interior, probably thinking that might be worse than the FBI, in Mongo's mind.

"An' you wanna see the mansion?" he asked.

"Yes, I'm curious. And I would like to see it from a place where the people that live there can't see us. From government land. Can you be our guide and show us the trail?" she asked sweetly.

"Sure can," he replied. "But there ain't no trail to the place to see the mansion. Ya gotta sidehill. The best place to start is from the Viking trailhead. Follow the trail for about three miles, then cross-country a couple miles more. Up and down a couple of ridges to get there. And cross one stream. Still flowin' but not much water, at least in the morning."

"Hey, remember, I'm really old," I said. "How long does it take to make the hike? And how difficult is it?"

"Couple hours for me," said Mongo. "Not as long comin' back. For you, maybe add an hour each way. You can make it."

Brenda asked, "Can you take us tomorrow morning?" I swear she batted her eyelashes.

Mongo's face lit up. "Sure can, ma'am. What time do you want to start?"

"As early as possible. Where's the best place to meet?" Brenda asked.

"Meamber Schoolhouse," said Mongo. "How 'bout seven o'clock?"

Out in the parking lot, as the three of us were standing beside my pickup, Brenda said, "I'm really happy to meet you Mr. Mongo, and looking forward to tomorrow's hike."

Mongo practically danced his way to his old, thrashed pickup.

On the way back to Yreka, Brenda asked, "Do you know where the Meamber Schoolhouse is?"

"Yep. From where we just came from, it's up the Scott River Road about seven miles or so, where it meets the Quartz Valley Road. It's an old schoolhouse building. Goes back, I think, to around 1870. Children first to eighth grades went there till around 1957. I think it might now be a private residence. I don't know where the Viking trailhead is, though. I guess we'll just have to let Mongo guide us. I think you've got a new fan."

"An interesting specimen," she said. "I like him. He's definitely different."

"Is that why you like me? One thing for sure, he's on his best behavior. You got his attention. He didn't utter a single swear word in your presence. Probably the first time in his life."

When we got back to my little house, I opened a bottle of red wine and poured some into glasses. We sat on the couch in my living room. I said, "I have a couple of day-packs. We should take something for lunch tomorrow, and some water bottles. Do you have hiking boots?"

"Of course. I came here to hike."

"Of course you did. How about a take-and-bake pizza tonight? I'll go pick one up, and get some sandwich stuff for tomorrow."

Brenda and I enjoyed our pizza on the couch, with Bebe relaxed on the carpet. We all crashed early. Normal procedure for me, the septuagenarian. Brenda was still operating on Eastern time, and Bebe could sleep anytime. But before I went to bed I assembled and prepared some things for the next morning's hike. I took individual bags of potato chips from the cupboard, and made sandwiches, which I left in the refrigerator. Then I rummaged through my large gun safe. I have collected guns for over fifty years, beginning when I was in the Air Force during the Vietnam War. My collection has the gamut: rifles, shotguns, revolvers, and semi-automatic pistols, some antique, some modern. It also includes scopes, holsters, loaders, and some gunsmithing and cleaning tools. I'm neither a hunter nor a competitive shooter, but I do like to shoot recreationally, either at a range or "plinking" in the boonies. I acquired the guns over the years, some by purchase or trade, and some inherited from my father. Mainly, I admire the craftsmanship that goes into a quality firearm. There is something satisfying about a fine piece of machinery that just gets better with use. I also consider my gun collection to be a good investment, notwithstanding the efforts of many state governments, especially California, to do away with guns. As a retired judge I have a concealed-carry permit, but I rarely carry unless I'm traveling in the middle of nowhere, or if it's a special occasion. I considered tomorrow's hike to be a special occasion. I took out my nine-millimeter Glock 19, loaded it, and also loaded two magazines. Remembering Mongo's statement that it was too far from his vantage point to read license plates or describe people, I also took out a high-quality Steiner one-thousand-yard rifle scope, minus the rifle, and an inexpensive Bushnell pair of binoculars. I would have taken a camera except I didn't own one that would work. My collection of antique cameras was of no help. Can a person even buy camera film anymore? Nowadays, all my photography is from my iPhone.

The next morning the three of us, Bebe, Brenda, and I, were on the road at 6:00 AM, headed for the Meamber Schoolhouse. It looked like it would be a nice day to spend at higher elevations; the temperature in Yreka was predicted to be one hundred degrees. Mongo was already there when we arrived. "Follow me," he said through the window of his pickup, and we followed him for about forty minutes. The road was paved for the first fifteen minutes, then deteriorated to gravel to dirt to two-track logging road; and we crossed a couple of cattle guards along the way. We finally arrived at an unmarked dirt parking area with no other cars. A gap in the brush surrounding the parking lot was the only indication of a trailhead. There was no sign or other marker. Maybe Mongo just made up the name "Viking" trailhead.

Once we strapped on our packs and got going along the trail, Bebe was in her element. She loved hiking in the mountains. For every step the humans took, she took fifty. Brenda, although a city girl, was in her element too, which didn't surprise me. I had seen her in action, four years before, when she took charge, leading a group of people including an injured woman on a stretcher and several goons who would have killed us if they could, down a steep mountain path from a mining cabin. Today our trail was a steady uphill, but not too difficult. After walking an hour-and-a-half we gained a thousand feet in elevation. Mongo in his unique style kept us entertained with tales. There was the one about the bear and her cub. "Most folks don't wanna get 'tween a mama bear and her cub," he said. "But me, I don't care. Last year, right here in this spot, I almost bumped into a mama, then saw her cub in the bushes right behind me. So, I jist kep' walkin' directly toward mama. Looked her straight into her eyes, I did. She got one look at me and she turned and run off, didn't give a goddamn about her baby. Hell, I had to pick up her baby, and run after her, carryin' her baby to her."

At another spot, he pointed at a campfire ring, and said, "One night I accidentally came up to some flatlander campers sittin' around a fire right here, smokin' weed. Actually, not accidental; I could smell the weed before I saw 'em. I jus' stomped right through 'em and roared. They was so scared, they run off in all directions. Hell, all I wanted was a friendly smoke, but they took off. Left behind a nice stash. Good quality, too. Made my day."

We were enjoying the hike and Mongo's stories. Except for the occasional "hell" and "damn," he didn't cuss. He must have worked hard on that. Brenda definitely had an influence on him.

The second hour-and-a-half was not so easy. The trail disappeared, and it was cross-country, and we climbed over rocks, pushed through thick brush, and crossed a stream. We finally arrived at our destination, and, what a spot! It was well worth the hike to get there. A clearing with nice shade; a spectacular view of the entire Scott Valley and the mountains surrounding it. If it had a stream or other water source, it would have been the perfect overnight campsite. For our purposes it *was* perfect.

Down below you could clearly see Ryder's entire spread. It looked to be a half mile or so as the crow flies. Hiking directly down looked impossible, but I suspected Mongo could do it without breaking a sweat. From this view, it was everything Hailey had described and more. Everything was first-class and magnificent, including the main house, guest house, pool, and tennis court. The grounds were perfectly groomed. It must have taken an army to maintain the whole thing. Still, there was something a little off about the place, something sinister. Mongo had a good point when he questioned the layout of the helicopter pad. It was too close to the main house. The noise of a helicopter landing or taking off would be loud from inside the house. And the short access walkway from the helicopter to the house was covered in such a manner that the walkway wouldn't be visible from any angle, even from an aircraft above or from where we were. Any person or object being loaded on or off a helicopter would be visible for only the brief second or two it would take to cover the distance between the chopper and the edge of the helipad, where the covered walkway began.

Otherwise, the property looked like a working cattle ranch, and there were several horses. We saw no other activity other than a guy driving a tractor in a distant field. I retrieved the food items from the day packs and passed them around. This was a nice place for a picnic, and the day was perfect. Pleasantly tired from the uphill hike, I felt a nap coming on, found a nice soft spot, and drifted off.

I was awakened by the chop, chop, chop of a helicopter rotor, and looked down in time to see a helicopter settling onto the pad. The once tranquil site down below suddenly turned into a frenzy of activity. Brown-skinned men disembarked from the chopper, and others streamed out from under the covered walkway. The door to a helicopter bay opened, and, working quickly, the men began off-loading large containers, four men to a container. I used the rifle scope to get a closeup view, and Brenda videoed the operation with her cell phone. Damn, I should have made the effort to get hold of a proper camera with a long lens, but it was too late now. Even zoomed in to the max, it was doubtful Brenda could capture any meaningful detail with her phone. I could see detail through the high-powered scope, but there wasn't much to see. The containers were brown in color with no identifying marks or labels. I counted nine men, four who came from the helicopter, four from inside the house, and one pilot, who never left the cockpit. The men carried six containers inside. Other than to say they were Hispanic, I wouldn't be able to describe any of the eight men. They were all dressed the same in olive-drab work uniforms. I don't know much about helicopters. It was big. Big enough to carry several people plus six identical large containers that were heavy, based on the way they were being handled. It was conventional in that it had one large rotor above the main cabin area, and a smaller one in the rear, not one of the banana-shaped choppers with large rotors at each end. It was dark gray in color, with no markings I could discern, not even an N-number. The whole operation took no more than fifteen minutes. They landed, off-loaded their cargo, took off, and immediately the whole scene was as tranquil as before. Very efficient.

"What do you think of that?" I asked.

"I don't think they were delivering furniture ... or groceries," said Brenda.

"I hope it was weed," said Mongo.

"If it's bulk cocaine, it's a hell of a lot," I said.

At around one-thirty we were pulling on our packs, preparing to head back down to the trailhead, when we saw a single truck come through the mechanical gate toward the main house. It went around the house onto the helipad, did a U-turn, and backed toward the covered walkway. It stopped before it was under the cover of the walkway, leaving a gap of a few feet. From where I was, looking through the rifle scope it looked like it could have backed all the way under, but didn't. This way we had a glimpse, although brief, of what was going into the truck. *Sloppy,* I thought. Two guys, also Hispanic-looking, climbed out of the cab, went around back, opened the back doors, and climbed in. The same four guys we saw earlier immediately started loading boxes, larger than bankers' boxes, into the truck. Using the scope, I could see the boxes reasonably well. They were identical brown wooden crates, the kind that fruit and produce used to be shipped in until the 1950s, when cardboard took over. Two sides of each crate had colored paper labels. The labels depicted two brilliantly colored oranges, and the word, "Sunkist." The other two sides had the words, etched or wood-burned into the wood, "Agriculture Supply Co." Crates like these are very popular, and sell for probably fifty dollars a piece on Amazon or at retail shops. The men maneuvered the boxes to the back of the truck using hand trucks, and lifted them up to the guys inside. I could tell by how the men handled the boxes that they weren't empty. This operation, like the one we had seen earlier, only took about fifteen minutes, and the truck was off, headed back in the direction it had come. I did get a good look at the truck. It was a white GMC cargo van, maybe two years old. It had California license plates, and I wrote down the number.

On the way back to Yreka, after we dropped off Mongo, I called Sheriff Brad Davis on my cell phone. I had forgotten that I still had his private cell number stored in my phone, from four years before. Brenda LeHane, now sitting next to me, had been with me the first time I used it.

Without saying hello, he went straight to, "You're scaring me. It was four years ago that you called me on my cell, and all hell broke loose."

I said, "What a coincidence. Brenda LeHane is seated next to me right now as we speak. We hiked up with Mongo to the location where he observed the woman being forced out of the helicopter at Ryder's house. We're headed back to town now." I described what we had seen earlier and read the license number I had jotted down. "Do you have enough for a search warrant?"

"Well," he said. "Maybe if we get a hit on the license number that is worthwhile. Let me check on that, and I'll call you back."

About ten minutes later he called back. "I've thought about this real hard," he said. "I don't know that we have enough for a warrant, at least so far. If the license plate were from a stolen vehicle, it would be a different story. But the vehicle is registered to an outfit called, 'Genuine Antiques Distributing,' in Sacramento. It advertises itself as a 'Wholesale Distributor of Antique Merchandise, the Real Deal.' A warrant is premature."

"But there's no way those are just empty wooden boxes," I said, frustrated and desperate. "That was obvious from the way they were being lifted up into the truck. I think there's enough. You've got an eyewitness who saw a woman being forced into the house. You've got a helicopter flying large containers to the house. You've got small containers being shipped from the house by truck. You've got a missing person, Hailey Madison. You've got a connection between Hailey Madison and Ryder and his sister to suggest a motive to do her harm. You've got a connection between Ben Thompson's father and Ryder to suggest a motive for Ryder to do harm to the father, and therefore to Ben."

"Well, the eyewitness was Mongo. Not the world's most credible witness to start with, and he was hazy about what he saw. Everything else they're doing is plausible. They could have a workshop manufacturing 'authentic' antique Agriculture Supply Company wooden crates. Hell, Agriculture Supply is still a major presence in Siskiyou County, even though they don't make wooden crates anymore. They own a lot of acres of timber here, some right in the Scott Valley, actually not too far from Ryder's ranch. Manufacturing 'antique' wooden crates with the 'Agriculture Supply' name on them at that ranch sounds like a good gig. We need more for a search warrant."

"Okay, let's accept that theory; they're making 'antique' wooden boxes." I think I was now whining, and the pitch of my voice was rising. And I was wondering if Ryder had "gotten" to Brad too. "I'll bet Ryder's property isn't zoned for manufacturing. That in itself is evidence of a crime, a basis for a warrant. And in the meantime, there may be a woman in there held against her will, subjected to unspeakable who-knows-what from two psychopaths."

"Yeah, right," said Brad, sounding exasperated. "A goddamn misdemeanor ordinance violation. And we're going to search the residence of the county's richest and most prominent citizen for that? I can picture the KTVL TV news coverage, and then the lawsuit. Look. We don't have enough right now, but we'll keep digging. I promise. I want to nail Ryder as much as you do. We'll follow up on the 'Genuine Antiques Distributing' angle.

"I'm really sorry. Give my regards to Brenda. Tell her I wish she would come visit us more often, but not when we're in the middle of a crime spree."

I didn't need to pass that on to Brenda. I was talking hands-free, and she heard the whole conversation, as did Bebe.

We got back to my little house around six. I gave Bebe some food and fresh water, and said to Brenda, "I'll buy you a glass of wine at the Wine Bar. That's where you and I first met, four years ago."

The Wine Bar was pretty busy, with Rusty Miller, a well-known local singer and songwriter, playing guitar. Brenda and I sat down at a large table with six other people, and I ordered house red wine for both of us. The crowd was upbeat, as were the people at our table. Both of us needed some uplifting of our spirits.

We were there about an hour when Rex Randall Ryder The Third made his grand entrance. He immediately was the center of attention. He sat at a bar stool, and held court, patrons fawning all over him. "Is that him?" asked Brenda.

"Yep," I said.

Except for Brenda, all of us at our table knew each other, but she easily got acquainted with the others, and we were all enjoying ourselves. An observer wouldn't know that she was with me, or anyone in particular. She was just part of the large group at the table. I saw Rex Randall Ryder The Third look in Brenda's direction more than once, which made me uneasy. They made eye contact at least twice, that I saw. Then, without warning, Brenda whispered, "I'm going to get acquainted," and she got up and sat at a bar stool next to him. If she realized that I was uncomfortable, and so was everyone else at our table, she didn't let it show.

Rex and Brenda were far enough away that I couldn't hear what they were saying to each other. But it sure looked like they were getting along just fine. I wasn't sure who was schmoozing who. At the beginning of their conversation their faces were two or three feet apart, but as the conversation progressed, their faces got much closer. At least twice Rex said something, and Brenda laughed and put her hand on his arm.

After about forty-five minutes, the two left their bar stools and came over to our table. Brenda cheerfully said to the entire group, "See you later. Nice to meet you all."

Then she bent down to me and started to say something, but I interrupted, and whispered, "Don't do this."

She whispered back, "This is too good of an opportunity. I've got to. Nothing can happen to me that's worse than what happened to me before. I've got my cell phone." And they both waltzed out the door.

Everyone at the table was puzzled, of course, and didn't know what to say. Most were probably embarrassed for me, thinking that I had been jilted by this beautiful woman less than half my age. I couldn't think of a clever explanation. I sat there for a few minutes, quietly finishing my glass of wine, and then left the Wine Bar.

CHAPTER 25

Brenda, Rex, and Melinda

Rex took Brenda by the hand as he led her to his vehicle, about two blocks away. His vehicle was a huge cherry red Dodge Ram pickup with lots of chrome, a rack of driving lights between the two factory headlights, and huge tires. Brenda was chatty and flirty with Rex, in stark contrast to the terror she felt in the pit of her stomach. She was aware of Hailey Madison's account of her frightening night with Rex and Melinda two years before, so Brenda knew what to expect. She wasn't disappointed.

He drove her to "his" ranch, regaling her along the way with enthusiastic descriptions of its beauty, and how she was certain to be enchanted. His verbal descriptions were accompanied with gestures with his hands, including touching her occasionally on the inside of her thigh, a little awkward given the huge console that separated them. He did ninety-percent of the talking, but did ask her to tell him about herself. This went on for the entire drive, and it was about ten o'clock when they pulled up to Ryder's house. The front door opened before they got to it, and standing in the doorway was a striking tall slender woman with jet black hair, flashing eyes, and a big smile. She was dressed in what looked like lounging pajamas -- two-piece, jet black like the woman's hair, and showing considerable cleavage. She stood at the doorway with her arms crossed and said, "Rex darlin', what have you brought us?"

"Melinda, I'd like you to meet Brenda LeHane. She came all the way out west to Siskiyou County from Washington, D. C. She likes to hike in our mountains. She is an important government official in the Department of Interior. Brenda, this is Melinda. Melinda and I share this beautiful home. We can hardly wait to show it to you, and all its wonderful features."

"I'm looking forward to it," said Brenda, cheerily, in contrast to the fear that was welling up inside her. *I'm positive I didn't tell Rex I work for the DOI. How does he know that?*

"Did you two get any dinner?" Melinda asked. Looking at Brenda, she said, "Rex can be so scatter-brained. He loves to go into town and get to know the locals. Sometimes he loses track of time and forgets all about eating. I'll bet you haven't had any dinner." Before giving Brenda a chance to respond, she went on, "I've got just the thing in the kitchen; follow me. The most wonderful King Ranch Chicken Casserole that Andre, our chef, put together yesterday. I can warm it up in a jiffy. In the meantime, Rex darlin', us girls need wine."

Melinda went to a walk-in refrigerator while Rex opened a bottle of Cabernet Sauvignon. He poured three glasses and passed them out, and Melinda kept on talking. "We'll get a bite to eat, then give you the tour. Wait'll you see our masterpiece bedroom, you'll be dazzled, just dazzled. You can sleep there tonight. Did you bring some things to wear? Well, no mind," she continued, again not waiting for Brenda to respond, "you won't need anything. We've got anything you need." She raised her glass toward Brenda. "Drink up. There's plenty more. This should be a fun night. I can hardly wait."

Brenda raised her wine glass and took a sip. *I've got to figure out how to go easy on the wine without being too obvious.* Then she remembered that Hailey Madison believed she had been drugged, and her level of fear rose another notch.

The three took their plates of King Ranch Chicken Casserole and their wine glasses to the great room, and sat on the big couch, placing their plates and wine glasses on the coffee table. Melinda chattered on, with Rex chiming in from time to time. Brenda did her best to participate in the conversation but found it hard to get a word in edgewise. Rex and Melinda were friendly and upbeat, continuously extolling the wonders of Siskiyou County and the Scott Valley, and the benefits of being so rich you can have absolutely anything you want. They both kept pressing her to drink up. Brenda's level of fear dissipated a little, probably because of the wine. She became more relaxed, but still wary. Melinda's hands were constantly in contact with Brenda's body, but never ventured to forbidden places, at least so far. Brenda tried to reassure herself. *Maybe Hailey Madison overreacted. After all, she was abnormally sensitive, because she was abused as a child. But then, what I went through was horrific, and it was only four years ago. I still haven't recovered. At least I was an adult, and a tough one at that, not a vulnerable child. I need to play along, and somehow minimize the alcohol. My sole mission is to discover if Hailey Madison is somewhere in this house. But what if they want sex? How far am I willing to go? I'm not sexually attracted to women, but Melinda is a hell of a lot less repulsive than Rex. What if they both want it? I'm not exactly a virgin, and it would be worth the sacrifice if Hailey is here and I can get her out. Wouldn't it? Anyhow, I need to keep a level head. Keep track of the amount of wine.*

They finished the casserole, and Melinda said, merrily, "Now for the house tour. Come along," and she took Hailey by the hand. They left Rex behind, and he collected the dirty dishes. "I'll show you first the *piece de résistance*, our fabulous master bedroom. Then I'll show you the rest of the house. We'll certainly be back to the master bedroom later."

Brenda was familiar with Hailey's description of the master bedroom but was still unprepared for what she encountered. It was beyond belief, but somehow consistent with the personalities of her hosts, as she knew them so far. She had never seen anything like it, anywhere, and she had traveled a lot. It was mind-numbing.

The tour of the rest of the house took forty minutes. There were, after all, three stories. Room after room, each uniquely magnificent, and Melinda had a story about each one, like a docent in a 17th century European chateau. Eventually, they worked their way back down to the first level, and Melinda directed Brenda toward the back of the house, through a spacious hallway to a large door, more like a garage door, which Melinda opened. The big door opened onto the covered walkway leading to the helipad. "This is *so* convenient for us," she said. "We commute a lot. We have lovely little places in Beverly Hills, Park City, Saint Malo, and Dubai. And some other places, too. On a moment's notice, we can summon our helicopter to pick us up and take us to the Medford Airport. We keep one of our jets parked at *Million Air* at the airport whenever we are here, so we can leave at a moment's notice, whenever we feel the urge."

Brenda noticed another large door and, right next to it, a large elevator in the hallway near the big outside door. "What are these?" she asked.

"They go downstairs," said Melinda. "We have a workshop down there. Back in the old days citrus and other fruit was commercially packaged and shipped in wooden boxes. Some of their labels were bright and colorful, works of art in their own right. We got interested because the Agriculture Supply Company manufactured those boxes, back in the day. They had a big mill and plant in Hilt, north of Yreka, just before you get to the Siskiyou Summit. The mill has been closed for years, but they still own lots of acres of timberland in Washington, Oregon, and California. They are very environmentally conscious. Their forests are sustainable, and they protect the wildlife. They own timber property right next to our property here, so they are our neighbors. We thought it would be cool to manufacture replicas of those old wooden boxes with the brightly colored labels. Kind of a tribute to them. They sell really well, but for us it's mainly just a hobby. Downstairs is where we build them."

"Wow!" said Brenda with enthusiasm. "Can I look?"

"Uh, not tonight." Brenda noticed a change in Melinda's demeanor; the color drained from her face just a little, but it was very brief. Then she brightened. "They are, uh, making some changes to the production line, and it's not accessible right now. But I can show you another day. I promise. It's fascinating."

They went back into the great room, where Rex was sitting on the couch. He immediately filled Brenda's wine glass. "Please, no," said Brenda. "It's getting late. I'm still operating on Eastern Daylight time. I'm already tired, and more wine will just put me to sleep."

"Well, we certainly don't want that, do we?" said Rex. "I've got just the thing to fix that." He went to a small desk, opened a drawer, and came back with a small baggie of white powder and a straw. He shook the white powder out of the baggie onto the top of the coffee table, and with his finger manipulated it into three lines.

Shit! I guess my life's been more sheltered than I realized, thought Brenda. *I've never done this. I don't want to do this. I don't know how my body will react. I've got to play along. I want to see what's downstairs.*

Brenda watched the other two. Rex went first, inhaling a line through each of his nostrils. He shuddered slightly and took a drink from his wine glass. Melinda performed the same ritual. Now it was Brenda's turn, and she copied what they did as best she could. It was horrible. It burned her nose, and her sinus hurt. Looking for relief, she also took a drink of her wine. The three were sitting on the couch, with Brenda in the middle. "You've never done that before, have you?" asked Melinda. "You can't fool me. I can tell. It doesn't feel good at first, but it gets better ... much better. Trust me. And I can help you feel even better yet." She put her right arm around Brenda's neck, and started unbuttoning Brenda's shirt with her left hand. Then, again with her left hand she took Brenda's hand and guided it up under her pajama top and onto her own bare breast. This activity went on for some time, with increasing intensity. Rex wasn't participating, just sitting next to Brenda in silence. Melinda talked, rambling on in a soft voice. "I have the greatest fantasies," she said. "Do you know what I fantasize about?" Brenda merely shook her head, without a word. "I fantasize that I'm in ancient Rome, an upper-class freeborn noble woman, and I can have slaves, as many as I want. Female slaves. My slaves would never be allowed clothing of any sort except for their metal collars. And I would have them branded on their butts, to identify them as mine. My slaves must do everything I tell them, perfectly. And if they hesitated in the slightest, or didn't please me to my satisfaction, I would have them punished. For a serious transgression, I would have a slave tortured publicly, mutilated and killed, if I so chose. After all, an example must be made for my other slaves. Sometimes I fantasize ordering the breasts to be sliced off from a screaming slave, to be sautéed and served to me while I make her watch me savor the taste." By now Melinda's left hand had unbuttoned Brenda's jeans, and was reaching inside. "Just thinking these thoughts makes me so horny I can't stand it. But if you are rich enough, you don't have to be in ancient Rome to own your own slaves, even here in the United States." When Melinda said that, Brenda immediately sensed that Rex, still sitting next to her, stiffened a little. But Melinda was on a roll, "In fact we just recently acquired a new one, didn't we Rex? Haven't had a chance to try her out yet, but she looks delicious. She's about ready."

Rex abruptly stood up and said, with unrestrained hostility, "Melinda, you're talking crazy! You've had too much to drink and your mind is addled with coke. I think it's time for you to escort our guest to the master bedroom, and enough of your made-up fantasy shit!"

Melina didn't skip a beat. "Oh, big brother. You're such a fuddy-duddy. They're just harmless fantasies, but they make me hot. C'mon honey," she said to Brenda, "Let's have some fun." She took Brenda by the hand and led her to the *piece de résistance* master bedroom.

Several hours later Brenda found herself in the giant bed, naked. She had no idea what time it was but could see that the sun was coming up. She felt horrible. Her head hurt, her joints and muscles hurt, and she felt nauseated. And, she was scared. Although her memory was hazy about what had happened to her, she remembered one thing, loud and clear. Melinda had said, "In fact we just recently acquired a new slave, didn't we Rex?" That was exactly what she said. *That should be enough for a search warrant. I need to call Bob.* She climbed out of the bed, trying to recall where her cell phone was. *It was in my purse. Where the hell is my purse?* She couldn't find it. Not only could she not find her purse, she couldn't find her clothes either. Naked, she walked around the bedroom, searching. Nothing. She went into the adjoining bathroom. It was magnificent, of course, with an amazing array of luxurious bath and body items: soaps, fragrances, salts, oils, and candles. But no purse and no clothes. Her headache and body aches were overshadowed by her mounting terror.

She grabbed a giant, plush bath towel that was folded atop the Jacuzzi soak bathtub and wrapped it around her body. She walked to the bedroom door and tried to open it. It was locked.

CHAPTER 26

Rex, Melinda, and Brenda

A few hours after she had ushered Brenda into the *piece de résistance* master bedroom, a totally nude Melinda walked into the kitchen, where Rex was brewing coffee. The sky outside was light, with the sun above the horizon. Rex was agitated and angry. "You've got to stop with the cocaine!" he said, in a sharp tone.

"Why? What did I do, big brother dear?" Melinda asked, innocently.

"What did you do?" He was shouting now. "What the fuck did you do? You told her that we have a kidnapped woman in our house! You have put us in an impossible situation. Now we're going to have to do something about this new plaything of yours, the black one!"

"Plaything of mine? Who brought her here? It didn't look like you minded too much what was going on. How long has it been since you had a black one? You were into it."

"That's not the point," he said. "I didn't tell her we had kidnapped a woman. Now we're in an impossible situation. What are we going to do with her? It's taken us years to get to where we are. We can live out our every dream. We can do whatever we want. We have built this world-class place here in the Scott Valley. We are where we've wanted to be all our lives. Now we can lose it all, not to mention go to prison, just because of your reckless stupidity!"

Melinda walked up close to Rex, and pressed her naked torso up against him. "Calm down, big brother," she said, touching his chest with her fingertips. "You're overreacting. This is not a big deal. We'll just deal with this one like we always have. She can just disappear, like the one downstairs. This is nothing new."

"The hell it's not!" He violently pushed her away, with enough force that she was slammed backward into the kitchen counter, hurting her elbow. "There were at least fifty people in the Wine Bar last night that saw the two of us leave together. And some of them surely heard our conversation." His face was now red, and he was shaking with rage. "Everyone in the place knew I was bringing her here. If she just disappears, I'll be arrested for sure, and you will too."

Melinda was shaken. She had seen her brother, the consummate glad-hander, become enraged before, more than once with a fatal result. But this was the first time his rage had been directed at her. She was genuinely frightened. "She doesn't have to 'just disappear.' She could be found somewhere a long way from here, an accident victim."

"Don't you get it?" he yelled. "She was last seen in public with *me* in *my* truck, headed to *our* house. She could be found in her hometown of Washington, D.C. and the finger would still be pointed at me! And at you too," he added. He made a fist and looked like he would hit her.

"Please stop," she pleaded. She had never been this frightened of her brother, and she was on the verge of crying. "What I said wasn't so bad. Analyze it. I was describing a fantasy, not an actual event. I didn't say we had kidnapped anyone. I said it was a fantasy, one that made me horny. We don't need to do anything. Business as usual. You can drive her back to Yreka. She spent a nice sex-filled night with us. What's she gonna say?" Melinda was getting her composure back. On a roll, she added, "Maybe we can grab her later, in Washington, D.C."

"That's probably the best plan, just taking her back to town, as though nothing happened." He was calming down, but felt compelled to continue, "You've got to be more careful. Keep yourself under control. We have too much to lose. Maybe we better make sure we have nothing but empty fruit boxes downstairs for a while."

"What about our little slave girl?" asked Melinda. Melinda had recovered from being slammed against the counter and moved her naked body until it was again in contact with her "dear big brother."

"They can search all they want. Never in a million years will they ever find where we are keeping her." He had definitely calmed down.

Melinda, who was also calmer, looked up at him with a smile, her fingertips again caressing his chest. "We are indeed lucky people," she purred.

Melinda, still naked, went to the master bedroom, unlocked the door, and walked in, without knocking. She encountered Brenda standing by the door, wrapped in the large towel. As if such an encounter were an every-morning-experience, Melinda asked, "Well, what do you think of our master bedroom?" Without pausing for an answer, she went on, "Isn't that bed *fabulous*? I'll bet you slept like a baby, didn't you?"

"I slept well," Brenda lied. "I didn't realize it's getting so late. I probably should go. Have you seen my phone?"

"I'm pretty sure you left it in the great room," said Melinda. "But you needn't go so soon, do you? This is the best time of day out here in the country. I *love* mornings this time of year. And I *love* the freedom this place provides. I can roam about the house without any clothes. I can even go outside, naked, without a care. It's *so* delicious. And exhilarating. I do it all the time. I guess I'm just a free spirit. Why don't you join me? There's some yummy Boston Coffee Cake heating in the kitchen. It's really nice outside. We'll grab some coffee cake and coffee, and go out to the pool." She took Brenda's hand. "You can wear the towel if you want, but it's so lovely out there, and the air feels so wonderful on your skin. We can hang out, swim, and enjoy a beautiful morning. Then I'll take you back to town. I took the liberty of putting your clothes in the washer, and I don't think they're dry yet anyway. You can take a swim, shower, and have fresh clothes to wear."

Brenda allowed herself to be pulled along by Melinda. She was at her mercy, so realistically she didn't have a choice. The only way back to town would be for Melinda or Rex to give her a ride. The knot of fear in her gut had subsided somewhat, but not entirely. Did they really intend to take her back? A lot of what had happened the night before was hazy, due to the cocaine and alcohol, but there was one thing she did remember clearly. Melinda said, "We just recently acquired a new one, didn't we Rex?" Brenda was sure those were Melinda's exact words. And she was also sure Rex responded angrily with, "Enough of your made-up fantasy shit!" Well, what was it? Was it fantasy, or did they have a captive in the basement of their home? Or more than one?

Brenda did find her phone on the coffee table in the great room. *I'm pretty sure this isn't where I left it. I think it was in my pocket I went into the bedroom. Well, I guess I'm glad it didn't end up in the washer with my clothes. But why was the bedroom door locked? And don't most bedroom doors lock from the inside?* She tapped her thumb on Bob's phone number. "Are you okay?" he answered.

Brenda knew that Melinda was listening to her end of the conversation. Merrily, she said, "Fine. It's beautiful out here this morning. What a great place. We're going to have coffee out by the pool and take a swim. I should be back in town early this afternoon."

CHAPTER 27

Bob

I was a basket case when I left the Wine Bar. The optics of what had just happened embarrassed me. I had entered the place accompanied by a drop-dead gorgeous woman, who then abandoned me, threw herself at Rex Randall Ryder The Third, and breezed out the door with him, right in front of all my friends. It *was* embarrassing, to be sure. If such a thing had happened when I was in college, I would have been so mortified that I might not have recovered. But I wasn't in college. I was a septuagenarian, Brenda was less than half my age, and I didn't have a romantic relationship with her, except maybe in my dreams.

Compared to the other emotions hammering me, the embarrassment was nothing. My gut was tight with fear and dread. The terror was crushing. That, and the feeling of helplessness. It was the fear and helplessness parents feel when their young child is suffering with a high fever and going into convulsions. I couldn't think rationally. *I should call the sheriff, but what will they do? They could track Rex's pickup and see where he takes her. But I already know where he's taking her; to his mansion in Scott Valley. So, then what could they do? Go up to their front door and inquire if they've seen a young black woman? That would be weird. It's not like she's a missing person. Everyone in the Wine Bar saw her happily go with him, like she initiated it. I should go after her. But what can I do? Go up to the front door and inquire? That would be as weird as if the police did it. And it would piss her off. Her mission was to see what the place looks like from the inside, and my presence would screw everything up. She would have a right to be pissed. And what can they do to her? Since everyone knows she is there, they can't allow anything to happen to her, right? She's a big girl; she can take care of herself; and she's got her cell phone. I'll sit tight for now.*

I went back to my little house and fed Bebe. I had eaten munchies at the Wine Bar, so I wasn't hungry. I picked up a paperback book, my *C.J. Box* mystery novel, and took it to my Lazy Boy. Usually, I can't turn the pages fast enough when reading *C.J. Box,* but this time, after reading a single page five times, I gave up on it. Bebe was sprawled on the carpet in front of the recliner. "What should I do?" I asked.

"I don't know," said Bebe. "That mansion is an evil place. Dogs can sense …"

"I know!" I snapped, interrupting her. "Dogs can sense things people can't. You're not helping me." Then I had instant remorse. "Sorry, Bebe. Didn't mean to take it out on you. I'm scared and frustrated. I'm sorry." She put her chin on my knee, and looked at me with a sad but quizzical look. I patted her on the head.

I tried unsuccessfully to fall asleep in the recliner until about midnight, then got up, went to the bathroom, and then to the bedroom. I stripped down to my underwear, which is what I usually sleep in; but before climbing into bed, I went to the kitchen and poured two shots of Gilbey's gin and some ice into a glass, thinking it would help me sleep. It didn't.

Twice I almost got out of bed with the intent to get dressed and drive to the Scott Valley, but talked myself out of it, using the same logic as before.

After the sun came up, my cell phone did its *Old Time Rock and Roll* thing and I saw that it was from Brenda. I almost dropped the phone trying to answer. "Are you okay?" I asked. After the conversation ended, I ran it back in my mind, trying to dissect it, examining the words for a coded message. I couldn't find one. She sounded cheerful. Happy. What's not to like about going for a morning swim in beautiful Scott Valley at a multi-million-dollar mansion?

I felt somewhat relieved after her call, but not completely. *They can't do anything bad to her now, can they? They can't not know they would be caught. But then, what if they really are psychopaths? The DSM-5 says psychopathy is an antisocial personality disorder highly correlated with crime and violence. Psychopaths don't respect social norms or laws. They don't consider their own safety or the safety of others. They don't feel guilt or remorse for having harmed or mistreated others.*

At about one o'clock my front door opened and in walked Brenda with another woman. The two were happily chatting; two college sorority sisters who hadn't seen each other for a while. *So, this is the notorious Melinda,* I thought. The woman was taller than Brenda, with striking black hair. She was jaw-droppingly beautiful.

Brenda introduced me as her "dear friend Bob." Melinda held out her hand, and I almost felt obliged to kiss it, but didn't. I took her hand, and said, "Nice to meet you."

"I *finally* get to meet you," said Melinda in her charming southern drawl. "I've heard *so* much about you, and I *always* read your newspaper columns." She was referring to the occasional opinion columns I began writing for our local newspaper after I retired. I was happy to know somebody out there actually read them. "And after hearing Brenda talk about you, I just *knew* I had to meet you," she went on. "This has been *so* wonderful. First, I got to meet Brenda, just yesterday for the first time, and I already feel like I've known her for years. And now, I get to meet you. I feel so blessed." *This woman is good. She actually makes it sound like she means it.* "I can't believe we haven't had you out to our house yet. You'll *adore* it. These fall evenings are *so* to die for. We *must* have you out for a barbeque before the weather changes."

The conversation went on like that for another ten minutes. Bebe, out of character for her, didn't go up and give Melinda her usual enthusiastic greeting. *She's a good judge of character.*

Finally, Melinda took her leave.

"Are you okay?" I asked Brenda.

"No," she said. The cheery disposition that came in with Melinda was now gone. Brenda's face crumpled up with pain, and I thought she would lose her balance and fall to the floor. She made it to the chair, and sat down. I went to the kitchen and got her a glass of water.

"I'll try to tell you what happened, if I can get through it. I believe those people are crazy … and dangerous." She then commenced a detailed chronological narrative, beginning with her conversations with Ryder at the bar the previous evening, and ending with when Melinda walked out my front door. Brenda took about an hour to get through her story. Although she said her memory was hazy from the wine and cocaine, her story was detailed and precise, except for her accounting of what happened to her on the large bed in the *piece de résistance* bedroom. When she got to that part of the narrative, she became vague and nonspecific, but highly emotional, and she wept, actually wailed. I didn't want to hear that part, yet at the same time I did, my anger and adrenaline rising. I asked a couple of questions, and the most I got out of her was that, whatever happened, it involved both Melinda and Rex, which raised my adrenaline to another level. Also, my remorse. What happened to Brenda four years ago was unimaginably brutal and was my fault. Now, four years later, it's happening again, and again it's my fault.

The other part of Brenda's narrative that made her emotional was her description of an exchange between Melinda and Rex. This time the emotion was one of fury, pure and simple. "Melinda was getting pretty drunk," she said. "The alcohol and cocaine were taking effect, and she was turning on the sex and careless with her words. She started going on about her fantasies, about being a noblewoman in ancient Rome and having slave girls, as many as she wanted. She talked about branding and torturing them. And then she said, and I did my best to memorize her exact words, 'If you are rich enough, you don't have to be in ancient Rome to own your own slaves, even here in the United States … we just recently acquired a new one, didn't we Rex?' When she said that, Rex got angry and told her to shut up. He said she was talking crazy; that she had too much booze and coke. He said, 'enough of your made-up fantasy shit.'

"But I don't think it was fantasy, at least that part. I've thought about this a lot, and I think they have someone locked up in that house, downstairs. Melinda gave me a tour of the whole house, except for the basement. There is a door at the back of the house, near the door leading outside to the helicopter pad. She said it went down to the basement, and that they have a workshop or something down there that manufactures boxes--fancy wooden produce boxes that they sell to antique stores. It jives with what we saw when we hiked up there. I told her I was really interested, and could I take a look? She said we couldn't go there right then, but later. Something about having to do repairs or something like that. I believe that the basement is the only part of the house she didn't show me, and it's a huge house. The house actually has an elevator. I felt like I was on a tour of a European castle. It took a long time just to do the tour.

"This morning I was really scared. When I woke up, they had taken my clothes, and the bedroom door was locked. I felt trapped. And I thought I could hear them arguing. The house is big and I guess well insulated, but I swear I heard Melinda and Rex shouting at each other, while I was still locked in the bedroom. I think he was yelling at her about what she had said about having a slave. Maybe they were trying to decide whether to let me go. I'm so glad to be out of there. I think there is something wrong with them. They're not normal. I think they are crazy and dangerous."

"People do crazy things," I said. "I know of an actual case where people captured a young woman and kept her as a sex slave for years. She had been a hitchhiker. They kept her naked, locked in a box under the bed. It wasn't my case--it happened in Tehama County, a hundred and fifty miles or so south of us. The county seat down there is Red Bluff. I was good friends with the judges who handled the case. Dennis Murray did the preliminary hearing and Noel Watkins did the trial. Also, a 'true crime' book was written about the case. But the perpetrators weren't like Rex and Melinda. They were husband and wife, poor white trash, who lived in a beat-up trailer out in the country. When the victim wasn't in the box, she was chained, always naked. Not only did they continuously rape her and force her to do things against her will, but they tortured her, hanging her up by her wrists. That went on for years. As the years went by, they gradually allowed her more and more freedom, and she didn't try to escape. It may have been a Stockholm Syndrome thing to some extent, but primarily they brainwashed her, and convinced her that there was a group of people, whom they called 'The Organization,' that would capture her if she tried to run, and torture and kill her. After years of that, she finally did get up the courage to escape. The poor woman's story was initially treated skeptically, and she wasn't believed at first. No one could understand why she stayed with them as long as she did. Finally, the authorities arrested the husband and wife. Prosecuting the case was difficult, because the victim's story was so far-fetched, even though they were able to find evidence, like the box and other paraphernalia, that corroborated her story. Fortunately, the jury believed her, and the perpetrators were sentenced to prison.

"I think you're right, and they do have someone imprisoned in the house. And maybe it's Hailey Madison. They got back at her for not playing along with their sex game. We need to talk to the sheriff and see if now he will ask for a search warrant for the basement. Actually, Rex and Melinda should be arrested for what they did to you."

When I said that, Brenda became emotional again. "I don't know if they actually committed a crime against me. They'll say that whatever happened was consensual," she said. I could see this was enormously hard for her. "And maybe it *was* … consensual," she went on. "I was in their house and realistically had no way of leaving. But I didn't ask to leave, either. I definitely felt the effects of the alcohol and cocaine, but I can't say I didn't have the will or freedom to say no. They didn't restrain me or threaten me or force me to do anything. The reason I didn't resist was because I was there to see what was in the mansion."

"Yeah, but you had already gotten the house tour before the sex started. That was no longer your incentive." I felt horrible asking her these questions, but I knew they were the questions she would be asked by the D.A. before he would file criminal charges. And if the case went to trial, she would be grilled by high-priced defense attorneys. "Why did you let it happen?"

"Because," she hesitated, "I guess it was a combination of things. There was some duress, of course. I was at their mercy and I didn't know how they would respond if I suddenly became obstinate. They could have physically hurt me, or threatened to, I suppose, and it would just be my word against theirs. They are pillars of the community. I'm just a black girl from out of town. Who's going to believe me? So, there's that. But maybe the real answer is that I didn't want to blow my cover, so to speak. I wanted to play along. Is that the same as consent? I feel like a character in a spy novel. If a spy consents to sex to obtain information, does that make it a nonconsensual assault? I don't think so."

By now, I wasn't sure which one of us was feeling worse. She had voluntarily put herself into a horrible situation over a problem that wasn't her problem. And I got her into it. "Maybe an arrest is premature," I said. "But there should be enough for a search warrant."

I called Sheriff Brad Davis's cell phone, well aware this was the second call to his cell in two days, after a four-year hiatus. "You again?" he answered.

"Yep," I said. Sorry, but I've got some new information you should know about, but not over the phone. Can we come see you?"

"We?"

"Yeah, Brenda LeHane and I. It's important."

"Are you at home?" he asked. "If you are, I can come see you. Fifteen minutes?"

"Okay."

When Brad arrived, the four of us, Brad, Brenda, Bebe, and I, sat down in my small living room. Three of us, the three humans, were sitting on chairs and the couch; and Bebe, the canine, was sitting on the carpet, obviously paying attention. I said, "Brenda spent the night at Ryder's place in the Scott Valley, and has some things to tell you."

Brenda recounted to Brad what she had told me earlier, in less detail, glossing over the sexual activities to some extent. Her delivery was less emotional, more businesslike. It came easier for her the second time, maybe because by then she had gotten some of the pain out of her system. The centerpiece of her story, and upon which any hope of a search warrant was based, was the brief dialog between Rex and Melinda concerning owning slaves. Melinda had said, "In fact we just recently acquired a new one, didn't we Rex?" Rex had done a good job of deflecting Melinda's incriminating statement when he said, "… enough of your made-up fantasy shit!" The dialog created an ambiguity. Either Rex and Melinda were imprisoning someone against her will, or a drunken Melinda was verbally expressing her fantasy.

"Don't you think, taken together with everything we talked about yesterday, that this is enough for a search warrant?" I asked.

The sheriff didn't look happy. "I don't know," he said. "There are reasonable explanations for their words that don't necessarily mean kidnapping or false imprisonment." He was clearly conflicted, not unreasonably. "Do you know what a clusterfuck this will be if we go in there and don't find anything?" He nodded toward Brenda when he said that, as if to say, *Sorry about the language.*

She nodded back, wordlessly implying, *"No problem."*

"I'll take it to Trampas, and if he buys into it, we'll go for it. If it goes south, it'll help that we've got an experienced team that agreed a warrant was called for. And at least you and Trampas are well respected around here."

"Thanks for the compliment," I said, "But don't sell yourself short." Mike Trampas had been our county's District Attorney for fifteen years, and indeed is well-respected, for good reason. He is a tall, good-looking, fifty-ish, athletic guy, having played college-level basketball, and who still coaches high school basketball. He was appointed District Attorney by the county Board of Supervisors after the former D.A. had resigned, and he has been reelected, unopposed, ever since. He is a good lawyer and reasonable, a testament to something I've always believed; that you don't have to be an asshole to be a good lawyer. And, he is a fair and professional District Attorney. A prosecutor's role is more than just to win cases. The prosecutor's role is also to seek justice, which means choosing with integrity which cases to prosecute and which ones not to prosecute.

Sheriff Brad Davis was also well-respected. If I commanded some amount of respect as a retired judge, it meant there were at least three of us that could stand together if execution of the search warrant turned to shit. Actually four, if you counted the judge who would issue the warrant.

Obtaining and executing a search warrant is not an easy task, and for good reason, thanks to the Fourth Amendment of the U.S. Constitution. There are a lot of moving parts. And a lot of risks. A law enforcement officer or prosecutor can't simply call a judge and say, "I think Rex Ryder and his sister have kidnapped a person and have her imprisoned in their mansion. Can you give me a warrant to search the mansion?" The most commonly used (and safest) process to obtain a warrant is with a set of written documents jointly created by a prosecuting attorney from the D.A.'s office and one or more law enforcement officers. The typical written application contains a sworn affidavit describing "with reasonable particularity" the property to be searched, and a statement setting forth the facts showing why there is probable cause to believe that the property to be searched is evidence that a felony has occurred or that a particular person has committed a felony. The application package also includes the proposed warrant itself. It takes time to create the paperwork. Once created, the application and proposed warrant then have to be presented to a judge who will review and issue the warrant, which takes more time. In our county, during normal court business hours, the warrant applicant goes to the courthouse and gives the paperwork to a clerk, who will schedule whichever judge is next available. On weekends and during non-business hours, the county's four judges rotate being on duty and available to review warrant applications. I recall instances before I retired when I received phone calls at my home from law enforcement people asking if I would review a search warrant. Sometimes it was quite an experience, such as when I had an entire platoon of drug task force officers in my living room at 3:00 AM, all in disguise, looking like gangsters, hookers, and druggies.

There are risks associated with search warrants. Serving the warrant can be dangerous. The people whose persons or property are being searched can be armed and dangerous criminals, who can respond violently. Another significant risk is that if a warrant isn't based on sufficient probable cause, or is executed incorrectly, a court can later throw out the evidence discovered by the search, and even evidence obtained later if it was derived from the search evidence. This is called "fruit of the poisonous tree." A worst nightmare of prosecutors and law enforcement officers is that their case against a dangerous violent criminal might be thrown out of court because of a bad search. Another risk, not as obvious or common, is the potential backlash that can occur when a warrant is served upon a prominent or influential person, especially if the search comes up empty. It was this risk we all feared at the prospect of searching the Ryder mansion.

CHAPTER 28

The Warrant

The warrant application for the Ryder mansion took time to prepare. The probable cause affidavit was lengthy and convoluted, and had to pull together disparate facts occurring over a period of time. It was necessary to include Hailey's experience at the mansion two years before, Mongo's "recon" observations, Hailey's relationship with Ben, Ben's father's interaction with Rex as a county supervisor, and Brenda's very recent experience at the mansion. Besides being complicated, the affidavit had to be prepared delicately, to minimize the danger to the people whose observations served as its basis. Brenda, particularly, was vulnerable. The only thing that kept Rex and Melinda from harming her more was that too many people saw her leave with Rex and knew where she was going. They could have done nothing worse to her under those circumstances, but what about later? When she got back home to Washington, D.C., anything could happen. A hit and run driver on a busy street? Mongo could also be at risk. The identities of informants need not be disclosed in a search warrant affidavit if doing so would put them in harm's way or jeopardize an ongoing investigation. Typically, such informants will be identified as "Confidential Informant #1," or "Confidential Informant #2," or "CI#1," or "CI#2," and so on. By statute a search warrant is confidential and not public record from the time it is issued to the time of its execution, but once executed it becomes a public record. Even so, under certain circumstances the court has the authority to order the warrant application, or portions of it, to be "sealed," to protect a person's safety, or to protect an ongoing investigation. When an affidavit doesn't present the actual names or other identifying information of informants, then that information is submitted to the court in a separate document under seal, and does not become public information, at least initially. The judge needs that information to determine the credibility of the informants. Although keeping information under seal may give some protection to vulnerable informants, that protection is limited. Upon motion, the sealed portions can later be court-ordered to be made public. Also, the unsealed portion of an affidavit may describe facts and circumstances that would give away the identity of the informants, even though not specifically identified by name. The search warrant for the Ryders' mansion in Scott Valley was fraught with many risks at every level, including personal risk to Brenda, and to Hailey Madison if she was still alive and in their basement.

The warrant application was taken to the courthouse the next morning by the D.A., Mike Trampas, himself, not one of his deputies, which was somewhat unusual. The clerk hand-carried the warrant application to Judge John Peterson's chambers. Judge Peterson took some time to carefully review it, then invited Trampas into his office. "Are you sure you want to do this?" he asked.

"There is nothing I'd rather do less," said Trampas. "I think this is the beginning of a nightmare. If we go in there and don't find anything, there will be hell to pay. And if the Madison woman is actually there, and alive, they will have every incentive to kill her. But we don't have a choice, as I see it. If she's in there, they can't let her go, no matter what; regardless of whether we search the place, it would just be matter of time. And what is she going through anyway? Why do they have her, and what are they doing to her? Brad Davis talked to the LeHane woman personally. She was in that house, and she's scared to death. She's convinced that the Ryders are crazy, psychopaths."

"But LeHane went there voluntarily, right? Why did she do that? She didn't have to go at all."

"Right," said Trampas. "But she's a pistol. I remember her from four years ago. She's brave and tough. What happened to her back then was unspeakably horrendous. You'd think she'd be frightened into submission, but actually it's just the opposite. I wouldn't want her after me."

"I have a bad feeling about this," said Judge Peterson. But then he went on, "Please raise your right hand. Do you swear under penalty of perjury that the statements in this affidavit are true and correct to the best of your knowledge and belief?"

"I do," said Trampas.

The warrant was in the hands of the search team by 10:00 AM that morning. The sheriff handpicked the team, which consisted of eight people and one K9. There were two deputy sheriffs, a sheriff's captain, two Etna police officers, one California Highway Patrol officer, and one officer from the Yreka Police Department. Although the Ryder mansion was not in any city limits, law enforcement for the cities of Etna and Fort Jones, the two main towns in the Scott Valley, was provided by the Etna Police Department. Sheriff Davis thought it imperative to have their officers involved. Because of the suspicion that the Ryders might be distributing cocaine, one of the deputies was a dog handler accompanied by his partner, Charlie, whose specialty was sniffing out drugs. The Yreka PD officer and the CHP officer were part of the county's inter-agency drug task force. The eighth member of the group was the Sheriff himself. He had mixed emotions about being directly involved, as this would put him in the line of fire if everything went south, but he wanted to be in control. This was a delicate matter, and he wanted everyone on the team to use utmost restraint.

The sheriff spent the morning briefing the team. Most of the briefing was actually conducted by Captain Gerald Franklin, head of the Sheriff's Office Enforcement Division. But the sheriff, himself, set the tone. "This is going to be an unusual search," he said. "I want it to be as unobtrusive as possible. Definitely not a SWAT operation. Unless something crazy happens, no firearms drawn and no detentions. Instruct the occupants of the house to sit quietly in a living room while the search is in progress. No handcuffs or other restraints unless, as I said, something crazy happens. The house has three stories and a basement. I want you to do a walk-through of every room in the three stories, but just to see if anybody's there. You can look in closets, but, unless you get permission from me, no opening drawers, containers, or rifling through anything. Don't seize anything. Leave all the rooms exactly as you found them. The primary focus of our search is the basement. Down there we will deploy normal search procedures and protocols, with two objectives in mind. One has to do with finding Hailey Madison, if she is there, so we will be looking for her and evidence that she is there or has been there at some point in time. The other objective has to do with the trafficking of illegal narcotics, especially cocaine. I want the basement search to be thorough, but, again, with restraint. This may be the most delicate and difficult search that this county has been involved with since I've been sheriff, and, as you know, that's been a long time. If we find someone or something important in the basement, then we can go back upstairs and do a more thorough search, but only if. Any questions?"

The team arrived at the wrought iron gate of Ryder's place at 1:00 PM. Two years before, Rex Ryder told Hailey Madison that the gate combination was "R-E-D-Y-R," Ryder spelled backwards. *Why not try it?* thought Brad Davis. It worked. The gate swung open, and the team drove their vehicles up to the main house. None of them had ever been inside the gate before, and they were awestruck. Nothing like this had ever existed in Siskiyou County to their knowledge. They pulled up to the main house and parked their vehicles along the semi-circular driveway, and were greeted at the front door by Melinda, looking drop-dead gorgeous in tight Wrangler jeans, cowboy boots, and a perfect-fitting western shirt with the top three buttons unbuttoned.

She was all smiles. "What can I do for y'all?" she asked, sweetly. Her eyes took in all eight members of the team, seven males and one female, looking them up and down, one at a time. Her gaze lingered a little longer at the female, a tiny red-haired young deputy sheriff. She would have been petite, except for the bulk associated with all the body armor and the belt she wore, complete with handgun, taser, radio, and all the other standard sheriff's paraphernalia. She looked overloaded by the equipment and didn't look like a law enforcement officer.

Sheriff Davis and Captain Franklin went up to Melinda, showed her the warrant, and explained why they were there. Melinda didn't bat an eye. "Well, c'mon in," she said, enthusiastically. "There's no one here today but little ol' me. Usually this place is buzzin', but today, I'm here all alone, and I'm happy to have some company. I'm sure Rex would have a fit if he knew what you're up to, but he's not here, is he? Can I get y'all something to drink?"

"No ma'am," said the Captain, "but thanks. I'm afraid we have to ask you to sit down in your living room while we conduct our business."

She looked crushed, "Is that really necessary? I can probably help you find whatever you're lookin' for."

"I'm sorry, but yes. We'll let you know if we need your help."

CHAPTER 29

Bob, Brad, Brenda, and Bebe

Late that afternoon, after the search team had completed their task, Brad came over to my little house to deliver his wrap-up of the events of the day. His audience consisted of Brenda, Bebe, and me, all of us sitting in my living room.

"How'd it go?" I asked.

"It went like I feared," he said. "A clusterfuck." He nodded toward Brenda as he had done before, as if to say, *Sorry.*

"Let me stop you right there. We need fortification," I said. I went into the kitchen, poured a glass of red wine for Brenda, a Jack Daniel's on the rocks for Brad, and a Gilbey's gin on the rocks for me, and returned to the living room. I didn't bother measuring the gin or whiskey with a shot glass.

"I can describe the result in one sentence. We didn't find shit." He nodded again to Brenda. "We were there for about three hours, max. Melinda was the only one home. In fact, as far as we could tell, she was the only live person on the whole ranch. We did go through every room in the upstairs part of the house, but quickly, not really to search, but to see if anyone was present. We spent most of our time in the basement, but there wasn't much to see. It was a workshop, like what a hobbyist might have who likes to do woodwork, but on a larger scale. Several workbenches, a couple of table saws, lots of tools. More like a workshop than a factory. There were three pallets with uncut lumber, and two pallets with cardboard boxes containing the labels to be applied to the finished product. There was a stack of the finished product, that is, old-fashioned wooden produce boxes with the bright colored labels glued on. But the boxes were open. No tops had yet been fastened on. There are two ways to get down there. There was a door with steps leading down, and right next to it an elevator."

"Did you seize anything?" I asked.

"Only one item, a finished produce box without a top. We didn't actually seize it. I asked Melinda if we could have one, and she said, 'Sure.'"

"What are your impressions? Anything unusual?" I asked.

"Nothing that really jumped out at me. But some things about the whole deal seemed a little off."

"Like what?"

"Well, one thing that struck me was that I had expected the basement to be bigger. You know, the house is huge. I've heard it has 10,000 square feet, and I believe it. The size of the basement doesn't correspond. Even with three stories, the house has a very large footprint on the ground. The basement doesn't fit the footprint, if you understand what I mean. For example, if you assume the first floor of the house occupies one-third of 10,000 square feet, or 3,333 square feet, you might assume the basement would also occupy 3,333 square feet. But it doesn't. We didn't measure it, but I eyeballed it. I'd say the basement area we saw had less than 1,000 square feet. I realize that a basement doesn't necessarily have to have the same square footage as an upstairs floor, but they commonly do. Also, I thought it was odd that there wasn't more stuff down there. Mongo described people carrying large containers from the helicopter. I didn't see anything like that, although I suppose the containers could have been discarded. The smaller packages of labels could have been inside them."

"You think there might be a hidden room?" I asked.

"It's possible. But I sure couldn't find how you would get into it, if there was one. I felt weird about asking our search team to look for a secret room, so I didn't. But I did my own search. I thought the most logical access point would be from the workshop area itself, but I couldn't find anything that could have been a door, a hatch, or a trapdoor. The workshop area, like most basements, is pretty much unfinished. The floor and walls are concrete. I checked out the elevator. I entered it from the first floor, using the elevator button. Inside the elevator there are two sets of doors, one in front and one in back, each with its own control panel. The front control panel has four buttons, three for each of the upper floors and one for the basement. The rear control panel has three buttons, one for each upper floor but none for the basement. I actually rode the elevator. I accessed all four levels, and opened both sets of doors at each level, except that the back doors don't open at the basement level. The front doors open into the workshop. Can you imagine having an elevator in your home? It's surreal.

"I also walked around the outside of the house, looking for some other entrance into the basement or some other underground room, and didn't find anything. But I can't rule it out either. The property is so big, you could have a whole team of people searching for days without finding anything like that.

"Oh, and Charlie was going nuts," he went on. "Charlie's our K9. I lost track of how many times he actively alerted. Dozens, probably. All over the place, mostly in the basement and in the elevator. But no drugs were found."

"What do we do now?" I asked.

"I don't have a clue," he said, shaking his head. "I thought it was curious that no one was on the property except for Melinda. You'd think the place would be overrun with people. It's supposedly a working ranch. And they are supposedly in the box manufacturing business. There must be all kinds of service people just to keep that big house going. Where was everybody?"

"Do you think they were tipped?" I asked.

"Could be. Melinda almost looked like she was expecting us. And she was way too friendly. I don't know what to do from here. And I expect the other shoe to drop. The shit is going to hit the fan, you can trust me on that."

It was dark, and we had consumed our second round of drinks, when Brad left my house. We were in a very worried frame of mind. I ordered a takeout pizza from Round Table and went to pick it up. Brenda was sitting on the couch when I returned, her wine glass refilled. Her eyes were red, and I could tell she had been crying. "I fed Bebe," she said, "and she's outside."

I placed the pizza on the coffee table, retrieved napkins, plates, and utensils from the kitchen, refilled my drink, and sat down next to her. After finishing the pizza in silence, Brenda scooted over until her body was pressed tightly against mine. She was crying again. She put her head on my shoulder, and I put my arm around her. The series of emotions coursing through my entire being were intense and all over the place. It wasn't lost on me that my body was pressed against the body of an amazing, beautiful woman less than half my age. It was thrilling and melancholy at the same time. Sometimes it's not so great being a septuagenarian. The worry about Hailey Madison hung like a cloud. Was she still alive, and what was she going through? And then there was the gut-churning fear of what lay ahead for all of us. The shit would hit the fan, to be sure.

CHAPTER 30

Bob, Brenda, and Bebe - Medicine Lake

The bad result from the search warrant was disheartening and frightening for both of us. Brenda and I spent the entire night on the couch, just hanging on to each other, not saying much or sleeping much. The following day was lost. It was like we had both been flattened by some horribly incapacitating disease. When we did talk to each other, it was to come up with a plan. Where do we go from here? But there were no answers. Even Bebe, with her usual Labrador Retriever enthusiasm, was lethargic, and had no ideas to offer.

"I should go home," Brenda said. "I've done about as much damage here as I can."

"Please stay," I said. "At least for a while. I need you. Let's try to sort this out. And maybe do something actually fun. The weather is perfect, and you said you wanted to see Medicine Lake in the daytime. The reason you came here in the first place was to see our beautiful country, and to hike. Let's get up early tomorrow morning and drive to Medicine Lake. We'll take Bebe and do a picnic. Bebe loves Medicine Lake. Actually, she loves any lake. She can't stay out of the water. It will be good for all three of us."

The three of us, Brenda, Bebe, and I, were in my pickup and on the road the next morning by 7:00 AM. We packed picnic lunches for the humans, and a baggie of Milk-Bones for Bebe. Also, I threw in my ultra-light spinning rod and tackle box. This trip was a good decision. It was a lovely fall day, and our dispositions were much improved from the day before. The drive to Medicine Lake takes a little over two hours, and we arrived around 9:30.

Years ago, early in my law practice career, a woman had come into my office and asked me if I would represent her about property that her family owned at Medicine Lake. I had never been to Medicine Lake and knew little about it. In the first office visit with the woman, I discovered that she was the mother of one of my wife's best friends from elementary and high school in southern California. The family used the property as a summer vacation place and continues to do so. Over the years, my wife and I visited them on several occasions, and Bebe and I still like to go occasionally.

About thirty miles north of Mount Shasta, Medicine Lake is mysterious and fascinating. Because of its location in the Cascade Range and its six-thousand-seven-hundred-foot elevation, the lake gets a lot of snow, and is only accessible for three or four months of the year. During the decades of their ownership, my client's family had built lake-front cabins on their property, very rustic.

Electrical power is created by their own generator. In the winter the snowpack is often so deep it covers the cabins. They fastened long uniquely marked rods or poles to the sides of the cabins pointing straight up in the air well above the roof lines to help the owners locate their cabins if they skied or snowmobiled in.

The lake is in the caldera of a collapsed volcano, similar to Crater Lake in Oregon. It is generally fairly deep with some places that are exceptionally deep. The water is cold, except for a few hot spots along the bottom, indicating that the volcano still has some life in it.

There is a small village of summer cabins along the southeast shore of Medicine Lake, and some Forest Service campgrounds along the north and northwest shores. The rest of the shoreline is private property with very few structures or improvements; isolated.

We drove around the lake until we arrived at the series of summer cabins I was familiar with. I hadn't called ahead, so had no idea if anyone would be home, but, as we pulled up, it was clear that people were there. My wife's school friend, Lorinda Fargo, was there with her extended family. It was great to see them. I let Bebe run free, and she was a happy puppy. There were two other dogs on the property, and once they got acquainted, they had a ball, romping and running together like cousins who hadn't seen each other for years.

I introduced Lorinda to Brenda. We went inside, and Lorinda treated us to some hot coffee and honey-cinnamon scones. The reason that Brenda wanted to see Medicine Lake "in the daytime" was a reference to a very dark night four years before, when we had an encounter we will never forget with Francisco Percival Coleccion. Also known as "The Collector," he personified the worst evil imaginable.

"Did you bring a fishing pole?" asked Lorinda. "We really aren't into fishing that much, but the reports are that the fishing is really good right now. Do you want to use our boat? It's tied up to the dock, and ready to go."

We sure do, I thought, *but not necessarily to fish.* I said, "Yeah, I brought my rod. That'd be great. Do you care if we just leave Bebe here? She'll drive us crazy if she's on the boat with us."

Their boat was a small aluminum fishing boat with a Honda five-horsepower outboard motor. The lake is small, and you don't need anything more than that to get around, although there are more powerful boats. Water skiing is permitted between 10:00 AM and 5:00 PM, a fact somewhat controversial due to the pristine quality of the lake and its small size. Brenda and I chugged out to a location familiar to us. I rigged my small spinning rod and reel and cast a Panther Martin spinner, not really expecting to catch anything. The most productive way to fish Medicine Lake is to troll.

Neither of us spoke for fifteen minutes. Then I said, "What do you think?"

"I'm glad we came. It sure is peaceful."

"Any remorse?" I asked.

"For four years hardly a day has gone by that I haven't reconstructed in my mind what happened out here. I've experienced just about every emotion imaginable. I don't know if remorse is one of them. Maybe remorse about having no remorse. I don't know. Today is good. Being here is good. It's settling, somehow, and I'm thinking more clearly. It's closure. It's so beautiful and peaceful here."

We were out there for an hour, in that same spot. Sometimes she would speak. Sometimes I would speak. In between, there were periods of silence. What we didn't talk about was that we were sure a young woman was being held against her will in a mansion in Scott Valley, a young man was in jail, falsely accused of her murder, and that we had no practical plan to do anything about it. And that the shit was going to hit the fan.

On the way back to town, I got a call on my cell phone from my son-in-law, David. "Most people, when they retire, just fade into the sunset," he said. "I think you are unclear on the concept. Have you seen today's paper?"

"No, I haven't."

"Well, it's a doozy. You'll probably need a drink when you read it. Come on over for dinner tonight. It'll be good for you."

"I've got Brenda with me. We're on our way back to town from Medicine Lake. Should be home around 5:30."

"Okay, come on over when you get back."

CHAPTER 31

Bob - The Aftermath

Our local weekly newspaper was on the front lawn when we arrived at my little house. The shit had hit the fan, for sure. The entire back page was filled with a paid advertisement that made my stomach churn. Under the headline, **"UNGRATEFUL COMMUNITY,"** was an announcement that read:

It is with great sadness and disappointment that I am writing this. Some ten years ago my sister, Melinda, and I discovered the beauty of Siskiyou County, and decided we wanted to become a part of such a wonderful place. We were fortunate to have sufficient resources to purchase our ranch property in Scott Valley, and build our wonderful home. We also wanted to become actively involved in the community and contribute our substantial resources to its betterment. Let's face it, with the collapse of timber harvesting, the economic health of our county has steadily gone downhill, and the future here is bleak. Ever since our first visit, Melinda and I have injected literally millions of dollars to maintain the county's beauty and its attractiveness as a tourist destination, and also to enhance its infrastructure, hospitals, and museums.

And how has the community demonstrated its gratitude? Melinda and I are shocked to inform you, dear citizens of Siskiyou County, that three days ago we were subjected to the most humiliating experience of our lives. A SWAT team of armed officers from the Sheriff's Office, the Etna PD, the Yreka PD, and the CHP, supposedly under the authority of a so-called search warrant, barged onto our private property and conducted a most intrusive search. What were they looking for? God only knows! As you would expect, they found nothing. The ostensible reason for the search was that they were looking for Hailey Madison, the local woman who unfortunately disappeared some time ago near Pineland and is presumed dead. We are sorry about that, and we extend our condolences to Ms. Madison's parents and family. It must be horribly hard on them. But a suspect is in custody and is being prosecuted. Why on earth would they use that as a pretext to trespass upon and ransack our home? The suspect's name is Ben Thompson, who, sadly, is a member of this very Siskiyou County community that Melinda and I have worked so hard to support.

Please forgive me, dear citizens. I am remiss in blaming you for the outrage that has been thrust upon us. Melinda and I should not be blaming you for the actions of a reprehensible few who for some reason have a vendetta against us. It's not you, dear citizens, who were responsible for this ridiculous and mean-spirited search warrant. The real perpetrators are a group of conspirators who belong to a ring dedicated to driving us from this wonderful county we have worked so hard to support. Who are these criminals? Here is the list: It is Sheriff Brad Davis. It is Dr. David Thompson, who did everything he could to prevent us from developing our lovely ranch when he was on the Board of Supervisors. And he is the father of Ben Thompson, an accused murderer in custody in Pineland and awaiting trial for Hailey Madison's murder. You can bet that if he would have been arrested here in our county, he would be out on the street, not in custody where he belongs. It is Judge John Peterson, who signed the travesty of a warrant. It is Mike Trampas, the D.A., who presented the warrant to the judge. And it is that retired judge, you all know who I mean, a constant troublemaker of the worst kind, and the African-American prostitute he brings from the east coast to do who-knows-what for him. These are the ones who are responsible for this, dear citizens, not you. They represent corruption in government at its worst.

Melinda and I were so devastated by this whole horrible experience that we have had serious and intense discussions about pulling up stakes and leaving Siskiyou County for good, and withdrawing all our support. But we came to realize that the evil being perpetrated upon us isn't coming from you, dear citizens, but from a corrupt few. We will never surrender to them. We will stay and fight. **And we will continue to give to this wonderful community all that we can!**

Sincerely,
Rex and Melinda Ryder

The "Ungrateful Community" ad in the local newspaper was, of course, only the beginning. This was the kind of thing that the big-city news media love to pounce on. And pounce they did. The San Francisco Chronicle's front-page headline read, **"RURAL SISKIYOU COUNTY OFFICIALS CONDUCT INTRUSIVE SEARCH OF HOME OF GRANDCHILDREN OF LEGENDARY MOVIE STAR – FIND NOTHING!"** This was the general theme of the nationwide media coverage, which only got worse. Rex Randall Ryder The Third was in his prime and was interviewed by several network anchors. Even usually reclusive Melinda had her opportunity to shine. The media loved them, and they basked in the glory. I had expected the worst, but still wasn't prepared for what I first read in the newspaper, and for what was to come. It was simply awful; there is no better way to describe it.

Erin and David and my two grandkids live less than a mile from my little house. Brenda and I got to their place at 6:30. The evening's guests also included their friends Carl and Donna MacGregor, husband and wife medical doctors, and their high school age daughter. It was Saturday evening, so no one had to worry about going to school or work the next day, and everyone was in a decent mood, despite the "Ungrateful Community" newspaper story. Although Brenda and I had an upbeat day at Medicine Lake, the feeling of euphoria was crushed by the newspaper story. Getting together with the group that evening was a much-needed spirit-boost for us.

After dinner, we talked about current events and, specifically, the Ryders, Hailey Madison, and Ben Thompson. My daughter and son-in-law were already in the loop, but the MacGregors, not so much. Brenda and I together gave them a detailed narrative, bringing everyone up to date. When we finished, the first topic of discussion was the newspaper article. Everyone was outraged, of course. "Can't you sue their asses?" was the universal question.

"Probably so," I said, "But that's the last thing on our minds right now. Winning a lawsuit would be little consolation. I've lived in this community almost fifty years. Being called corrupt by such a prominent and important figure as Rex Ryder is devastating. It's going to be hard for me to walk down the street and wonder what people are thinking about me. And what about Brenda? What they said about her is awful."

Brenda said, "Right, I'm a prostitute. Don't they have to prove that what they said is true?" Then she said, with a laugh, "They can't prove it because I don't take money. But, on the other hand, isn't there a presumption that all black women are hookers?"

"If we sued them, what we would have to prove, and what they would have to prove, is a legal question that hinges on whether or not we are considered to be publicly-known figures," I said, pleased with myself that I remembered some law after being out of the loop for so long. "We were in the public eye four years ago, at least here locally, when we fought with The Collector. Because of that, we might be considered public figures as a matter of law, which would mean that the burden of proof would be on *us* to prove that they knew their statements were false, or that they recklessly disregarded their falsity. In any event, the statute of limitations for defamation is one year, so we've got time to think about suing them, and that's not what's urgent right now. Hell, after this whole thing is over, maybe we can sue them and end up owning that big mansion of theirs." I laughed at my own comment. "Think of all the things we can do with that place."

"But when is this whole thing going to be over?" asked Erin. "Do we really know for sure that Rex Ryder and his sister are doing anything illegal? What evidence is there of that? Maybe it's just weird stuff they're doing, not criminal. Their ideas about sex and threesomes, and maybe even incest, sound crazy to us; but they come from a different world, Hollywood and all. There's nothing illegal about that, except maybe the incest part. And the idea they have kidnapped Hailey Madison and are keeping her against her will as some sort of a sex slave? That's really bizarre."

"Well, there *is* evidence," I said. "Mongo saw it, or at least, saw a woman who was restrained and forcibly being led from the helicopter."

"Yeah, but *Mongo*?"

"Hey, sometimes the most unusual people can be great witnesses, and juries often find them believable. I personally believed every word of what Mongo told me. And, trust me, far-fetched as it sounds, sex slave cases do occur." I told them about the 'woman in the box' case in Tehama County.

Then I said, "And I had my own case here in our county, about twenty years ago. The guy was a British citizen, whose real name was Robert Martin Lloyd, but he called himself 'Master David.' Initially, during his court proceedings, I refused to call him 'Master David,' and insisted on referring to him by his correct name. But his defense attorney convinced me that his client had legally changed his name, and showed me the documentation, so I called him Master David from then on. The investigation started when a woman was treated in our hospital's emergency room and reported that a man had held her against her will, raped her repeatedly, and broken her leg with a rock. She said she escaped from an RV park where she and other followers had been staying with a man who had taken the name of 'His Holiness Master David,' an ordained minister with the 'Essence Church of the Fields.'

"'His Holiness Master David' escaped being caught by local authorities but was finally arrested while attempting to deliver a teddy bear to the governor in Sacramento. He was extradited to Siskiyou County where he initially insisted on representing himself in court, proclaiming that he was Jesus and 'knew all.' Shortly after his arrest, he filed court papers against his victim, claiming he was suing the woman who brought the false charges against him. He wrote in the court documents, 'If I could spend a few hours with her no doubt she would apologize.' And then he wrote, 'unfortunately she is the perpetrator.' He claimed the 'womyn' (he spelled it w-o-m-y-n) signed a binding contract as did his other followers, and that she had broken that contract by leaving the path of 'truth and love.' He also wrote that the victim took his training course willingly for two-and-a-half years, explaining that, 'under the intense strain of the program one aspires for perfection.' He described her 'training' to be part of a program that 'teaches someone to respond to violence with love while finding peace within.'

"When in custody, he ate nothing but candy bars at the jail and was seen drinking water from puddles on the floor of an exercise area of the jail. I ordered psychological examinations, and the shrinks determined him to be mentally incompetent to stand trial. He was transported to Atascadero State Hospital, but after about a year, the hospital proclaimed that he had been 'restored to competence,' and sent him back so his court proceedings could resume.

"I sentenced him to state prison, and supposedly he was to be deported to England after serving his time, but I heard that years later he was seen around here. I don't know what, if anything happened after that. I've been out of the loop.

"Obviously Master David was an entirely different character than Rex and Melinda. His psychopathy was obvious for all to see. But there are a hell of a lot of psychopaths in this world who can appear perfectly normal in their day-to-day activities."

Erin said, "Yeah but they searched the house, and didn't find anything or anyone. Not really a surprise. But the idea of some secret vault or dungeon or something sounds pretty sketchy, like a B horror movie."

Now David jumped into the discussion. David was a contractor, and had done a variety of construction jobs, residential and commercial. "Let me show you something," he said, and opened his laptop. He went to YouTube, and searched for "Underground Survival Shelter." He clicked on a video which depicted an animated, talking sepia photograph of a bearded miner, a geezer from the 1800s. The geezer voice said, "Hey Everybody, I want to introduce you to my new show, where I buy everything to prepare for when the shit hits the fan." The video was one of a series of episodes where he and others, self-proclaimed "preppers," would review and demonstrate the latest in survivalist gear and gadgets. The video was actually an advertisement for a company that manufactures and sells underground survival shelters. The company is one of several engaged in that business, which, I learned, has become a major industry. The video was interesting, and very funny, and raised our spirits, but after it was over, instead of moving on to another episode, David switched to the company's website. It was fascinating and enlightening. It wasn't a surprise to me that there are companies that manufacture and install bomb shelters. I have been aware of that for years, ever since the post-war fifties when the Russian nuclear threat was on everyone's mind. As a child, between kindergarten and the third grade, I lived in the heart of Los Angeles. I still have frightening mental images of the atomic bomb drills we did at school. The teacher would bark a sharp command, and we were all required to duck under the desks, heads down, protecting our necks and the backs of our heads with our arms and hands. Maybe what scared me the most was that I had seen newsreel pictures of the detonation of nuclear bombs and the damage they could do. I thought ducking under a desk was a futile gesture. We would already be, literally, toast.

The website was a real eye-opener. The company manufactures and installs modular shelters of all shapes and sizes, for many purposes, some starting below the $10,000.00 range. Some units are designed to be built into or under the home, some with hidden entrances. One example has an entrance hidden under a kitchen island. The island counter-top slides open, revealing a door to stairs to an underground room with a seven-foot ceiling that can be used for just about anything: bomb shelter, tornado shelter, fallout shelter, wine cellar, or gun storage safe.

Besides the modular lower-end shelters, at the upper end of the scale the company can provide made-to-order shelters custom designed to suit the buyers' needs. These can cost millions of dollars. For example, the website lists one model floorplan with a price exceeding $5,000,000. The uses for these underground shelters are limited only by the imaginations of the buyers. I'm not suggesting this company, or any other supplier of similar products, intentionally sells their products for illicit or immoral purposes. If someone misuses the product in a manner not intended, the company should not be legally responsible, any more than Ford Motor Company should be legally responsible if one of its customers intentionally runs over and kills someone with a Ford automobile.

What the website did for me, and for everyone else at our dinner party, was to open our eyes that it is feasible for people, especially if they have unlimited wealth, to surreptitiously design and construct an underground compound to be used for illegal purposes, including distribution of cocaine, or imprisoning people against their will. The design and construction of the Ryders' mansion was done by their own people, and, as a practical matter, without oversight by any local government officials.

We concluded this whole idea wasn't something out of a science-fiction novel or a fantasy action/adventure movie, but real life. Having come to that realization, thanks to David's indoctrinating us into the world of survivalists and bomb shelters, we had to figure out what to do next. Going back for another search warrant was not an option. There was no new evidence to offer supporting that. That we now knew more about underground shelters and their hidden access doors was not new evidence. The officers conducting the disastrous search had no idea what to look for. The result might have been different if the search team included an expert on underground shelters.

Unfortunately, no one at the dinner party came up with a specific action plan. We finally gave up, thinking, we'll consider it again in the light of day. For tonight, lets just enjoy a Saturday night dinner among friends. We had a grand time with another round of drinks, watching more episodes of the guy demonstrating what you need "when the shit hits the fan."

CHAPTER 32

Rex and Melinda

The same evening that Bob and Brenda were having dinner at Erin and David's house, Rex and Melinda had finished their own meal, and were relaxing on their big couch, sipping Remy Martin Louis XIII Cognac. They were watching Hailey Madison on their giant television screen. The TV was cycling through live feeds from closed-circuit cameras directed toward Hailey from various angles. Their victim was in terrible distress, a circumstance that provided pleasure and enjoyment to Rex and Melissa. Unlike her condition the last time they had watched together, this time the chain from the ceiling connected to Hailey's neck collar had been shortened, preventing her from moving off of the bed, and preventing her head from making contact with it. She couldn't lie down. A bowl of water was placed on a night stand next to the bed, which Hailey could barely reach with her mouth. She had access to nothing else. No food. No toilet.

"It's her own fault," cooed Melinda, as she rubbed her hand along the inside of her brother's leg. "I visited her this afternoon and explained to her how delicious her life could be if only she would be a little more reasonable. She can be our pampered pet, you know, and have a wonderful life. But rather than be our contented little puppy, she chose to be a complete bitch. Do you know what she said? She said, 'Fuck you' six times, and she tried to kick me, the ungrateful little bitch. I quietly explained to her that we were losing our patience, and that we would give her some more time to come around, but if it didn't happen soon, some bad things would start happening to her.

"I also explained to her that I was concerned for her mental health and feared she might harm herself. I shortened her chain for her own good, to minimize the risk of suicide. I told her I'd check back again tomorrow. But all she said was, 'Fuck you,' over and over. Can you believe that? I don't know. I just don't know. I don't know what to do with her if she doesn't improve her attitude by tomorrow. Do you have any ideas, big brother dear?" she asked salaciously.

"I'm sure you'll think of something," said Rex with a smile. "You always do." He felt Melinda's hand working its way toward his crotch and leaned his head on the back of the couch when his reverie was interrupted by the electronic sound of a cell phone behind him on the kitchen bar. By the time he got to the phone it had stopped sounding its alarm. The phone was not the one he normally used. This one, a blue burner phone, was special, and used only on rare occasions. On the phone's display were the words, "I will call you tomorrow at 10:00 AM Pacific time. Be ready. Both of you."

"Shit!" muttered Rex. "She's going to call tomorrow morning at ten. She wants to talk to both of us." The mood cast upon these two unusual siblings by

144

the cognac and the pornographic spectacle they had been viewing on their gigantic television screen had quickly vanished. He turned off the television, leaving the despondent naked woman downstairs to suffer unobserved. Then, using his regular cell phone, he made a call. "Margaret," he said. "We need complete privacy in the house tomorrow, probably till noon, but I'll call you. Nobody in the house until I call. Everything on the outside, business as usual, including ranch hands and groundskeepers. But no one inside. Thank you." Margaret was the Ryders' Chief of Staff. Rex couldn't remember how long Margaret had worked for them. Actually, Rex and Melinda didn't hire Margaret, they inherited her. Or maybe she inherited them. Margaret had worked for their father, Rex Ryder, Junior, until he died, some twenty years before, then transitioned seamlessly to Rex and Melinda. Generally, neither Rex nor Melinda dealt directly with the huge staff that managed and maintained the Ryders' empire. The staff answered to Margaret. Rex and Melinda merely communicated to Margaret whatever they wanted, and she took care of it. Margaret was paid an ungodly amount of money, more than the CEO's of many Fortune 500 corporations. Margaret knew almost everything there was to know about Rex and Melinda, including their penchant for acquiring and keeping unusual pets, and their illicit business activities. Margaret was one-hundred-per-cent loyal and would never betray them. Her loyalty was assured by her outrageous salary, and also, maybe to a greater extent, by the fact that she had a few secrets of her own that no one knew about except Rex and Melinda. The perfect business relationship. The only person who knew more about Rex and Melinda than Margaret was the possessor of the female voice that had just dictated the text message they received on the blue phone, a person that neither Rex nor Melinda had ever laid eyes on.

"I'm going to bed," said Rex, and he headed to his own bedroom, alone.

The next morning Rex and Melinda were sitting at the kitchen table when the blue phone made its electronic sound, exactly at ten o'clock. They were the only ones in the house and Rex turned on the speakerphone feature.

"Good morning," said the voice in the phone. The voice sounded like it had been electronically generated, but also sounded female. The voice was very businesslike, unemotional.

"Good morning," said Rex and Melinda simultaneously.

"You sound like you are on the speakerphone," said the voice. "Are you alone?"

"Yes. No one is in the house but us," said Rex.

Rex and Melinda did not know the name of the person they were talking to. The voice in the phone had never identified herself, and they never asked her name. All the calls were initiated by her, not by them. If they wanted to initiate contact with her, they had a phone number they could text with a one-word message, "Call," followed by the number of their current burner phone. They could then expect a return call later. The text number they used was changed periodically, hidden in **postcard** advertisements for an auto repair shop in Phoenix, Arizona, which they received occasionally in the mail. She was the only person they talked to on the blue phone. This hadn't always been the case. Until four years before, their phone contact had been another electronically altered voice, this one male, who identified himself as "The Collector." Like Margaret, they had inherited The Collector from their father. But The Collector had suddenly stopped calling. Two years went by with no contact, and then they received another text number hidden in a postcard. They sent the text and thereafter received a call from the new female voice. There was never a conversation about the change. They never asked, and she never volunteered.

"What on earth possessed you to pull off that stupid stunt?" asked the voice, with no preliminary introduction or pleasantries.

"What are you talking about?" asked Rex.

"The full-page piece in the newspaper, of course. What do you think I'm talking about? Did you do something even stupider?"

"What's so stupid about the newspaper ad?" demanded Rex.

"If you don't know, you're stupider than I thought. Smart people usually lay low when they are under scrutiny by police authorities. But never mind, that is not the reason for my call. I called because I have a task for you."

Those words triggered immediate and intense fear in the hearts of Rex and Melinda. Rex, particularly, was visibly shaken and broke into a cold sweat. It was not unexpected, however, that she had a task for them. This was part of their arrangement. Rex and Melinda received great benefit from the organization. But it didn't come without strings. It was the *quid pro quo.* It was expected of them. The organization didn't ask very often, but when it did, immediate and full compliance was expected. Refusal or failure were not tolerated. Rex and Melinda had heard plenty of war stories about what happened to people who were unwilling or unable to satisfactorily complete a task they were assigned by the organization. The stories were horrifying and brutal. Death was a blessing for people subjected to the organization's wrath. In keeping with what little they knew about the electronic female voice on the phone, neither Rex nor Melinda knew anything about the organization. They had no idea how the organization was structured, its principals, or if the organization even had a name. It was always referred to simply as "the organization," or "our organization."

The electronic voice continued, "As you know, the organization for years has been aligned with the *La Peninsula* cartel. The arrangement has been mutually beneficial. *La Peninsula* has always been powerful and has always fully and satisfactorily carried out its promises to us. Our organization has benefited greatly from their professionalism, and, of course, so have you. But now it's time to give back. *La Peninsula* is being challenged by a new cartel, *Costa Oeste.* The confrontations have turned into bloodbaths. Our organization has dedicated itself to giving its support to *La Peninsula.* Two days ago, *La Peninsula* captured the wife and two children of *Costa Oeste's* top leader, and currently have them in custody. They need a secure and secret place outside of Mexico to hold them. That is where you come in. They will be brought to your house tomorrow by helicopter, and you will give them secure lodging in your unique downstairs accommodations.

"The organization was very much distressed that your house was searched by the police as a consequence of your recent stupid carryings-on, but the search brought some good news as well. First, they didn't discover your downstairs facilities, which is comforting; and second, having found nothing, it is unlikely they will search again. Still, it is worrisome that you have conducted yourselves in a manner to attract the attention of the local authorities so much that they felt it necessary to conduct the search in the first place."

Listening to the message being delivered by the voice in the phone was having a bad effect on Rex and Melinda. They had always feared the organization and the *La Peninsula* cartel. But they always had a mutually beneficial working relationship with both. Harboring these people in their basement brought an entirely new concern, fear of another cartel, *Costa Oeste,* with whom they did not have a working relationship. This would be extraordinarily dangerous. They were in panic mode.

"Relax. Don't worry," continued the voice in the phone, "you won't have to do anything. You won't have to actually entertain your new guests. All you have to do is provide the space. Our people will take care of everything else, including security, food, clothing, and amenities for the guests. They will be completely provided for."

Swell, thought Rex. *Providing for their comfort is the least of our worries.* "How long will they be here?" he asked.

"As long as it takes," said the voice. "It should be no problem for you. As I said, our people will take care of everything. But I think you can understand how useful it will be to *La Peninsula* to have the Rodriguez wife and two children in its custody and control. Lisa Marie Rodriguez is the wife of Juan Riccardo Rodriguez, the number two man in the *Costa Oeste* hierarchy. Señora Rodriguez and their two children were taken just yesterday. The two children are fraternal twins, fifteen years old, a boy and a girl. Their names are Miguel and Carmella. The two children and their mother are all quite beautiful."

Melinda asked, "What do you mean, 'as long as it takes?' As long as *what* takes?"

"As long as it takes to neutralize the *Costa Oeste.*"

"What will happen to them? The mother and two children?" asked Melinda.

"That is none of your concern. Hopefully there will be a happy ending. Americans always like happy endings. But you know how it is with the cartels. And right now, there is much bloodshed. But you are asking too many questions. The less you know, the better."

"But they will be staying in *our* house. They will be in danger, and so will we." Melinda was whining now. Not her usual persona. "And, we already have a guest downstairs."

"Enough!" said the voice, obviously losing patience. "The organization asks very little of you, and you get much in return. But when the organization does ask, it does not accept anything less than complete and unwavering compliance ... and loyalty. The helicopter will deliver your new guests tomorrow at 1:00 PM. Of course, we know about your current guest. Your current guest may have to ... check out." And the line went dead.

CHAPTER 33

Lisa Marie, Miguel, Carmella, and Martinez

At precisely 1:00 PM the next day, Rex and Melinda heard the chop, chop, chop of the helicopter as it settled onto the helipad. They went to their back door and observed passively as the helicopter's door opened. The first to disembark were two Hispanic guys carrying large duffel bags. Without a word, they walked right past Rex and Melinda to the elevator. They pressed the elevator button; the door opened and they entered, the door closing behind them. *Just like they own the place!* thought Melinda, with disgust. In truth, the organization *did* own the place, the entire ranch, although the only names that would show up on a title search were the names of Rex and Melinda Ryder. The organization owned Rex and Melinda too, and Rex and Melinda knew it, although they tried to drive that thought out of their minds. A few minutes later, more people disembarked. The first down the steps was a dark-haired woman, whose face would have been beautiful had it not been that her dark eyes were puffy, with one slightly blackened. She wore an expensive black cocktail dress and high heels. She descended the steps with some difficulty, due to the high heels and also because her ankles were connected by a one-foot lightweight chain, almost inconspicuous. Behind her was a pretty fifteen-year-old girl, dressed in a Catholic school uniform: a plaid pleated skirt and oxford dress shirt with a school emblem. She was followed by a handsome fifteen-year-old boy, also dressed in a Catholic school uniform. Both kids had dark hair and dark eyes. Neither appeared to be shackled or restrained. The girl was visibly crying, with her head down, obviously frightened. The boy looked straight ahead, defiant.

Next down the steps was a tall muscular Hispanic man, well-groomed and well-dressed in a navy suit with a vest and tie. He gave off the appearance that he was in total control. He was followed by two other guys who could only have been bodyguards. The woman and the two children were marched by the bodyguards past Rex and Melinda toward the elevator, but the tall Hispanic man stopped to talk to them. "My name is Martinez," he said, in a quiet, even tone. "I am now in charge. My primary mission is to maintain the security and custody of Señora Rodriguez and the two children. But to carry out that mission, I have been assigned the command of this entire ranch, including the residence house. Nothing is to occur here, not so much as taking out the trash, without my express knowledge. I have already spoken to Margaret, and she has been advised that she answers only to me. One of our people will be stationed at the front gate at all times. No one will enter or leave the ranch without my knowledge and express permission. We will also have our people on patrol throughout the ranch at all times. No one except me will know how many there are or their locations at any given time. Do you understand?"

"That doesn't apply to us, of course?" said Melinda, half asking a question and half making a statement. "We, of course, can come and go as we please?" Again, was it a question or a statement?

"My apologies, but my instructions are that no one leaves or enters without my permission," said Martinez in a gentle voice laced with a trace of menace. "That includes you."

"That's ridiculous!" said Melinda, raising her voice. "You need to contact your superior, whoever the fuck that is, and get it straightened out. This is *our* house."

"It has already been, as you say, 'straightened out,'" said Martinez, with a look of impatience. "I have my orders, and they are specific. *No one* leaves or enters without my permission, including you. If it is any consolation, I will do everything in my power to limit our intrusion on your privacy, and on whatever, ah, activities you do here in the house. We know, for example, that you have a houseguest down below, and we have no intention of interfering with your entertaining your houseguest. I am aware that yesterday you were informed that your guest's visit should be terminated, but the organization has reconsidered that. There is plenty of room downstairs to accommodate your houseguest and the Rodriguez family. You may do whatever you wish with your guest, except that we *do* want to be involved if it becomes your intent to terminate your guest's life. It does not appear, at least for now, that your guest's presence will unduly conflict with our mission here. Now, if you will please excuse me, I have important matters to attend to. Don't worry, I won't be staying here in the house. I will have my things carried to the guest quarters. Oh, and by the way, I think it's only fair to advise you that all of your telephones, including your personal cell phones, are being monitored. Have a nice afternoon."

Rex had remained silent throughout the conversation. Melinda had started to object further, but Martinez departed before she had the chance. "Fuck!" she said to nobody in particular.

Unknown to Rex and Melinda, and also unknown to Martinez and his entourage, a pair of eyes peered down from above. Mongo was doing his "recon," and this time he had binoculars.

CHAPTER 34

Bob, Brenda, Bebe, Mongo, and Brad

The morning after our dinner at my daughter's house, Brenda, Bebe, and I were enjoying a rare quiet time in my little house. Brenda and I were sipping coffee at the kitchen table, checking our emails. Bebe was snoozing on the carpet when she raised her head, jumped up and headed toward the door, tail wagging. She was already at the door when we first heard footsteps on the front porch, then the doorbell. I opened the door and immediately my senses of sight and smell were impinged upon by the sheer size and aroma of Mongo. I invited him in and led him to the same kitchen chair he had occupied previously. It had held up under his bulk before and appeared to be up to the task again.

"I got more intel for ya," he said, "and I think it's important. I was doin' my recon yesterday 'bout one o'clock when I seen another helicopter land. This time it was carryin' what looked like a Mexican family. Not really Mexican. More high-class. More like, whatcha call 'em, Spaniard. There was the mama, dressed in black, elegant-like. But she had trouble walkin', like maybe her feet was shackled. Then there was two kids, a boy and a girl, both dressed in school uniforms, the kind kids wear that go to them parocal schools. Then there was a big guy with a suit. I thought maybe he was the dad, but the way he was dressed, he looked like a gangster. Then there was other guys, I didn't count 'em. They just looked like thugs. All Mexican."

"What were they doing?" I asked.

"Looked like they was movin' in. I stayed up there all afternoon and part of the night. The goddamn helicopter stayed about an hour, then took off. All them people stayed. Most in the main house, 'cludin' the mama and two kids. It looked like the gangster guy moved into one of the other buildings. After a while, one of the thug guys went out to the main gate, and stayed there, like he's some kinda guard. And the others spread out, like they was some kinda soldiers on patrol. It's fu--, darned weird." Mongo almost slipped. He was determined not to swear in front of Brenda. He caught himself just in time. "The place looks like an army camp, with soldiers on guard duty, 'cept they wasn't wearing uniforms, and they's all Mexicans."

"What do you suppose that's all about?" I asked, to no one in particular.

Mongo said, "I sure don't know. The mama and kids looked scared. I only saw 'em a few seconds, when they got off the helicopter, but I felt like they was, what's the word, hostages. Do you want me to keep on doin' recon?"

"Well, sure," I said, "if you have time. I believe Hailey Madison is still there, but I have no idea what this new development is all about. Mongo, you should be really proud of what you're doing. If we can get her rescued, much of the credit will go to you."

He looked genuinely pleased. "Just doin' my civic duty," he said as he rose from his tiny chair. He headed to the door, with Bebe following, her tail wagging enthusiastically.

After he was gone, Brenda and I again fell silent, and went back to checking our emails. But my mind wasn't on my emails; it was still trying to conjure up a plan of action, while at the same time processing this new information. Although she said nothing, I was sure that Brenda was going through the same mental exercise. There *had* to be something we could do. But what?

I switched from my emails to the *National Review*, a conservative on-line publication I read every day. I was half-heartedly scanning it when something caught my eye, under the "Breaking News" banner. The headline was, **"Mexican Cartel Wars Escalate. Family Members of *Costa Oeste* Gang Boss Taken Hostage."**

"Listen to this," I said to Brenda, and read to her from the article. "In a bloody skirmish yesterday at a cocktail party at the posh Mayan Nayarit Hotel in Nuevo Vallarta, Mexico, Lisa Marie Rodriguez, the wife of *Costa Oeste* cartel kingpin Juan Riccardo Rodriguez, was forcibly abducted and taken away in a speeding vehicle. At least six people, mostly partygoers, were reportedly killed in what appeared to be a shoot-out between members of rival gangs *Costa Oeste* and *La Peninsula*. It has also been reported that, at the same time as the Mayan Nayarit Hotel incident, the two teen-aged children of Juan Riccardo and Lisa Marie Rodriguez were kidnapped from a Catholic school they attended in the Mexican state of Nayarit. The current whereabouts of the wife and two children are unknown. The motive for the abductions is also unknown." Brenda came over and looked over my shoulder at the iPad screen. There was a photograph of Lisa Marie Rodriguez, dressed in a black cocktail dress chatting happily with a couple identified in the story as the host and hostess of the event.

"We need to catch Mongo!" said Brenda, urgently. "I sure wish he had a cell phone."

I called George Jackson at the **Salmon/Scott River Ranger Station**. Fortunately, he was in his office. "Hey Jackson, Mongo left here an hour or so ago," I said. "I'm not sure exactly where he was going, but I suspect he is headed your way. Could you try and track him down? I am going to email you a photograph from a news clipping. Could you show it to Mongo and ask him if he recognizes anyone in the picture? I know it sounds kind of crazy, but this is really urgent, and could be important, a matter of life and death."

"If it has to do with Mongo, it's probably crazy, but sure, be happy to do it."

"Give me a number or email address where I can send it, and I'll get it to you right away. Then please call me immediately with his answer."

"Okay," Jackson said, and gave me a phone number, to which I forwarded the *National Review* article.

Brenda re-read the *National Review* article, and asked, "Do you really think the family members of the cartel leader are right here in Siskiyou County? If that's true, then that means Melinda and Rex have some kind of a connection with the *La Peninsula* cartel. I don't know anything about Mexican cartels, but even I have heard of *La Peninsula*. They're huge. And they kill people. And they are right here in Ryders' mansion? The basement under that house must really be something, if it can accommodate all those people. But how do you get to it?"

"Mongo saw the woman who we think is Hailey Madison being led from the helipad to the back door, where the elevator is. Then he saw the woman and two kids yesterday, being led to the same back door. The access has got to be the elevator. Maybe there's another level, not accessed by a button, but by a key. Or maybe some kind of a sensor that reads a control device, like how a TV reads a remote."

Our conversation went on for about forty-five minutes, but was leading nowhere in terms of developing an action plan. My cell phone rang. It was George Jackson. "I just saw Mongo," he said. "I showed him the picture, and guess what? He positively identified the woman in the photograph as a woman he saw yesterday. What's that all about?"

"I'll tell you," I said. "But is Mongo still there with you?"

"Yes. Do you want to talk to him?"

"Yes."

"I'm positive she's the same goddamn woman," said Mongo's voice. "No question."

"How can you be so sure?" I asked. "Weren't you a long way away?"

"Yeah, but I had binoculars. I was prepared, just like a goddamn boy scout. It was quick, but I got a good look. It's her. It's the same goddamn black dress. The same white beads around her neck."

"White beads?" I asked.

"Yeah, like rich people wear. Ya know. Pearls."

"Would you be willing to give a statement to that effect, under oath, to the District Attorney? For that matter, if the woman is who we think she is, would you be willing to give a statement to the feds, like maybe the FBI or CIA? And be willing to testify in court if necessary?" I asked.

"Sure as shit! Why wouldn't I? It's my civic duty." He almost sounded offended that I would have to ask.

"Okay. Please don't tell anyone what you saw, or what you just told us. These people are very bad people. It could be dangerous for you."

"Shit, I ain't scared o' them bastards. Do I sound scared?"

"No, you don't. And I know you aren't. But if the word gets out, it could put Hailey Madison in danger, and also the mother and two kids you saw yesterday."

I called Sheriff Brad Davis's cell phone for an unprecedented third time. It rang four times before he answered. I figured he probably wasn't going to answer it at all, but then had a last-minute change of heart.

153

"Now what?" he answered.

"Probably even worse than the last time," I said. "I really need to talk to you immediately, but not over the phone. I think it really is worse than last time."

"I don't see how that could be possible. Please don't mention Mongo's name."

"Sorry, can't help it."

"I know I'm gonna regret this. Are you at home? I'll come right over."

He showed up at my front door about twenty minutes later. I offered him a seat at the kitchen table, and asked, "Coffee, or whiskey? You might need the whiskey."

"Let's start with coffee," he said. It's not five o'clock yet."

I got him a cup of coffee, refilled Brenda's cup, and sat down. Bebe was sitting on the floor next to Brad, her ears perked up. I asked, "Did you read about the kidnapping of the wife and children of a major Mexican cartel leader?"

"Yeah, I did. Just yesterday, or maybe the day before, wasn't it?"

"Yes. The cartel boss's name is Juan Riccardo Rodriguez. He's the number two man in the *Costa Oeste* hierarchy. His wife and two children, a boy and girl, were kidnapped. Apparently, the wife was taken after a shoot-out at a luxury Mexican coastal hotel, where several people were killed. The two children, fraternal twins, were taken from their school."

"So, what about 'em?"

"I think they are now being held at the Ryders' mansion in Scott Valley."

"And why do you think this? And please don't say Mongo's name."

"Afraid so," I said. "He was doing his 'recon' yesterday and saw them being off-loaded from a helicopter."

"How does he know who they are?"

"I showed him a newspaper clipping that had a photo of the wife. Her name is Lisa Marie Rodriguez. Mongo says he's positive it's her."

"From up there on the government land?"

"Yep."

"Shit!"

"You got that right." I recounted for Brad everything that Mongo had told us, including the telephone conversation with Mongo facilitated by George Jackson, and Mongo's positive identification from the *National Review* photo. "Brenda and I have been trying to come up with a strategic plan, with no success, but I'm leaning in the direction of getting the federal government involved; the FBI or whoever deals with cartel kidnappings and stuff like that. I personally don't like the FBI, based mostly on how they handled, or mishandled, the murder that I witnessed four years ago. I also don't want to get them involved because I can picture a raid with lots of shooting and lots of collateral damage. It would put Hailey Madison's life in danger, if she is even there, and also the lives of the wife and children of the cartel mob boss. But, on the other hand, what choice is there? If the place is now being guarded by an army of cartel thugs, as Mongo suggests, how else is there any chance at rescuing them? And their chances of survival are pretty low in any event, no matter what we do."

Brenda spoke for the first time. "Melinda has taken a shine to me," she said. "Maybe I can get in there and soften things up a bit, before the FBI army stages their invasion."

"Bullshit!" I said. "There is no way you're going back in there. It would be suicide."

Brad said, "And what makes you think you'd be welcome? If I remember right, Rex and Melinda called you Bob's 'African American prostitute.' It doesn't sound like you're on good terms with them at the moment."

"Maybe not Rex," Brenda said, with a smile. "But Melinda is quite attracted to me."

"She wants you, all right," I said. "She wants to own you. She wants you to be her black slave. I won't let you go back in there."

"So ... now I'm *your* slave?" Brenda had some attitude in her voice when she said this.

Brad interrupted. "This absolutely calls for FBI involvement. Although it scares me, I need to contact them immediately. What scares me most is when I explain to them that Mongo is our primary informant. I can imagine the reaction I will get when I tell them all about Mongo, although working with unsavory informants is something the FBI is quite used to. And Brenda, don't even think of going in there. It will just make the FBI's job more difficult. One more person they will have to look out for."

"Yes, Massa," she said, with no humor in her voice.

Brad went back to his office. About two hours later he called on my cell phone. "I just talked to the feds. They are salivating over this one, and will be here en masse tomorrow. They want to talk to you and Brenda first thing tomorrow morning. Oh, and Mongo, too. 6:00 AM in my office."

"6:00 AM? They *are* salivating."

"Yes. I was dreading making the call. I thought they would just laugh at me when I told them about Mongo. But they didn't. It seems they already had some intel--god I love using that word--intel of the possibility the Rodriguez family might be in Siskiyou County. What I told them just corroborated their suspicions."

"Where do you suppose they got their, quote, intel? Mongo seems to be the source of all intel, and I can't picture him talking to them."

"No, but for some reason they had heard of him. They made a big deal of having him available tomorrow."

"That may not be so easy," I said. "Especially if he's up there in his recon spot collecting intel. I don't know how to contact him directly. I've been going through a forest service guy at the Salmon/Scott River Ranger Station. He's now their best buddy, and they seem to be able to track him down at will."

"Well, they *really* want to talk to him tomorrow."

"I'll see what I can do. But they may have to send their own people out to find him."

The sheriff got a good laugh at that. "I can just picture three FBI guys, dressed in black suits and Florsheim shoes traipsing through the forest, wading through streams, and crawling through brush."

I laughed, too. "Okay, I'll try to find him. See you tomorrow morning."

I reached Jackson, and asked him to try and find Mongo, giving him the details of the next morning's meeting. "It's important," I said. "The FBI wants to talk to him."

"Wow, the FBI? To Mongo?"

CHAPTER 35

Bob - The Feds

Brenda and I were in Brad's office the next morning at 6:00 AM. I hadn't heard from George Jackson, so I assumed he had located Mongo, but Mongo wasn't present when we arrived. Brenda and I were ushered into the conference room, which was already crowded with people. There was Brad, Captain Gerald Franklin, head of Brad's Enforcement Division, and two people in Sheriff Department uniforms I didn't recognize, one male and one female. Then there were four people who might as well have had the letters "FBI" stenciled on their outfits because it was obvious who they were. Three men and one woman. The men were dressed in black suits, white shirts, innocuous ties, and, you guessed it, Florsheim shoes. The woman wore a gray skirt and matching gray jacket, with the skirt length just above her knees. She didn't wear Florsheims but her shoes looked equally uncomfortable. The FBI agent clearly in charge and who did most of the talking was the woman, named Silvia Shorenstine. About 5'6" with medium length brown hair, she looked extremely fit. She would have been very attractive, even sexy, except that her demeanor was harsh, all business. There was nothing soft or tender about this woman. The great line from the Tommy Lee Jones character in the original *Men in Black* movie came to mind: "No, ma'am. We at the FBI do not have a sense of humor that we're aware of."

After a brief introduction, but with no explanation as to what information the FBI already possessed, Agent Shorenstine asked questions of Brenda and me, the beginning of what turned out to be a six-hour marathon. At the outset, one of her questions was, "Where is Mr. Ray, the gentleman you call Mongo?"

I said, "Mongo lives in the forest, and he's hard to find. He's an unusual guy, and doesn't believe in things that the rest of us take for granted, like a phone. I asked a forest ranger to find him, but don't know if he has made contact yet. I'm sure Mongo will show up if he gets the word you want to see him."

About two hours into the question-and-answer session, Mongo showed up. After introductions, he said, "Sorry to be late. I just found out you was lookin' for me. I was doin' recon."

"Did anything unusual happen at the Ryders' house?" I asked.

"Well, there's nothin' there that ain't unusual. But I didn't see no more helicopters, if that's what ya mean. And there was no delivery trucks."

The tone of the FBI's interrogation process took a dramatic turn when Mongo entered the room. The agents focused their questioning primarily on Mongo, which made sense, of course, as Mongo was the only one who actually witnessed the arrival of Hailey Madison, if she was the woman, and the arrival of the Rodriguez family and their *La Peninsula* guards. The interaction between the FBI agents and Mongo was like watching an *Abbott and Costello* comedy routine. The four well-educated, articulate, sharply-dressed federal law enforcement agents versus Mongo, the smelly, uneducated gentle giant dressed in rags. Surely, they were experienced at interviewing witnesses from all walks of life, but they clearly didn't know what to make of Mongo and were having a hard time assessing his credibility. To their credit, the agents didn't come across as arrogant or paternalistic. They were genuinely mystified. They would need a warrant to gain access to Ryder's mansion, and they were worried about what kind of presentation they would make to a judge to obtain such a warrant, based on eye-witness accounts from someone like Mongo.

It was past noon when the agents had finished their interrogation session with Mongo, Brenda, and me. Once they were done, they thanked us and let us know, without elaboration, that we were dismissed. "Can you tell us what you plan to do?" I asked.

"I'm sorry, we can't do that," was the response from Agent Shorenstine. "But we'll be in touch. Thank you again for your cooperation. Please do not interfere in any way with our operation. And don't go out to the property or have any communication with the Ryders or anyone else involved."

Brad walked us out the door. "I'll keep you in the loop, if I can," he said. "But I honestly don't know how much they are going to keep *me* in the loop, or how much participation they are going to want from my department, if any."

Out in the parking lot, Brenda, Mongo, and I talked. I said, "They probably intend to obtain a search warrant and raid the Ryders' property. I believe they will get their warrant from a federal judge. That's way out of my area of expertise, and I don't have any idea what the process is, or how long it will take to do that. I guess we'll just have to wait and see what they do. Hopefully they will keep the sheriff involved."

Mongo asked, "Do you want me to keep doin' recon?"

"I don't want you to get in trouble," I said.

"Well, the FBI lady said 'don't go out to the property.' I ain't goin' to the property. I'm goin' to federal guv-ment land. It belongs to the people."

"I guess that's true," I said. "But listen, if you do go there, I want you to indulge me. Take a phone. Let's go to Walmart. I'll buy you a phone and teach you how to use it."

The three of us went to Walmart, where, even there, Mongo, got a lot of double-takes. Back out in the parking lot, Brenda and I showed Mongo how to use the phone, including the camera app. After he got the hang of it, we did some practice calls between our three phones, so that all our numbers were stored in each phone. Mongo headed back toward Scott Valley in his beater truck, and Brenda and I drove back to my little house. About forty-five minutes later, my cell phone rang. It was Mongo, with a selfie photo. "Just practicin'," he said. He sounded like he was proud of himself.

Later that afternoon, there was a knock on my back door. It was the sheriff, who never used the back door before. "They got the warrant," he said. "Gerald Franklin and I are part of the search team. Everyone else is FBI. It's going to be a big deal; I'm not sure how many personnel, but a lot. Probably the biggest search ever conducted in the history of Siskiyou County. It's not every day we have the kidnapped family of a Mexican cartel boss here. We rendezvous at 1:00 AM in a secret location outside of Fort Jones, with the objective of being on the property at 2:00 AM."

"Holy shit, a nighttime search. I hope they have someone on the team who knows how to locate and access secret underground bomb shelters," I said.

"I hope so, too. I told the FBI lady all about our earlier search, and what we think went wrong. Actually, I think that's the only reason Gerry and I are invited. It's because we've already been on the property, and they think we can be of help. Otherwise, their choice would be to limit it to their own people, for fear of a leak."

"Probably justified," I said, with a laugh.

"Probably, so please promise me you won't do anything stupid enough to get me in trouble."

"Okay," I said, knowing I hadn't been sworn, and that the "okay" was not under oath. "Thanks for the heads up."

Our conversation lasted less than three minutes, and then Brad furtively went out my back door. I watched him head for the back alley, then toward the street in the next block.

"What do you think?" I asked Brenda.

"I think we should ask Mongo to observe the search while it is in progress. I'm afraid this search will turn into something really bad, with Hailey Madison being a victim of the carnage. The cartels don't mess around, and neither does the FBI. But I don't know what else we can do. Even asking Mongo to watch could be considered to be obstruction of justice, a crime which the FBI is notorious for getting people to plead guilty to."

The experience Brenda and I had with the FBI four years before was horrible, so neither of us trusted them, based on our own personal experience. They had said that they were vigorously investigating the brutal murder of a young woman, when they did the opposite, and engaged in a coverup. But every organization can have corrupt bad apples; and that doesn't mean the entire organization is corrupt. The country needs the FBI. But still ...

"I'll call him," I said. "But I'm paranoid when it comes to worrying about calls being tracked. Can they track my call? The technology is way over my head."

"Mine, too," she said.

Not knowing if it would make a difference, I drove back out to Walmart and bought another burner phone. Then I drove north on Interstate 5 until I crossed the state line into Oregon, pulled into a rest area, and called Mongo. He answered on the second ring.

"Hey Mongo, are you liking your new phone?"

"Yeah, but somethin's different. The ring's different"

"I'm calling you from a different phone. Do you want to do some recon at 2:00 AM in the morning?"

I told him about the planned FBI search, and warned him that his involvement could be considered a crime. "Fuck yes, I'll do it!" he said with enthusiasm. "And I'll keep ya posted. It looks like a good night to be out, a full moon. I should be able to see real good."

"Okay. Please don't say anything about this to anyone. And don't do anything to interfere. Just stay in your spot and be, like, you're on a stakeout."

CHAPTER 36

Bob - The Second Search

It was around 6:30 PM that evening, and I felt somewhat refreshed after a later-than-usual septuagenarian-required afternoon nap. Brenda had spent the afternoon reading a few chapters from a James Lee Burke *Robicheaux* novel. "Hungry?" I asked.

"Starved."

"How about some take-out? I'll make a run. Do you like Thai food?"

"Love it," she said, not a surprise. Brenda likes food.

"Not exactly collard greens, cornbread and grits," I said. "Do you have any requests?"

"Fuck you," she said sweetly. "I'll eat whatever you gives me, Massa."

I went to Natalee's Thai House and picked up some grilled salmon with mango curry and, for an appetizer, an order of shrimp tempura. When I got back to the house, Brenda had set the coffee table in front of the couch with plates, napkins, and silverware, and had poured two glasses of white wine. She was watching the news. I served the food onto the plates, sat down, and we watched the evening news while we ate. She had the remote, and periodically surfed several news channels. She said, "I don't know why I even watch this crap. I don't believe most of it. It doesn't matter which channel it is."

"They shouldn't be called *news* channels," I said. "They should be called *propaganda* channels. All of the news sources, conservative and liberal, have erased the distinction between opinion and news. And now it's worse than ever. There is virtually no *news* anymore, it's all opinion, with a political spin. But they present it like it's news."

Brenda said, "Yeah. And the two sides are so far apart, it's like they aren't even reporting the same events. It used to be that if you visualized a Venn Diagram the circles would overlap in the center, where the actual truth might be. But now the circles are so far apart they don't overlap at all, so it's impossible to extrapolate the truth."

"Well, you don't have to *watch* the news. You make your own," I said.

"What do you mean by that?"

"Well, who was it that went voluntarily with Rex that night at the Wine Bar? You did that on your own. And look what that stirred up. The good news is that you did it with such a flourish that Rex and Melinda had to let you go. Otherwise, you would be with Hailey Madison right now, alive or dead, or maybe worse. It's good the FBI is executing a search warrant tonight, otherwise you'd be out there doing it on your own. I know you would do that. Let's change the subject. I'm scaring myself. Let's watch some mindless comedy on Netflix."

We binged on several episodes of *The Big Bang Theory,* laughing heartily, enjoying the wine. She was pressed tightly up against me on the couch, and I had my arm around her shoulder. It felt good. I remembered similar feelings from high school, on a first date with a girl, thinking, *she likes me, what should I do now?*

At 3:30 AM Brenda and I were asleep on the couch, still pressed against each other, when my cell phone rang.

It was the sheriff. "It's done," he said. "And it was ugly."

"What happened?" As I asked that, I turned on the phone's speaker so Brenda could hear the conversation.

"It turned into a shoot-out. Gunfight at the OK Corral. Gerry and I were ordered to stay back, so we weren't directly involved, thank God. But we were close enough to see most of what happened. At least four people got shot that I'm aware of, two FBI people and two of the cartel's thugs."

"Are they dead?"

"I honestly don't know. I do know that they were able to rescue the Rodriguez woman and her kids, and that they're okay. I was able to actually see them before the FBI lady ordered me off the property, so I know they're okay. They also rescued the big guy that Mongo described, but I couldn't tell if that was a rescue or a capture. I don't know if he is a good guy or a bad guy. I've already told you too much, I've got to go."

"Wait a minute! You didn't mention Hailey Madison, or the Ryders!"

"That's the weird thing. There was no sign of them, any of them, or for that matter, any of Ryder's people. It was like, none of them were there, anywhere."

"You're shittin' me!" I said. "Poof, they are gone?"

"Poof! It's the damnedest thing. I don't know what to tell you."

"Well, the shit is going to hit the fan tomorrow. Half the news people on the planet will be here in Siskiyou County before the sun comes up."

"I don't think so. And here is where it gets even weirder. Gerry and I were given direct and explicit orders by the FBI lady not to disclose anything that happened out there. Not to anyone. They said it's a matter of national security. I can be arrested for obstruction of justice just for saying what I told you. So, you can't tell anyone, either."

"You think they're not monitoring your call?"

"Maybe so, but I don't give a shit. If Rex and Melinda and their people are unaccounted for, then you and Brenda may be in danger. If they can simply disappear into thin air, especially with the FBI after them, then they can do anything. It's no secret that they don't like the two of you, especially Brenda. I wanted to warn you. You may need to hide, or at least be aware. I've really got to go."

He hung up before I could respond.

"Wow!" said Brenda.

"Yeah. But why would they come after us? I would think we'd be the last people on their minds, especially if the FBI is after them. They could be *en route* to one of their offshore villas or somewhere. They must have gotten a heads-up and gotten the hell out of the county before the feds did their raid. They're long gone. With Hailey Madison, apparently. And how can the FBI keep this under wraps? They must have put out some kind of bulletin to be on the lookout for the Ryders. And for Hailey Madison."

"You'd think," said Brenda. "But they're not here for the Ryders, or for Hailey Madison. They came here for the cartel family. Maybe the Ryders were their informants. Maybe they are giving protection to the Ryders. Or cut them a deal."

"Okay, but what about Hailey? The FBI isn't going to conduct a raid and simply ignore a kidnap victim. Kidnapping is a crime; actually, a federal crime."

"Collateral damage?" asked Brenda. "In furtherance of the larger objective?"

"I thought about that, but it seems far-fetched. Of course, this whole thing is far-fetched. I still don't see how we are in danger."

"You didn't spend the night in their house." she said. "I did. And I haven't told you or anyone what they, mainly her, did to me that night, and I never will. I can't ever tell anybody. It was mostly her, Melinda, but it was facilitated by Rex, and he was definitely getting his jollies. It was horrible." Brenda was becoming agitated. As she talked, the intensity of her voice rose, and tears started flowing. She was having an abrupt, violent, emotional breakdown. I grabbed her, fearing she was about to collapse. She continued to talk, with difficulty, "They are both crazy, but she is worse. She is sadistic. She derives pleasure from hurting and humiliating people and has no remorse or human compassion." Brenda's entire body was shaking now, and she could hardly talk through heaving sobs. Four years before, I saw her through a rough time, but never like this. "What is scaring me is that I have now become her. I am her, maybe worse. I want to hear her scream and plead for mercy while I take my time killing her." She was fighting me now, hitting me and trying to push me away. I didn't know what she would do, and was holding on with all my strength, but couldn't hold on much longer. She shrieked, "Let me go, you bastard!"

I squeezed her harder, with my arms around her back, grabbing the back of her head with my hands. I pulled her head tightly next to mine, cheek to cheek, and just held on. I kept holding on, saying nothing, as her violent body movements slowly subsided. We must have stayed like that for a full five minutes, and I gradually released the pressure of my arms and hands. I guided her toward the couch, and released her, gently allowing her to slide down onto it. She sat down and put her face in her hands. I sat next to her and put both arms around her. I don't recall exactly how long we remained like that, but it was a long time, until my cell phone rang again. It was Mongo.

"Where are you?" I asked.

"Still in my spot," he said. "I got a goddamn good view."

"I'm turning the speaker on. Brenda is with me. What did you see?"

"The whole goddamn thing. When I was a kid, I used to go to cowboy movies at the Broadway Theater, before they kicked me out. They was all shootin' at each other an' shit, just like cowboys."

"Who was?" I asked.

"I dunno who most of 'em was. I recognized the sheriff and one of his guys, but they wasn't in the middle of it. They was in the back. It was these new guys, in SWAT outfits. Their clothes said FBI in big yellow letters. Against a bunch of guys that was in the house, Mexicans. They was all shootin' at each other. I saw at least four guys get shot. On the ground. At least two of 'em looked bad. Two guys down for each side. Then the Mexicans surrendered. They was ordered to the ground. Some of the FBI guys went in the back door of the house. They came out in a little while with the Mexican family, mama and the two kids. The big Mexican guy in the suit came out with 'em. I couldn't tell which side he was on, the FBI guys' or the Mexicans'. The FBI guys wasn't shovin' him around. And he didn't have his hands up. The whole thing didn't last long, but it was wild. Hundreds and hundreds of shots. Like a war. There was two helicopters roarin' around, too. But I think they was just observin'. They never landed, and they never got into the gunfight. Most everybody's gone now. They took the Mexican family and the big Mexican guy away in a couple big black wagons. There was four different meat wagons that come and got the guys that was shot."

"Are there still people there?" I asked.

"A few. All FBI guys. I tell you, it was a real goddamn shootout, just like the cowboy movies."

Brenda asked, "What about the Ryders, and their people. And what about Hailey Madison? Did you see any of them?"

"None of 'em was there at all. Not a single one."

"The whole time?" I asked.

"Yep. The whole goddamn time. I been here since a couple hours after you called me, and I ain't never saw any of them. It's fuckin' strange. Oops, sorry ma'am.

"I've been doin' recon enough lately, that I'm startin' to recognize the people that work for 'em. Ain't none of 'em was there this time. What do you want me to do now?"

"You probably need to get some sleep," I said. "Why don't you go on home for a while."

"Okay, but I'm happy to do whatever you want. This is kinda fun. Like goin' to the movies when I was a kid. I'm glad they got the Mexican lady and her kids out of there alright. I'm afraid that if it looked like they was goin' ta get hurt, I woulda gone down there and helped 'em, even though you said not to."

"You did great, Mongo," I said. "What's really strange is, where are the Ryders? Do you want to hang around there for a while, and see if they show up?"

"Shit, I can hang around here as long as ya want. I brought stuff to eat, and water. And weed. Hell, I can hang around a few days if I'm needed. It's my civic duty."

"Well, that could be really useful, but it's your call. I'm happy to pay you for your services."

"Don't fuckin' insult me," he said. "Like I said, it's my civic duty."

"Okay, thanks. Make sure to keep your phone with you. And please call if you see any sign of the Ryders, or of Hailey Madison."

"Roger," he said.

CHAPTER 37

Bob and Brenda

We were still on the couch when the sun came up. I got up, went into the bathroom, then to the kitchen to make some coffee. Brenda took a shower, then came into the kitchen.

"Are you okay?" I asked.

"Better than last night. I'm really sorry. I totally lost it last night. It came on all of a sudden, and you were very sweet. Thanks for putting up with me."

"Putting up with you? You came to Siskiyou County for some R and R, and look what you've gotten yourself into. Some vacation this turned out to be, and you don't have a dog in the fight. I'm worried about you. It's really distressing to not know where the hell the Ryders are. I don't think you are safe. It may not be safe for you to stay here in Yreka."

"Well, I *have* thought about going back home. After all, I do have a job I eventually need to get back to. I feel that we, you and I, need to do more to find out where Hailey Madison is, if in fact she is alive. But I don't know what we can do."

"The likelihood of her being alive is now pretty thin," I said. "But the situation is more muddled than ever, and I don't have the slightest idea of what we can do either, or what we should do next. I've got a medical appointment in Medford later today that I really need to keep, so I'll be gone for about three hours. I'll think about it while I'm on the road. Maybe you should come with me, and we can brainstorm."

"You go on ahead. It will give me a chance to think about what I want to do, and whether I should go back home."

"I don't know if I should leave you alone."

"I'm a big girl. I can take care of myself."

I've seen her in action, I thought. But I was alarmed nonetheless. I went to my gun safe and retrieved a Walther PPK/S .380 caliber semi-automatic pistol I have had for over thirty years. I inherited it from my father. I handed it to Brenda, with two loaded magazines. "Do you know how to use this?"

"Of course."

I headed up toward Medford, Oregon at around 11:00 AM.

CHAPTER 38

Brenda and Hailey

After Bob left for his medical appointment in Medford, Brenda LeHane went into the bedroom and sat down on the bed. She was troubled and indecisive, and felt helpless. Indecisiveness was not a sensation she was accustomed to. And she didn't like it. Or maybe it was the helplessness. She didn't like that either. Her style had always been to enter the ring swinging away, and she had the scars to prove it. But this time it was all indecisiveness and helplessness. Was Hailey Madison actually a captive in that house, or was it all just a bizarre apparition, fueled by bits and pieces of fragmented information, none of which was authenticated? And there had been no progress, despite two raids; one by the sheriff and one by the FBI! Even though she hadn't actually met Hailey Madison, Brenda felt like she had known her all her life. They shared the same awful experiences. Brenda knew, from four years before, what it was like to be held against her will, totally at the mercy of a remorseless sadistic psychopath. Although she had worked through it to some extent the last four years, the healing process wasn't complete, and it never would be. Her nightmares persisted. And the horrible night she had spent at the mercy of Rex and Melinda in that grotesque house had set her back, maybe beyond repair. *I need to get away from here,* she thought. *I'll go crazy if I stay here any longer. I'm not accomplishing anything worthwhile, and I haven't a clue what to do next. I should go home, back to my job.*

Brenda was preoccupied with these thoughts. She vaguely heard Bebe barking outside, but it didn't register. From the bedroom she thought she heard the front door open, but that didn't register either, she was so deep in her thoughts. Suddenly two men crashed through the bedroom door right at her. One tackled her with brutal force, knocking her to the floor and was on top of her. The second man remained on his feet but held a semiautomatic pistol with both hands pointed at her face. She fought with the man on top of her, trying to hit him with her fists and knees, but he was all over her, and she couldn't get leverage. The man with the gun hit her with it, sharply on the side of her face, creating an instant welt. He said in a staccato but not loud voice, "Stop fighting or we will seriously hurt you!"

She stopped struggling. The man with the gun said, "My friend here is going to get off of you, but do not move. Remain on the floor and put your hands behind your head." She did as she was told, and the other man got off of her. He then fastened cuffs on her ankles, allowing her feet to move only about four inches apart. The man with the gun said, "You have fifteen minutes to get all your things packed. Everything. You are not to leave a single item behind that is yours, not even a toothbrush. We know you want to find Hailey Madison. Well, you are going to get your wish. But if you try to escape or act out in any way, or if you aren't ready to go in fifteen minutes, it will not go well for Hailey Madison. Every minute you delay will make it worse for her. And it will be your fault. You will be the cause of her discomfort. Now, get started. The clock is ticking."

Brenda retrieved her travel bags and started to pack, moving as quickly as she could with her ankles shackled. Almost as penetrating as her fear was the humiliation of shuffling around in the shackles, at the mercy of her captors. But she persisted, throwing her things in the bags as fast as she could, not taking the time to fold or organize. Besides thinking about the packing job, her mind was also on the gun, the little Walther .380 that Bob had given her before he left for Medford. She had put it in the drawer of the nightstand next to the bed. One or the other of the two men kept his eyes on her at all times, watching every move she made. She had placed her large suitcase, opened, on the bed, to make it easier to pack. As she was tossing things into the suitcase, she worked her way to the nightstand. She opened the nightstand drawer, as if to retrieve something for the suitcase. The gun was gone! "Looking for this?" said the other man, with a smile, as he walked into the bedroom. Brandishing the Walther in his hand, he walked over to Brenda and hit her hard with it, this time on the other side of her face. "I'm afraid this is not good news for your friend Hailey Madison," he said.

Brenda didn't get it done in the prescribed fifteen minutes, but was close. The man still holding the Walther walked over to her, looked at his watch and said, "Pretty good, but not quite good enough. I'm afraid your friend will be sorry. But now we have another task for you, before we leave. Sit down at the table." He produced a single sheet of computer paper and a pen, and said, "Write a note to your geezer lover, telling him how much you love him, but you can't stay. The age difference is just too much, make it sound heartfelt. What's it like for someone as hot as you to screw an old geezer like that, anyway? Can he even get it up? You're just a gold digger, aren't you? He probably won't last but a couple more years anyway. You can put up with him that long, right? And then you end up with everything he's got."

Brenda, seated at the table, took the pen and attempted to write, but her hand was so shaky, she couldn't do it. "Time's a-wasting," said the man with the Walther. "Get it done, quick! Think of your friend."

Brenda took three deep breaths, clenched her teeth, and wrote the note. The man with the Walther inspected it and was apparently satisfied. "Okay, we're out of here," he said, as he pulled Brenda off the chair and pushed her toward the door.

Forty miles away, Hailey Madison was in agony. She was still naked, and still limited in her range of motion due to the metal collar around her neck and the chain connected to it from the ceiling. Melinda, in a fit of anger, (or was it sadistic pleasure?) had caused the ceiling chain to be shortened to a length that prevented her from resting her head on the bed. She couldn't lie down, and she couldn't move but inches in any direction. She could barely get her mouth to a bowl of water on a nightstand next to the bed, but had no access to food, or to the toilet. She had no idea how long she was left in that condition but believed it to have been at least twenty-four hours. The pain was brutal, and her body and the bed were wet and filthy from her own excrement. The temporary relief of sleep was denied to her, and she was awake when Melinda paid her another visit. "Look at you," she cooed. "Aren't you a sight? Sleep well?"

Hailey's defiant resistance was gone. She was broken. She whispered, "Please, no more. I'll do what you want."

"Well, now. Let's see. I will lower your chain enough for you to prove it. Melinda did that, then unbuttoned her shorts and panties, letting them fall to the floor, and presented her body to Hailey's face, making it obvious what she expected from her. Afterward, she said, "That's pretty good, but I'm sure you'll get a lot better with time and practice, and you'll have plenty of that, before we sell you. We want our customer to be satisfied." As she was leaving the room, Melinda turned toward Hailey and said, pleasantly, "Oh, I meant to ask you, are you lonely?" Before waiting for an answer, she went on, "You're going to have some company soon, a delicious chocolate morsel. I'm sure the two of you will get along just fine." Melinda turned and went out the door.

Later, a couple of men came into Hailey's dungeon room. One of them disconnected the chain from her neck collar, released her hands from behind her back, and manhandled her into a walk-in shower in a nearby room. "Get yourself clean," he commanded, and watched her do so. Afterward, he manhandled her back to the bed and reconnected the ceiling chain, but not her wrist cuffs. The bed had been changed and the room cleaned, and a tray of food on the bed actually looked pretty good.

CHAPTER 39

Bob and Brad

My drive to Medford was uneventful. The appointment was with my dermatologist. I am skin cancer prone, paying the price for spending too much time in the sun as a youth. Back then the objective of summer vacation was to soak up as many rays as necessary to build up a tan that would allow you to spend all day in the sun with no sunscreen protection, and still not burn. Most young people today are more careful; at least I hope so. Over the years I have had more than a hundred lesions removed, including Basal Cell Carcinomas, Squamous Cell Carcinomas, and even some malignant Melanomas. Fortunately, the malignant ones have all been caught before they metastasized and spread to other parts of my body, but the concern is great enough that I go every six months for an examination. My dermatologist goes over my body with a magnifying glass, like Sherlock Holmes, and often detects spots barely discernable to the naked eye. I probably owe my life to him. I missed the last appointment and was overdue. The appointment this day lasted only about thirty-five minutes, and the doctor spotted nothing that looked suspicious, thank God, so I was on my way home by 12:45 PM. I hoped to use the driving time constructively to come up with a plan regarding Hailey Madison and the Ryders, but my septuagenarian brain wasn't cooperating. It was too consumed with dread and worry about Brenda, and, I have to confess, about me.

When I got home at 2:00 PM, I didn't see Brenda's rental car parked in front.

I walked into my little house, and Brenda wasn't there. Bebe was outside in the backyard, barking furiously. I went out to see what was bothering her. "Hey, Bebe, what's the matter?" Before I finished the question, she was on me, pouncing on my chest. She never does that. She was agitated, barking and whining, and then ran into the house, as if she wanted me to follow her. Usually, I understand her language quite well, but I wasn't picking up on it this time. She was distraught. I followed her into the house. She was running around like crazy, inspecting every room, with me following behind.

Brenda's clothes and personal items were gone from the bedroom and closet, including her travel bags. The bathroom had similarly been emptied out. She had packed up and left! She wouldn't have done that without telling me, I was sure. This was all wrong. Trying to calm myself, I began methodically to survey the house, again going from room to room, but in a more deliberate manner. Except for the fact that neither Brenda nor her possessions were present, the house looked normal. There were no indications of a physical struggle or altercation. Then, on the kitchen table, I saw the note.

It was a white 8 ½ x 11-inch sheet of printer paper with handwritten text in blue ink.

> *Dear Bob*
>
> *I'm so very sorry to leave in this manner, but frankly, I just didn't have the heart to tell you in person. I truly do love you, but more like a grandpa than the way you want me to love you. What you want from me is destined to failure. It just can't happen. Our age difference is too great. It's hard enough for me to tell you this today, but it will only get harder if I put it off into the future.*
>
> *Please don't try to contact me. I think it is better for both of us if we end this once and for all.*
>
> *Lov*
>
> *Brenda*

I was standing up when I read the note, but felt my legs trembling so much I had to sit down. Bebe came up to me and put her head on my knee, much less frantic now. It was as if she was satisfied that I had now gotten the message she was trying to give me. "This is terrible," I said to her. "I knew I shouldn't have left her alone. It's my fault. It was my fault four years ago when she was dragged through hell, and now it's happening again. I wish you could tell me exactly what happened, but I already know she didn't leave on her own volition. She would never write a letter like this. It doesn't describe our relationship. Whoever took her, forced her to write the letter; but they wouldn't know of the true nature of our relationship. They wouldn't know that Brenda would never write a letter like this. And they certainly wouldn't know of our secret code. By signing off with 'Lov,' she signaled to me that she's in trouble and needs help. The Ryders are behind this. They wanted her, and now they've got her. But where the hell are they? Wherever they are, what they've done is diabolical. It's just like what they did to Hailey Madison and Ben Thompson. If Brenda disappears, the existence of the note gives me a motive to harm her. I will be the prime suspect. It's a convenient way to get rid of two people who have become irritants to them. But it's so damn obvious, no one in their right mind would believe they could get away with it. But the Ryders are psychopaths. Enough said."

Bebe looked up at me as if she understood and agreed with everything I had said. Bebe, like most Labradors, looks you right in the eye. Not all dogs do that. "What do you think?" I asked her.

"They have both Brenda and Hailey Madison in that house," she said. "That house is an evil place. I'll help you get them out."

"How do we do that?"

She didn't have an answer.

I called Brenda's cell number. It rang in the normal manner and went to voicemail. "This is Brenda. Leave a message."

"It's Bob. Please call me."

I called the sheriff, using his personal cell phone. "Brenda's gone," I said. "Can you come over?"

He arrived at my house about fifteen minutes later. I showed him the note and told him about Mongo's "intel" report.

"The Ryders and their entourage had to have been tipped, somehow," said Brad. "I'm sure it didn't come from my department. Hell, no one in my department even knew anything about the raid, except Gerry and me. Gerry's rock solid, and you know I wouldn't leak it. That raid was one-hundred-per-cent controlled by the feds. They just took Gerry and me along for the ride. And they didn't fill me in on any information they had. For all I know, the Ryders could have been informants. Maybe they have already been whisked away to some safe house. Part of a witness protection program."

"Sure, but where is Hailey Madison? And where are the Ryders' people? I'm not talking about gardeners, house keepers, and people like that. They must have people on the property that are in their inner circle. And who kidnapped Brenda? You do believe she was kidnapped, don't you? You don't take Brenda's note at face value … Do you?" I was desperate.

"Calm down," he said. "I'm on your side. I think she was taken against her will. I've gotten to know her pretty well myself, you know, and she wouldn't write a note like that voluntarily. One thing I have to say about her. Every time she comes to town, all hell breaks loose. I may have to ask the Board of Supervisors to pass an ordinance prohibiting her from entering the county."

"It would make your job boring," I said. "But she's a missing person, what do we do?"

"Well, you and I know she's a missing person, but it might be a tough sell to others, considering her note. Did you recognize her handwriting?"

"Yes. It's hers."

"I'll handle it with standard 'missing person' protocol. Other agencies may not get too excited about actively pursuing it, given the note, but I'll do my best to persuade them."

"What about going back out to the property?"

"What for? The FBI's already been there. Nobody does a better job conducting a search than the FBI. Trust me, I'll put everybody on it that I can." He headed for the door.

I followed him out. "Thanks, I know you will, but I'm really scared."

After he left, I sat down and put my head in my hands. I couldn't remember ever having felt so devastated; terrified, angry, frustrated, and alone. Bebe rested her head on my leg. It helped a little.

CHAPTER 40

Bob - The Posse

I had dinner that evening with my daughter, son-in-law, and the grandkids at their house. Many septuagenarians aren't fortunate enough to have their grandkids so close. Watching your grandchildren grow up and participating in their lives has all the benefits of raising children without the burdens. Another advantage is that my daughter and son-in-law have their own circle of friends, a younger generation. They are kind enough to include me in their social events and activities, keeping me in the loop. Their group of friends is diverse. It includes school teachers and administrators, hunting and fishing guides, contractors, small business owners, lawyers, cops, firefighters, doctors, and ordinary working people. They, like most people, don't live in our county for the money. They live here for the lifestyle. They appreciate the mountains, forests, rivers, and streams. They are fiercely independent and take pride in that. They resent big government and bureaucrats from Washington, D.C. and Sacramento telling them how they should live their lives. Four years ago, this group of people, who I called "the posse," helped me fight the leader of an international criminal organization engaged in human trafficking that was conducting its obscene and vicious operations right here within our rural peaceful county.

I brought Erin and David up-to-date, and showed them a copy of Brenda's note. I had made a copy before giving the original to the sheriff. We were having a spirited conversation that, unfortunately, was not leading toward a workable plan of action, when my cell phone did its Bob Seger ring tone.

It was Mongo. I put him on speaker. "This is the goddamnedest thing I ever saw," he said. "They're still here."

"Who?'

"Ryder, the cowboy movie star grandson, and his sister. They was in the house the whole time."

"What do you mean? How is that possible?"

"Beats the shit out of me," he said. "I been here the whole fuckin' time and been watchin.' I never seen 'em leave, and I never seen 'em arrive. They must've been in the house durin' the shootout. And their people, too."

"What people?"

"*Their* people. Ya know, the people that works for 'em. I recognize 'em, 'cause I seen em' come and go before, while doin' my recon. They're not the Mexicans. The Mexicans is all gone. They was rounded up by the FBI. These're Ryder's people. I seen some of 'em outside the house a few hours ago. A couple of 'em drove up in one of them delivery trucks. They drove to the helicopter pad and backed up to the house. Two of 'em got out of the front seat and walked around to the back of the truck, but it was under the roof and I couldn't see if they took nuthin' from the back of the truck. They was parked there a few minutes, then the two got back in the front seat and drove off. But just now, I seen both the Ryder guy and the sister. They came outside the house for a few minutes with another of their guys and went back in."

"What were they doing?" I asked.

"I dunno. They was just walkin' around the house, like they was lookin' for something. Then they walked over to the guest house. Then back in the big house.

"Is anything going on there right now?" I asked.

"Nope. Everyone's inside."

"I don't understand how the Ryders can be there," I said. "Are you sure they didn't come to the house sometime after the search?"

"Sure as shit. I ain't never took my eyes off the house. They had to be inside the whole time."

"Okay," I said. Then I remembered I hadn't told him about Brenda. "Brenda's missing. You didn't see her there, did you?"

There was a pause, then a shaky voice, "No she ain't been here. What do you mean she's missing?"

"When I got back home from Medford this afternoon, she was gone. I think she may have been kidnapped. She left a note, said she was going home. But I don't think it's true. I think she was forced to write it."

"You think Ryders got 'er?" He sounded like he was about to cry.

"I think maybe so. We've got to find her."

"Fuck! This is horrible. Ya know, they coulda took her in the house when I seen the truck on the helicopter pad. She coulda been in the back of the truck. I couldn't see."

"That's possible," I said. "Look, we're working on a plan to get her out. What you're doing right now is the most important thing. Can you stay there and keep watch?"

"Damn right. But if she's in there I should go in and get her."

"I don't think that will be possible. Too dangerous for her and for you, too. Our best bet is to send a posse out there. And it is very important for you to maintain your position. You can be the posse's eyes and ears."

"Okay."

"Okay," I said. "Now promise me you will stay right there, that you won't try to do anything on your own."

"Okay."

"And call and report everything you see."

"Okay."

After Mongo hung up, David said, "They're underground. In the bomb shelter."

"Sure," I said. "But wouldn't the FBI have found them? They found the cartel family."

"There could be more than one underground vault, separate from the other. Hell, there could be more than one level. A basement under the basement. Since the last time we talked about this, I got really interested and have done a lot more research about underground bomb shelters. I've actually been thinking about building one. You never know when you might need one. The Ryders built their place from the ground up. Actually, maybe from the underground up, or the under-underground up. They could have built anything they wanted, and no one was looking over their shoulders. Here's a hypothesis. Suppose there are two -- maybe even more, why stop at two? -- separate underground vaults. Suppose the Ryders weren't happy having to be hosts to the kidnapped family of a Mexican cartel. Suppose they tipped the FBI that the family was there and gave them enough information for the FBI to get to the family, but not to the Ryders, in a completely separate underground vault. The FBI may not even have known about another vault, or cared, as long as they got what they came for."

"That makes sense," I said. "But the Ryders may be on thin ice with the cartel they work with. Let me try to get this straight. Two rival cartels are fighting with each other, *Costa Oeste* and *La Peninsula*. The Ryders have a connection to, or are maybe owned by, *La Peninsula*. Maybe *La Peninsula* decides now is the time for the Ryders to pay their dues, and the cartel calls on them to provide secure quarters for the kidnapped *Costa Oeste* family. The Ryders aren't happy with the arrangement, so they tip the FBI. Well, *La Peninsula* can't be happy about *that*. They'll get revenge on the Ryders. That's where the hypothesis breaks down. The Ryders surely are smart enough to know there will be consequences. Why would they do it?"

David answered, "Because they are the Ryders. They've spent their whole lives doing whatever the hell they want, with no consequences. Why should this be different? But they may have gone too far this time. Those cartels are Mexico's most powerful and ruthless. They're used to doing whatever they want, too. The Ryders might be in the unfortunate situation of having both cartels after them, *Costa Oeste* for assisting in the kidnapping, and *La Peninsula* for tipping the FBI. I think the Ryders are toast."

Erin entered the discussion, "When you guys started this conversation, I thought you were crazy. This is Siskiyou County, for God's sake, peaceful rural Siskiyou County. But now you've got me convinced. Frankly, I don't care what happens to the Ryders. They'll get what they deserve. But what about Hailey Madison and Brenda? I think we all believe they are being held in that awful house. What will happen to them?"

David responded, "They are toast, too, if we don't do something to help them. We can't rely on the cops, or the FBI. Let's face it, there already have been two raids on the house, one by the sheriff, and one by the FBI. And what have they accomplished? Nada. We can't wait for them to do something else. We've got to go in there tonight, before the Mexicans get to them first. I'm calling the posse. I'm going to see how many people I can round up and get them here in an hour. We'll meet here at the house, as our staging area."

"You think you can get people here in an hour?" I asked. "It'll take longer than that to just explain what's going on."

My son-in-law looked at me with more than a little contempt; out of character for him. "You have a better idea?"

I was more embarrassed than pissed. "No, I don't. Divide up the names; we can all start calling."

An hour and a half later there were eleven people at the house, seven men and four women, including David, Erin, and myself. I didn't count the firearms, but was sure that the firearms outnumbered the people by at least two to one. Hey, this is Siskiyou County! David had initially objected to including women, but the ladies quickly disabused him of that notion. As I may have said earlier, the folks of Siskiyou County are fiercely independent. That includes the women-folks.

After an organizational briefing session, with David in charge, by 2:00 AM the eleven of us were on our way to the Scott Valley in four heavy duty four-wheel-drive vehicles. The briefing had been short, primarily devoted to assembling a list of equipment items each person should have, in addition to the firearms. Several members of the posse were on the volunteer fire department. One of the four vehicles was a truck "borrowed" from the fire department, containing an assortment of equipment and tools normally used for firefighting. When I saw the fire truck, I immediately started counting the lawsuits in my mind, but kept my mouth shut. Also "borrowed" from the fire department was a set of walkie-talkies, all set to the same frequency; enough to go around. We launched our invasion, long on firepower and equipment, but short on an actual plan.

It was not a particularly dark night. The moon wasn't full, but close enough. The visibility was fair, which worked both ways.

CHAPTER 41

The Basement

Rex and Melinda hadn't tipped the FBI. They were unaware that a raid was imminent. They weren't happy about being the unwilling hosts of Señora Rodriguez and her children, and the idea scared them. It would not go well for them if the *Costa Oeste* discovered where the family was being held. They feared the cartel, and had made arrangements for a hasty getaway if necessary. But the fear was not so overwhelming that they were in panic mode ... yet. Getting away, if it came to that, was entirely within their means. Actually, Melinda had already been warming up to the thought. They had been in the Scott Valley too long. A change of scenery would be nice, and they certainly had pleasant places to go. They would take their downstairs captive with them. Melinda had plans for her. The thought made her body tingle.

The FBI raid caught them by surprise but dealing with it was easy. Rex and Melinda considered their underground domain to be their masterpiece, even superior to the mansion itself. With its three self-contained units, it was world-class. These were in addition to the more-accessible space which contained their produce-box "factory." After Señora Rodriguez arrived, all three units were in use. She, her children, and their cartel handlers occupied one unit. Hailey Madison, and *maybe soon the black bitch*, mused Melinda, occupied another. The third was primarily for Rex and Melinda's personal use and their illicit "business" operations. They both realized they had gotten carried away when they built their underground complex. It hadn't originally been planned to be so extensive; rather, it evolved. As construction progressed, they kept coming up with new ideas, until they kept adding more rooms and high-tech gadgetry simply because they could. It was a challenging game. They wanted to have the best in the world, and they may have succeeded. Also, they wanted their facility to be able to accommodate their darkest fantasies, and they accomplished that as well. Hailey Madison was not the first of their unwilling "guests." Although the FBI raid was unexpected, its occurrence wasn't much of a setback for Rex and Melinda. It was actually somewhat of a blessing, because it got rid of the *Costa Oeste* family. Rex, Melinda, and their key staff people merely sat out the FBI search in the third unit of the underground vaults. They weren't sure how the FBI figured out how to access the unit that housed the *Costa Oeste* family, and that was of concern. Maybe someone in their own organization tipped them, and Rex and Melinda would have to look into that, in due course. Of more immediate concern was whether the FBI knew about the other two units. But, as their search progressed, it became clear that the FBI had no idea that the other two units even existed, allowing Rex and Melinda to wait it out. The FBI didn't know they were there, or that Hailey Madison was there.

Their comfort level received a massive jolt the morning after the FBI raid, and it caused them to seriously begin thinking it was time to leave. The jolt was in the form of a call on the blue phone, and the electronically distorted female voice. Rex answered the phone and put it on speaker for Melinda to hear. "You have no idea what you have done," said the voice. "You have angered *La Peninsula* because you let the Rodriguez family get away. You have angered *Costa Oeste* because you imprisoned their family in your basement. And you have angered us because you have caused a breakdown in our very beneficial working relationship with *La Peninsula*. There is a colorful phrase that describes your situation, and it is this: you are royally fucked."

"Wait a minute!" shouted Rex, attempting to sound defiant. "It wasn't our fault. It wasn't our responsibility to guard them. It was *La Peninsula's* responsibility, and they had their people here to do it. We did nothing wrong! Guarding them was never our responsibility. We didn't want them here in the first place." There was a catch in his voice that betrayed his effort to sound bold. "And we certainly had nothing to do with the raid itself. There must have been a leak in the *La Peninsula* organization. None of our people would have done that."

"Ah, but I fear that both cartels will see it differently. And our concern, of course, is our excellent relationship with *La Peninsula*, which I fear has been damaged."

"But, we didn't ... What should we do?" whimpered Rex.

"I'm at somewhat of a loss to give you advice. It would help if somehow you could return the Rodriguez family back to *La Peninsula*, but it's not likely you have the resources to do that. Your resources, compared to those of *La Peninsula* and to ours, are paltry, miniscule; so, I don't realistically expect you to be able to pull that off. My primary reason for calling you at this time is simply to give you a heads-up. Our organization has worked with your family for generations, and I feel an obligation to express our disappointment, to warn you of danger, and to set you on the right track. Like a parent speaking to a child. And also, to let you know that, whatever happens, I, and the organization I speak for, sincerely wish you the very best. We have your best interest at heart." And the line went dead.

The shards of terror in Rex and Melinda's hearts gradually gave way to other emotions; anger, then rage, then focus on a course of action. "Paltry and miniscule?" said Rex. He wasn't asking a question. "Paltry and miniscule!" said Rex again, rage building up. "Our place here in the Scott Valley is just the tip of the iceberg of our resources. I think it's time to leave this back-woods hillbilly dump. We aren't appreciated here anyway. We will leave tomorrow morning. I'll have Margaret set it up right now. She can get the helicopter here late tonight, and we'll leave at the crack of dawn tomorrow morning. We won't use the airplane that's in Medford. If anyone's watching us, that's what they'll expect us to do. We'll bring in the Los Angeles jet. Our pilots can fly it to Eureka, and we'll catch it there. How does Dubai sound? It's been a long time since we've been to Dubai. We can fly there and stay a while. I've been wanting to get back there anyway. We'll have the black bitch by then, and we can take her and the white bitch with us. They can entertain us on the long flight. That'll make you happy, dear sister, and I'm sure the eyes of our discerning friends in Dubai will light up when they see them."

"Adios, Siskiyou County, we're out of here!" exulted Melinda, with no remorse.

CHAPTER 42

Bob - The Posse

Our four vehicles arrived at the front gate of the Ryder compound at 3:30 AM. While we were *en route,* Mongo called me on my cell. "What's going on?" I asked.

"Not a goddamn thing," he said, "'cept for the helicopter. It just landed a few minutes ago. It's a big sombitch. And I lost track of the number of people that climbed out of it. They all went inside the house, and nuthin's happnin' right now. It's quiet. The chopper's shut down. Nobody's outside the house."

"How well can you see it?" I asked. "Can you see its N-number?"

"Its what?"

"There should be a number on the side of the helicopter, big letters. Combination of letters and numbers; the first letter is an 'N.'"

"Shit yeah. Pretty dark, but I can see it. It's 'N41221.'"

"Okay," I said. "Good job. We're getting close to the front gate. You should be able to see us pretty quick. Keep us posted if there are any changes."

"Roger."

As the four vehicles approached the gate, my anxiety level peaked. We had no plan; no strategy. What were we going to do, just boldly drive right up to the house? That didn't seem like a good idea, but did anybody have a better one? There was some comfort in knowing we had our eye in the sky, Mongo. Mongo was our secret weapon. I was riding with Erin and David in their pickup. The fourth passenger was Charles Black, their good friend. He was a big guy, about forty-five years old. Now a physical therapist, he played NCAA Division I football while in college. I was glad he was on our side. I was happy that our whole crew was on our side. They weren't cops or soldiers, but, except for me, all the participants were in their forties, and physically fit. Our vehicle was the first to reach the gate. Remembering what Hailey had told me a long time before, I told David, our driver, "Try R-E-D-Y-R."

He did, and the gate slowly swung open, remaining open long enough for all four vehicles to zip through. We trundled along the Ryders' lane toward the house, with no opposition. When we were within sight of the house, David announced on his walkie-talkie, "No resistance so far. The main road connects with the circular driveway that goes around the house to the helipad. Let's leave one rig to guard the main road, to prevent anyone from getting away that direction. Then we'll surround the house with the other three. My truck and the fire truck around back, and the other rig in front of the house. Everybody just stay with your vehicles while we come up with a strategy." All the vehicles were moved into position, still with no resistance. It was unnervingly quiet.

My cell phone came alive. Mongo. "I see all of you, but don't see nobody else. It's fuckin' weird. I know there's lots of people in the house. I seen 'em go in. I don't know where ..." He spoke too soon. Before he finished his sentence, the back door and front door of the house suddenly burst open and shots were fired. Shots were also coming from two of the windows at the back of the house. It was a barrage of fully automatic machine gun fire that lasted a full minute, although it seemed like ten.

Bullets tore into the four vehicles, causing major damage. The four of us were crouched low behind the pickup. Suddenly Charles, right in front of me, yelled and spun around, grabbing his right shoulder as he was slammed to the ground. About the same time, I heard a female scream from behind the fire truck, although I couldn't see what happened or recognize the voice. At least two of us had been hit. Possibly more; we couldn't see what was happening with the vehicles on the other side of the house. Then it got quiet again, although Charles was moaning and the sound of a woman crying came from behind the fire truck.

A full five minutes passed, with no activity. It was a standoff. The people inside the house were trapped. We had them pinned down, so they couldn't come out. But similarly, we couldn't emerge from behind our vehicles. I grabbed my cell phone and called the sheriff's cell. He didn't answer, but before it could go to voice mail, my phone signaled an incoming call, from him. "Now what!" he said after I connected with his call. "You do realize it's four o'clock in the morning."

"I do realize that," I said. "Sorry to bother you, but we have a situation here and need some back-up."

"A situation where? No, please don't tell me. I don't want to know. I'm going back to sleep." Then there was a pause, and he went on, "Please don't tell me you're at the Ryder place?"

"I'm afraid so. Whether we are right or wrong, it doesn't matter. The situation here definitely needs a law enforcement response. We have four vehicles and eleven people who have surrounded Ryder's mansion. They have opened fire on us from inside the house. Fully automatic firearms. We have the people inside the house pinned down, but they have us pinned down as well, so no one is going anywhere. It is a hostage situation. At least two of our people are injured, I don't know how seriously, and there may be more. So, we need a medical response, as well. I'm positive Hailey Madison and Brenda LeHane are inside. There's helicopter parked on the helipad, but it is currently unoccupied. Its N-number is N41221."

"Shit! OK, we'll get rolling, but it's going to be a while before we can get there. I'll see if we can get some air support. Give me the N-number, again."

I gave him the N-number and hung up. We hadn't been disconnected more than thirty seconds when my cell phone notified me of another call, an "unknown caller."

"This is Rex Ryder," said the caller. "I assume you are one of the people outside, trespassing on my property. You need to get your people the hell off of my property. Right now!"

"I'm afraid we can't do that," I said, trying to mask the fear and sickness I was experiencing in my gut. "We know you have kidnapped two women, and that they are your hostages. We can't leave here without them!"

"You have no idea what you are talking about. You are full of shit. By the time we get through suing you, all of you, you won't have a pot to piss in. You'll be ruined, and you'll deserve it. We have two guests who came out here to have a good time. If you haven't noticed, we have a beautiful place here, despite your efforts to destroy it and us. People like coming out here. People come here from all over the world for what we have here. We don't kidnap people." His voice was devoid of any trace of a southern or western drawl. Also, although his words were tough-sounding, the tone of his voice didn't match the words. He sounded scared shitless; like a frightened kid.

I interrupted him. "So, you admit the women are here. Your people have injured two of our folks, good people in our community. They need medical care. We may have trespassed, but if we did so it was under the belief that you committed the crime of kidnapping. This is a volatile situation. We have you surrounded, and I just talked to the sheriff. Your place is about to be invaded by every law enforcement officer in the North State, with helicopters. There is no way you can win. If this doesn't stop right now, people are going to be killed, and it will be your fault. You have the power to stop this. If the women are here voluntarily, all you have to do is send them out so they can tell us themselves. If we are satisfied, then we'll back off, and you can sue us all you want. The ball is in your court."

He didn't respond. Two minutes went by, and we were still connected, but neither of us said a word. Then the line went dead. "Shit!" I said to David and Erin. "I don't know what the hell to do, except wait for the sheriff's people to show up. Maybe they've got someone who is a trained hostage negotiator. We've got them surrounded, so they can't go anywhere. But it would be a disaster if we tried to storm the house. They would kill us all with their fully automatic firearms." Erin and David just looked at me, silently nodding.

Then David spoke into his walkie-talkie, "We have reinforcements on the way, and need to hold our positions here. Don't anyone try to do something heroic, like charging the house. We have one injury here, Charles. He's hit in the shoulder, but he's going to be okay. Are there any other injuries?"

"It's Donna," said the voice of Dr. Carl MacGregor, sounding shaken. "She has a leg wound and is hurting. We have first aid supplies here in the fire truck, and I can stop the bleeding, but she's in shock. I hope I have what I need to help her."

"Okay, do what you can. Help should be on its way," said David. A trained paramedic, he bent down to see what he could do to help Charles, who was on the ground clasping his shoulder.

Ten minutes later, my cell phone came to life. It was Rex again. "You need to listen to me and do exactly what I say." His voice sounded more authoritative than before; less frightened. There was still no drawl. "These women are here voluntarily, because they want to be. But we know you won't believe us, because you are so narrow-minded and ignorant, and have no idea what is actually going on. We know you will kill us if we come out. So, you leave us no choice. We have to protect ourselves from your murderous stupidity, and these women are the only means we have to do that. We feel bad for them, but, again, you leave us no choice. If something bad happens to them it will be on you, not us. I have instructions for you. Are you listening?"

"Yes," I said.

"Ten of us are going to leave here on that helicopter. The ten people include two pilots, Melinda and me, Margaret, our chief of staff, our two guests, who you claim are here against their will, and three of our trusted men. Although we deplore the thought of harming them, it will be our two guests who will insure our safe passage away from here. We have no choice. In one minute, our two pilots will walk out to the helicopter, do their preflight, and prepare it for takeoff. Once the aircraft is ready to go, Margaret, Melinda and I will board it. We will be followed by our two guests, accompanied by three of our men. The three men will have guns pointed at our two guests. Also, we have men in the house with rifles that will also be pointed at them, until they are actually inside the aircraft. Your job will be simple. You will make no move to stop us. You will fire no weapon. You will do nothing to hinder our aircraft. If any one of your people so much as breathes, our men are instructed to kill our black guest instantly. If that happens, we will still have our white guest to guarantee our safe passage. If it becomes necessary to kill the white one also, then of course our cause is lost. But we don't think you will want to have the killing of either one on your consciences. You have one minute to give the necessary instructions to your people, then our two pilots will start walking toward the aircraft. Any questions?"

"No," I said, nodding to David, who had heard Rex's voice. David picked up the walkie-talkie and instructed the posse to comply.

The two pilots, both armed with holstered pistols, walked calmly and deliberately out the door, along the covered walkway, onto the helicopter pad, and climbed up into the chopper. We could see them through the windscreen, as they spent a few minutes settling into their seats, putting on headphones, and manipulating controls. Then, slowly the machine's rotors came alive. The next person to walk to the helicopter was a woman I didn't recognize. Presumably she was Margaret, the chief of staff. Behind her, walking side-by-side, were Rex and Melinda. They weren't wearing their usual pricey Western garb. They looked like they were going to a celebrity cocktail party in Monte Carlo. Rex looked like James Bond in a black tuxedo, and Melinda was striking in a slinky long black cocktail dress with a neckline down to her navel, and black shoes with spike heels at least four inches long. They both looked like they were strolling down the red carpet at the Academy Awards, until they ducked while approaching the spinning rotor blades and climbed single-file up the steps into the helicopter. After Rex and Melinda were well within the chopper, the final five members of the procession made the same journey, single file, all dressed in non-descript casual attire. The first was thug number one, carrying an AK-47-style automatic rifle, followed by Hailey, who didn't appear to be cuffed or shackled. Behind her was thug number two, pressed up tightly against her back, shoving her toward the chopper, with his left arm around her neck. With his right hand he pressed the muzzle of a handgun into the side of her head. Brenda, also unshackled, was pushed along behind them, with thug number three and his handgun pressed up against her, similar to the one with Hailey.

I watched this procession with such a sinking feeling I had to fight hard not to vomit. The feeling of helplessness was overwhelming. It would be impossible to get off a shot at either guy holding onto a woman without a risk of hitting the woman. But, even more important, any attempt to do so would be a death sentence for the woman from a sharpshooter inside the house. *We can't just do nothing*, I thought. *If that helicopter takes off with them inside, we will never see them alive. If we are going to make a move, it has to be now.*

Suddenly, a very large human-like figure came roaring around from the other side of the helicopter and crashed into the guy holding Brenda, causing him to release his grip and fall away from her. Brenda reacted by breaking loose and jumping onto the back of the guy holding Hailey, and screaming, "Run Hailey, run!" Her impact caused him to lose his balance and caused the muzzle of his gun to be deflected away from Hailey. The gun did not fire. Hailey started to run toward us. Brenda, still clinging to the guy's back, maneuvered him around so his body was between her and the house when a burst of bullets ripped into his chest, causing him to be slammed backward, and causing Brenda to shriek. I thought maybe she had been hit, too. As he was going down, the guy in front with the AK-47 in one hand pulled her off him with his other hand and physically dragged her up into the helicopter. Rapid-fire shots came from the house, apparently aimed at her, but instead ripped into the large human-like figure, who was attempting to grab Brenda and prevent her from being pulled up into the chopper. Hailey still had some distance to reach us, so the posse fired a continuous blast of bullets at the people inside of the house, to give her cover. Thug number three, who had been knocked to the ground by the large human-like guy, was picking himself up, the gun still in his hand. He was taking aim at Hailey as she was running away, when the posse's bullets tore into him. As we pulled her to safety behind our vehicle, the helicopter began slowly rising from the pad. Brenda was somewhere inside, but the door was still open, and the guy with the AK-47 was firing down on us. Someone in the posse – I couldn't see who – shot him in the chest, causing him to fall backward inside the helicopter, putting an end to his threat. The copter rose and then moved in a westerly direction, toward the ocean. The shooting stopped, and it was quiet.

CHAPTER 43

Bob - The Cavalry

As the helicopter disappeared from view, I called Brad's cell. He answered immediately. "The helicopter took off," I said, breathlessly. "They've got Brenda. It took off and is headed west. Where are you?"

"Okay, slow down," he said. "Tell me what's going on."

"Okay, sorry. It's bad here. Rex and Melinda and some of their people boarded the helicopter and took off. They had Brenda and Hailey Madison at gun point and tried to get them into the helicopter. We had the house and helicopter surrounded, but they had the two women as hostages, so we couldn't stop them without risking the two women. But some big guy came from out of nowhere and started a scuffle. I think it's Mongo, but it's still pretty dark. Mongo was up above, watching the house, and I think he decided to come down and join in. But he got shot, and I don't know how bad. We can't get to him. Because of him, Hailey was able to break away, and she's now okay. She's with us. But they've got Brenda. She's with them in the helicopter.

"In addition to Rex and Melinda, four of their people are in the helicopter, plus Brenda. But I think we may have shot one of them. So that makes three, the two pilots plus a woman named Margaret. Two of their people didn't make it into the chopper and are on the ground. They've been shot; I don't know if they're still alive. So, we've got a total of five injured or dead people on the ground. Some of Ryder's people are still in the house, don't know how many, and there may be some injured people in there, too. We have a standoff, with them inside, and us outside. We need ambulances and help. How far out are you?"

"Probably about forty-five minutes."

"Okay, I don't think anyone's going anywhere. We've got a doctor with us, and by the way, we stole a fire truck, which has emergency first aid equipment and supplies. Can you track the helicopter?"

"We'll do our best, but we don't know exactly where it's going. The N-number is phony. That registration number was decommissioned long ago."

After the helicopter had disappeared beyond the horizon, the frenetic activity at the Ryder mansion came to a standstill. There was no more shooting. But the atmosphere was highly charged. It was like the proverbial calm before the storm, except that the storm never materialized. Hailey Madison was safely behind our truck and uninjured, at least from the gunfire. She was shuddering violently, crying and sobbing, generally hysterical. Erin had her arms around her, trying to calm her down, with little success. She looked pale and emaciated, but I saw no obvious signs of trauma or physical abuse. Her injuries were much deeper, and would take a long time to heal, if ever.

The first to appear from the sheriff's forces were two helicopters. They did not try to land; rather, they hovered overhead, as if keeping the whole scene under surveillance. Shortly after, a procession of official vehicles streamed onto the property, lights flashing, and took up positions around the main house. The vehicles included patrol cars and trucks from various agencies, and three ambulances. At least a dozen officers, male and female, emptied out of the vehicles, including six in full SWAT garb. Shortly after the vehicles had established their positions, but well before any effort was made to storm the house, the back door opened, and two men walked out nervously, their hands raised high in the air. They looked pathetic. They walked slowly toward the sheriff's vehicle, yelling, "Surrender!" repeatedly, until they felt comfortable that they wouldn't be shot.

Sheriff Brad Davis held a bullhorn, "How many are inside?"

"Five more," said one of the men. "They are surrendering, too. They will be coming out the back door in a few minutes. Give them time, please." The guy was whimpering and looked sincere. A few minutes later, five more people filed out, all males, their hands raised high.

"Is there anyone else in the house?" called out Brad.

"No. I'm the last one," said the man at the end of the procession. "No one else is inside, I swear."

That turned out to be true, although it was several hours before the sheriff's forces could be sure. Once the surrendering men were cuffed and secured, the SWAT team cautiously entered the house and began to clear it. Paramedics checked out the people who had received gunshot wounds. The two thugs who had walked Brenda and Hailey out of the building were both dead, their bodies shredded by countless bullets. Charles Black and Donna MacGregor were in considerable distress, but stable. After being ministered to for fifteen or twenty minutes, they were loaded into ambulances and transported to the Fairchild Medical Center in Yreka. Mongo was alive, but barely. He had suffered an unknown number of bullet wounds to his chest area and was critical. The paramedics thought it highly unlikely he would survive, but his vital signs hung on by a thread. "This is one tough dude," they said to each other. One helicopter landed on the pad, and Mongo was loaded onto it, and on his way to the hospital in Medford.

It did take several hours for the sheriff's troops to clear the mansion. The hang-up was getting access to the subterranean vaults. The rest of the house, although massive with many rooms, was relatively easy, but the officers were unaware how to gain entry to the underground areas. After two hours, they still didn't know. All but two of the Ryders' surrendering soldiers had already been loaded into patrol cars and were on their way to the Siskiyou County jail. The remaining two, who appeared to be the highest ranking, were still on the property, cuffed in the back of separate patrol cars. The sheriff went to the patrol cars and talked to each one. Those conversations gave him what he needed. I didn't ask him what he said or did to persuade the men to disclose the secret to gaining access, and he didn't volunteer the information. "Let's just say," he said quietly, "that they weren't appreciative of the fact that their employers took off in a helicopter, leaving them hung out to dry. Frankly, I was surprised that the Ryders didn't kill them, or at least cut off their fingers or gouge out their eyes, but maybe they realized it wouldn't make any difference in the long run. We know that the underground rooms exist, and we would eventually figure out how to get to them. It would just take more time."

"Fingers and eyes?" I asked.

It was discovered that there were three ways to gain access. One was from the elevator. The second was from a secret door remarkably well-hidden in the wall of the room with the workbenches, table saws, tools, and pallets. The third was from a secret panel in an interior wall of the workshop away from the main house. That involved an expensive and elaborate engineering feat of its own, the construction of an underground quarter-mile tunnel connecting the workshop to the main house's basement.

Each access point had small, well-disguised biometric sensors that performed a fingerprint and retinal scan. It would open the secret access door only upon recognizing both a fingerprint and a retina simultaneously. In the elevator, it activated the appearance of a previously-hidden touch screen. The touch screen facilitated further control of the elevator, allowing it to descend to levels not otherwise apparent from the main control panel.

Using an eyeball and finger so graciously provided by one of the Ryders' left-behind thugs allowed the sheriff's team to clear the entire underground complex in another two hours. There were no other people on the premises. The two-hour sweep gave the members of the search team enough of a glimpse to demonstrate that what they were witnessing was out-of-this world, like a science-fiction movie. George Lucas couldn't have created a set with more high-tech detail and visual impact. It was also enough to convince the search team that there was an incredible amount of incriminating evidence that the Ryders left behind. They were satisfied, for the time being, to secure the entire complex as a crime scene. They would leave it under guard, obtain search warrants, and come back another day to conduct an extensive search, a task which would take weeks, and would necessarily involve the invasion of an army of federal agents.

There were thousands of pieces of evidence to be logged and cataloged that linked the Ryders to crimes up and down California and other states, much of it involving the distribution of cocaine. But there was evidence of other crimes as well, clandestine and not readily identifiable, possibly international in scope. Regarding the cocaine operation, the agents found a massive inventory of product, and packaging materials and equipment designed for its distribution. It became apparent that the product was shipped in "antique" Agriculture Supply Co. produce crates. Back in my law practice days, Agriculture Supply Co. was a client, and I was personally acquainted with many of its people. They would be horrified to find out how their company's logo was being used.

There were massive volumes of records. When applying to a judge for a search warrant to locate narcotics, it is standard for drug task force officers to include a request to search for "pay and owe sheets." This is police lingo meaning accounting records that document transactions with suppliers and customers, including names, addresses, prices, method of payment, quantities, delivery dates and locations. With most garden-variety drug busts "pay and owe sheets" are just that, mere scraps of paper with information hand-written on them. That was not the case with the accounting records of the Ryders' vast illicit empire. These records, consisting of digital and hard-copy files, occupied a large room in one of the underground vaults. It would take an army of accounting and IT experts to sift through the data and gain an understanding of the big picture.

After the warrants were obtained, a few days into the search the officers made an interesting, and horrifying, discovery. It was a bomb. More accurately a series of high-tech explosives planted throughout the entire underground complex. This discovery brought the search process to a screeching halt until a bomb squad, consisting of federal agents, could fully examine and disarm it, a process that took two days. The bomb people were mystified as to why the explosives hadn't been activated. Initial impressions of the "pay and owe sheets" suggested that, besides their connection to the *La Peninsula* cartel, the Ryders were also connected to a domestic criminal organization, possibly the same organization, or an off-shoot of it, that the posse, Brenda, and I encountered four years earlier. It had been that organization's *modus operandi* to blow up and destroy their own facilities when the pressure got too great, obliterating incriminating evidence. Why that didn't happen this time was a mystery. Theoretically, the whole place should have been blown to smithereens once the Ryders' helicopter was a safe distance away.

CHAPTER 44

Bob - Murphy

After the last of the Ryders' followers had surrendered, I called John Dickenson, Ben Thompson's lawyer. "How's Ben's defense going?" I asked.

"Not well," he said. "And I'm really frustrated. I don't think there's sufficient evidence to hold him, let alone convict him, but the D.A. is going all-out, and isn't reasonable. There's a bigger picture that I can't get a handle on. Someone is pulling his strings. Or maybe he's being blackmailed. I don't know. But there is something more than just prosecutorial zeal, or even the desire to be re-elected. The whole thing stinks. I think we can win the case, but it's going to take an ugly jury trial to do it. Even if we win, Ben loses. He will always be tainted. People will never look at him the same again, they will always be suspicious. I've had contact with his medical school, on his behalf. I can only hope to get him reinstated, so he can complete his residency and get his license to practice medicine. But they are unwilling to make a commitment. Understandable, I guess, at this stage. He *is* in custody, charged with a heinous crime. But I don't know if their attitude will change if he is acquitted. And what if he does get his license? Will people want him to be their doctor? Would *you* want him to be your doctor? If Murphy loses the case, you can bet he will give a press conference refusing to acknowledge that Ben didn't commit the crime. He'll blame the defeat on something other than Ben's innocence. It'll be 'because of jury misconduct,' or 'because of a technicality,' or something like that. In the meantime, Ben is going through hell, and so are his parents. They all look terrible. Ben is young and can probably hang in there, but I'm worried about David and Lillian. I don't know if they can physically or emotionally survive this."

As I listened to him go on, something got into me, I'm not sure what; maybe lack of sleep, maybe I had become unhinged by the violent events that had unfolded, but I felt a perverse desire to string him along. "I've done a little investigation on my own, and I think I've uncovered some helpful evidence that may provide him a defense. But it's a bit complicated."

"I'll take anything I can get," he said. "I plan to go down to Pineland tomorrow, to follow up on some things, and to talk to Ben. Shall I stop in to see you on the way?"

"Yep," I said.

"So, what have you got?"

"I have something that can demonstrate reasonable doubt," I said. "Do you remember the legendary jury trial story? The one where the defendant was being tried for murder of his wife but her body had never been found? The defense attorney tried to plant the seeds of reasonable doubt in the minds of the jurors by pointing out that the prosecution had failed to demonstrate that the victim was even dead. During his argument, the defense counsel dramatically pointed toward the back door of the courtroom, and said, 'Why, she might walk through that door any second now!' The entire jury and just about everyone else in the courtroom turned their heads toward the door. This made the jurors realize that if they themselves had expected the dead wife to burst through the courtroom door, how could they be sure beyond a reasonable doubt that the defendant had killed her?"

"Sure, that's a great story," said Dickenson. "But you know how it ended. The prosecutor was sharp. He also dramatically gestured toward the door, looked the jurors in the eye, and said, 'Every head in this courtroom turned toward that door just now – every head except one, that of the defendant. He didn't bother to look because he knows she's not going to walk through that door. He killed her.' I'm pretty sure the defendant got convicted in that case. What's your point?"

How far should I draw this out? I wondered, and then I said, "I have evidence that can convince the jury that Hailey Madison actually will walk through the door."

Dickenson was now getting impatient. "And, what's that?"

"Hailey Madison."

"Holy shit! Is she okay?"

"Yep."

"What the hell happened?"

I gave him an abbreviated version of the chain of events, and assured him that Hailey Madison was indeed alive, but had been through a lot. She probably looked as bad, if not worse, than Ben. I also told him that Brenda had been taken along with the Ryders in the helicopter. "I'm sure you're disappointed that you won't be able to try the case and make the big bucks. But you'll just have to suck it up."

"Yeah, I'm devastated! What great news for Hailey, and for Ben. I'll call D.A. James Murphy right now and let him know, and hopefully get Ben released. Stay by your phone, though, in case I need to get more information. Murphy's such a jerk, he may not believe me when I tell him his victim is alive. He may want documentation."

"Okay," I said. "Actually, you might be able to get some substantial civil work out of this whole thing, if you want it. It's going to be interesting to see what they come up with when they do a complete comprehensive search of the property here. I think the Ryders have connections to major criminal organizations involved in illegal activities. From what we know of Murphy, I'll bet he is connected to them as well. That's why he's pushing so hard. Maybe they put pressure on him. At the very least, Hailey Madison has a compelling civil action against the Ryder family's fortune for what the Ryders did to her. There's a secret underground basement, or vault, under the house. When they begin a serious search, who knows what information might turn up? There might be a treasure trove of records."

"Well, we will see. I've got plenty to keep me busy. Honestly, I was beginning to get stressed because Ben's case was taking my time away from my day job, and I was getting behind. It's good that it's over. And no amount of money can equal the pleasure I will get when I inform Murphy that his dead victim isn't dead. That alone will make it worthwhile."

CHAPTER 45

Reunited

It took two more days to get Ben Thompson released from jail, which incensed John Dickenson. The jail, understandably, wouldn't release him until the D.A. dismissed the charges. Murphy stubbornly refused to dismiss until he personally interviewed Hailey. Hailey expected that she was in for a long haul of police interviews and medical and psychological evaluations, but an immediate interview with Ben's accuser was hard for her to process. Dickinson was viscerally angry at Murphy's intransigence. There was no reason for it. Sure, it made sense that Hailey should be interviewed extensively. Many crimes had been committed, very serious ones, and she was a material witness. But there was no reason she had to be interviewed with such immediacy. And there was no reason that Ben's release should be conditioned upon a personal interview with Hailey. You can't hold someone for a murder when the victim isn't dead. That she was alive didn't necessarily rule out that Ben may have been guilty of *something* connected to Hailey's abduction, but that could be ruled out easily by some means other than subjecting her to an in-person interview in Murphy's office. His demand was unconscionable, but realistically she had no choice but to comply. She would have gone to his office right then to get Ben released, but Murphy was suddenly "far too busy" for that. He couldn't possibly take the time to see her until two days later, and he'd try to squeeze her in then. Two days later the interview did proceed, and turned out to be a relentless five-hour long ordeal that took its toll. Over Dickinson's vehement objections, Murphy grilled her heartlessly and viciously, accusing her and Ben of all manner of conspiracies against Rex and Melinda Ryder. He suggested that she wasn't really kidnapped, or tortured, or raped, or held against her will, but it was all a hoax. A hoax she and Ben dreamed up together solely to harass and destroy Rex and Melinda. It was more an inquisition than an interview. Horrible as it was, Hailey held up admirably and made it through, but was emotionally bruised and scarred when it was over. Mercifully, at the end of the day Murphy formally dismissed the charges, and Ben was released. When he walked out the main door of the jail, he was met by Hailey, his parents, and his lawyer. After a happy but tearful round of hugging -- and in Hailey's case, kissing -- the Thompsons, Ben, David, and Lillian, and Hailey all climbed into David's car and headed up I-5 for the three-and-a-half-hour drive back to Yreka. They were all planning to spend the night at the elder Thompsons' home, with Hailey invited to occupy the guest bedroom. It was late when they arrived, and it had been a long day. David and

Lillian retired, leaving Hailey and Ben alone on the living room couch. They were pressed close together, with Ben's arm around her shoulders. They sat in silence for a half-an-hour. Then Ben asked, softly, "Do you want to tell me what happened to you?"

"Yes, I do. I want to tell you everything, but not tonight. I just can't tonight. But I promise I will. I'll tell you everything."

"Are you okay?" he asked.

"Now that I'm sitting here with you, I'm okay. More than okay. I don't honestly know how long I was in that awful place, but the only thing that kept me sane and kept me from not giving up, was to picture myself with you holding onto me, like right now. It feels so good, but I'm still scared."

"What are you scared of?"

"I'm scared that after what they did to me, I'm a different person, one that you won't like."

"I will always love you no matter what. Don't even think that. I think I've changed, too. We both have been through hell and have changed. We have to be honest with each other and talk it through."

"I know we do. And we will. I promise I will tell you everything, but tonight, I don't want to talk anymore. I just want you to hold me. Hold me tight."

They didn't talk any more that night. They just held onto each other, for dear life. When David and Lillian came into the living room the next morning, that's how they found Ben and Hailey. They were asleep on the couch, still dressed in the clothes they had worn the day before, and still hanging on to each other for dear life.

CHAPTER 46

Bob and Bebe Back Home

At around 9:00 PM the evening after our invasion of the Ryders' property, I arrived back at my little house, exhausted. The day would have taken its toll on a younger man in his prime. As for me, the septuagenarian, by the time I got home I was a physical and emotional wreck. Bebe of course was there to greet me, but not her usual enthusiastic self. It was as if she already knew something horrible had happened. "Where's Brenda?" she asked. Before answering, I put some ice cubes into a glass, and, without measuring, poured some gin, a healthy amount. I sat down on the couch. Bebe sat on the floor in front of me, her eyes fixed on mine. Her eyes were sad. I described the events of the day, ending my story with the helicopter pulling away with Brenda LeHane inside. Bebe was visibly shaken. "That's horrible," she said. "You didn't take me with you. Maybe I could have helped." I had nothing to tell her in response. Maybe she was right.

I climbed into bed at 10:30, and fell into a fitful, uncomfortable sleep.

As usual, the next morning my clock radio popped on at 5:00 AM tuned to NPR. Also, as usual, I was half-sleeping through the newscast, until I heard this, which brought me immediately awake:

> The Federal Aviation Administration has reported early this morning that a private jet aircraft, owned by Rex Randall Ryder The Third and his sister Melinda Ryder, has disappeared over the Atlantic Ocean. The Gulfstream G650, reportedly carrying the two grandchildren of famed 1940's western movie singing cowboy icon Rex Randall Ryder reportedly had departed from the Arcata-Eureka Airport in far northern California about mid-day yesterday. Before departure, the pilot had filed a flight plan indicating an ultimate destination of Paris, France. Government sources indicated that the aircraft made a short stop at a small airport in Florida, and then resumed its flight, ostensibly to Paris. The pilot continued radio contact with international air traffic controllers until approximately ninety minutes from the flight's Paris destination. At that time, radio contact ceased, and according to traffic controllers, the aircraft inexplicably changed its course to a more southerly heading. Thirty minutes later, with the flight still over water, the pilot broke the radio silence and advised air traffic control he was experiencing engine problems and might have to make an emergency water landing. Minutes after that, the pilot issued an urgent "Mayday" message.

That was the last radio communication from the aircraft, which then disappeared from the air traffic control's radar. A multinational search team has been dispatched to the area where the plane disappeared, but neither the aircraft nor any signs of wreckage or debris have yet been spotted. Sources at California's Arcata-Eureka Airport reported seeing the Ryders and several others arriving in a large helicopter and then quickly transferring to the Gulfstream jet, which took off without delay.

Flamboyant Rex Randall Ryder The Third and his reclusive sister Melinda are well-loved philanthropists who have donated millions of dollars to many worthwhile charitable organizations world-wide, including foundations which support National Public Radio. Despite his flamboyant personality, Rex Randall Ryder The Third, who appears to be the primary administrator of his and his sister's wealth, has routinely kept the true extent of the family's net worth a well-kept secret. But many experts believe that their assets, if known, would put them on most lists of the ten wealthiest people in the world. In the last decade the Ryders became enamored with the beautiful countryside and laid-back lifestyle of northern California's remote Siskiyou County, home of 14,000-foot Mount Shasta. They built a mansion in the scenic agricultural Scott Valley region of the county, where they spend most of their time, although they reportedly own properties all over the world. One of their neighbors in the Scott Valley recently said this of Rex and Melinda to a reporter from our affiliate Jefferson Public Radio in southern Oregon: "They are great neighbors, and I sure hope they're okay. When they first came here, the locals were skeptical, as you can imagine, but since we have gotten to know them, they have become just like us. Very generous. They would give us the shirts off their backs. Our county's a much better place with them here."

Our hearts and prayers go out to Rex and Melinda and the others on their airplane, and hope that their plane will be located, and that they all are safe.

I sat upright in bed with a jolt, and Bebe, who was sleeping on the rug beside the bed, came up to me and put her chin on my knee. She looked up at me, crestfallen, as if she had heard and understood every word of the NPR broadcast. "She's not coming back, is she?" she asked. Then, "Rex and Melinda are evil. The guy on the radio is full of shit." I don't think I ever heard her swear before.

CHAPTER 47

Mongo

The staff at Providence Medical Center in Medford, Oregon, had never experienced a patient like Christopher Ray, AKA Mountain Mongo. Mongo was the talk of the entire hospital. He was in ICU recovering from a seven-hour surgical procedure that removed three bullets from his chest. The scuttlebutt was that he had been airlifted to Providence after having been involved in a wild-west shootout at a remote cattle ranch down in Siskiyou County. He had been all but pronounced dead, but somehow had pulled through, thanks, according to the rumor mill, to his supernatural size, strength, and toughness.

Although there was no formal count, Mongo probably had more visitors than any other patient in the hospital's history. The visitors weren't the kind you normally expect, friends and family members. They were people who didn't even know him, mostly people who worked at or were otherwise affiliated with the Providence Medical Center. They weren't there on official business. They came from all of the hospital's departments; the cancer center, the cardiology center, the birth center; you name it, they showed up. The word was out, and they just wanted to get a look at him. They weren't disappointed. Just a look was worth it. His body was at least a foot longer than the longest hospital bed. And the hospital gown was ridiculous. They weren't quite experiencing the "real" Mongo, however, because by the time he got to ICU, he didn't smell like the "real" Mongo. He smelled more like … a hospital. Too bad.

If they arrived when he was awake and talking, the visitors really got their money's worth. For a guy who recently had three bullets in his chest, he was quite cheerful. He loved the attention, and rewarded his visitors with colorful stories, mostly free from his usual bad language. But sometimes the bad language just slipped out, he couldn't help it. No matter, his visitors loved him all the more for it.

When he got going on the events leading up to three bullets in his chest, his audience was captivated.

CHAPTER 48

Brenda

Brenda LeHane was having trouble figuring out where she was. She emerged from a deep sleep and was disoriented. Her brain was processing sensory perceptions one at a time. The first was her general feeling of physical discomfort. Her body ached, and she tried to move her limbs to relieve the stress, and realized she was restrained. She was sitting in a seat, an airline passenger seat. Her movement was restricted because her wrists and ankles were immobilized. Her ankles were cuffed underneath the seat to its legs. Her arms were pulled up and behind her over her shoulders, causing her back to arch painfully. Her wrists were cuffed to something behind the aircraft seat. Her situation was slowly coming into focus, and the terror rose a little more with each new realization. She was dressed in the same clothing she had been wearing when two men came into Bob's house and abducted her. She could tell from the familiar humming sound and vibration that she was in an airplane that was airborne. She was alone in a small compartment which had two rows of seats facing each other on each side of a small table. Her inner-ear told her she was facing forward, but she couldn't verify that, as the shades had all been pulled down, covering the windows. As she sat in that uncomfortable position, one-by-one images of the events of the last several hours materialized in her mind, each causing her level of terror to rise. How many hours had it been? She realized she had no idea how much time had passed since she was roughly dragged up into the Ryders' helicopter.

She froze as the door in front of the cabin slowly opened, and Melinda appeared. She was dressed in the same long black cocktail dress she wore when they had boarded the helicopter. "My, my, my, what have we here?" clucked Melinda, tauntingly. "Look at you, you *are* a sight. Those nasty restraints just don't look very comfortable. But they're for your own good, you know. We have your best interest at heart. We are afraid you will do something self-destructive if your hands and feet are free. We certainly don't want you to hurt yourself, do we? If you hurt yourself it might decrease your value. We wouldn't want that, would we?"

Brenda stared at Melinda but said nothing, biting her lip.

"Nothing to say?" continued Melinda. "Well, I'll bet you have a whole *slew* of questions. You're a world traveler now, and I'll bet you're just *dying* to know where you are headed, aren't you? Well, on the other hand, maybe you don't really want to know. I think if I were in your shoes, I would prefer dying to going where you're going."

Melinda sat in the seat facing Brenda, reached across the table, and touched her on the cheek. Brenda immediately snapped her head away, still saying nothing. "Now don't be that way," said Melinda. "Don't make it hard on yourself. Don't worry, even though you aren't talking, I know that you *really do* want to know where you're going, and you have every right to be informed. So, I will be the one to inform you." Melinda trailed her hand from Brenda's cheek, down her neck toward her chest, causing Brenda to squirm as much as her bonds would allow. She still remained defiantly silent.

"First, I need to compliment our fine pilots. They are indeed excellent. You should feel safe in their competent hands. They have successfully completed a very complex aeronautical maneuver that has caused the whole world to think we are all dead. Isn't that a *hoot*? The whole world thinks our airplane is under the sea, having crashed *en route* to Paris. They are mourning for us. Well, maybe not for you, but for Rex and me. Every newspaper in the world is talking about the tragic demise of two of the world's most beloved people. Our pilot made a 'mayday' call and skillfully guided our aircraft off their radar screen. We will be landing at a small private airport in the United Arab Emirates within the hour. Ah, Dubai here we come! I *love* Dubai and am *so* excited! Aren't you excited?" Melinda's hand drifted to Brenda's left breast and flicked the nipple with her middle finger through the cloth of her shirt. Brenda flinched, but said nothing.

"You know, it's been *ages* since we've been to Dubai, and I'm *so* looking forward to getting back. It was actually Rex's idea to move to the Scott Valley, and I went along with him. I suppose it was okay while it lasted, but it really wasn't my thing. I'm happy to be done with it. But not Rex; I guess it's the cowboy in him. He *loved* the ranch life, and he's *really* upset that it didn't work out. And he's angry, really angry. One thing I've learned about my big brother, when he gets angry, he's capable of doing just about anything. He gets his payback, no matter how long it takes, or how much it costs. He obsesses over it. He's obsessing right now, up in front of this airplane. As we speak, he's making a list of the people he intends to deal with. Unfortunately, all but one of those people are back in California, so it'll take some doing, but he'll just take his time. No rush.

"In the meantime, one of those people is not back in California. Any idea who that might be? Do you have any idea?"

Brenda continued her silence.

"I'm sure Rex will come back here and pay you a friendly little visit before we land, but that shouldn't be anything for you to worry too much about. For you, the real fun will begin when we get to the UAE. He already has plans for you. There is an auction coming up in the next few months. Underground, it is highly classified and guarded. The clients are high-rollers from the Arab world. *Really* high rollers. You will be one of the auction items for sale. We will have plenty of time to get you prepped to bring a fabulous price. I'm getting excited just thinking about it, the idea is *so* delicious. I'll bet you're excited, too. I'll bet you're just *dying* to know what price you will bring, aren't you?" With that, Melinda gave Brenda's nipple a little squeeze, stood up and walked toward the door. In the doorway, she paused, looked back and said, cheerfully, "Enjoy the rest of your flight. See you in Dubai," and closed the door.

CHAPTER 49

Bob

For about a week, the airplane crash and Rex Randall Ryder The Third and Melinda were headline news on every mainstream media outlet and all the social media. The stories I heard were all the same. Nostalgia about all the wonderful albeit corny movies their famous grandfather starred in back in the forties; and the hit records, particularly the countrified Christmas songs. I never heard a negative word; every story gushed the wonderfulness of the original Rex and his descendants. Rex The Third and his shy but beautiful sister Melinda carried on the family tradition of wonderfulness, unlike so many of the troubled descendants of rich and famous people we read about nowadays. Rex and Melinda blessed the earth with their wonderfulness and their charities. It was enough to make me puke. Every passing day more examples of their wonderfulness were unearthed and made public. A great deal of attention was directed toward how much they did for the people and communities close to them, especially the simple folks of the idyllic but backward rural northern California valley where they had settled. It was unfortunate, declared the media, those folks didn't appreciate just how important Rex and his sister were to them. You couldn't blame them though; they just didn't know better. Provincial in their ways, those folks just didn't understand. The full-page letter that Rex and Melinda had published in the local newspaper was read repeatedly, and excerpts reprinted in the national press. The so-called "shootout" which drove them to flee from the wonderful ranch and home they had created in the Scott Valley was "alt-right" terrorism organized by local rednecks and good-ole boys, aided and abetted by local police. Alt-right? I wondered how they came up with that.

But there is always a silver lining. Our local folks began to realize how much Rex and Melinda's unfortunate and tragic deaths could do for them economically. Local businesses were picking up. A new business was created, "Ryder Country Mansion Tours," which packed ten tour buses every day with tourists for a visit to the now famous "Ryder Mansion in the Scott Valley." It apparently didn't matter much that the buses couldn't actually get close to the mansion itself, still being treated as a crime scene.

Three months after the "Shoot-Out at the Ryder Ranch," I felt like I aged ten years. Aging ten years is one thing for someone who is, say, twenty-five. But when you're a seventy-eight-year-old septuagenarian, it definitely takes its toll. The stepped-up aging process began when I saw the helicopter disappear over the ridge with Brenda on board. A lot of things happened during the three months since, some of it good, slowing down the accelerated aging process. I hoped if things kept heading in the right direction, the process would reverse itself.

The outlook for Hailey Madison and Ben Thompson was bright. They both had their demons to deal with, but were doing okay. They got professional counselling, which helped, but mainly they had each other. They talked to each other, sharing what they had been through, which was probably the best thing, surpassing the counselling. Hailey wore an engagement ring, a lovely but not ostentatious diamond. No date had been set, but there was no hurry. They would know when the time was right.

Once he convinced Pineland District Attorney James Murphy that he couldn't continue to prosecute a murder charge when the alleged victim wasn't dead, John Dickenson turned his attention to other matters. One was getting Ben reinstated into medical school. It wasn't a tough sell, as it became clear that Ben had no culpability in anything criminal. He did lose a few months in his quest to become a doctor, but he was still young. John Dickenson then went after James Murphy.

Law enforcement's crime-scene processing of the Ryders' compound in the Scott Valley was still ongoing, even three months after they gained access to the underground areas. Federal agents were doing most of the work and discovered records that were indeed a treasure trove of information, linking the Ryders to a domestic criminal organization and two Mexican cartels. Cocaine distribution was only one of their business ventures; but it was a significant one, especially in rural northern California. Records painted a picture of a huge cocaine distribution network that included Morrow County, in which James Murphy played an important role. Although he was an outsider, his election as district attorney was guaranteed because of the campaign funding provided by the Ryders' organization, and because of the political pressure it exerted on local leaders and potential challengers. He won the election handily, but he owed his soul to the organization. Although Murphy's role was primarily to give aid and assistance to the Ryders' cocaine distribution operation, he could help them in other ways. For the Ryders it was a stroke of luck that when Hailey Madison pulled off I-5 that night with a flat tire, she was still in Morrow County, Murphy's jurisdiction.

The records retrieved from the underground vault were voluminous, meticulous and detailed, describing the activities of major players as well as people in the trenches with minor roles. A name that showed up from the latter category was Harold Watson. The name caught the attention of the authorities because his listed home address was the same as Ben Thompson's apartment complex in Sacramento. The file described Watson's occupation as a lab technician who worked at UC Davis Medical Center's pharmacogenetics laboratory. But that was his day job. He moonlighted as a low-level drug dealer for the Ryders' organization. During their investigation, the authorities determined that Harold Watson was the person described as confidential informant "CI#2" in a police report the Pineland District Attorney relied on in his case against Ben. Watson was uniquely positioned to be of great value to Rex and Melinda. Being acquainted with Ben, he could deliver the credible lie that Ben had told him Hailey was pregnant and that Ben was "pissed" about it, thereby furnishing a motive for Ben to murder her. But the fortuitous circumstance that he also worked in the medical center's pharmacogenetics lab was a major windfall. His job gave him daily access to the lab's records, and doctoring them was easy. He also had access to the stored blood samples. The information in the file didn't specify how much the Ryders paid Watson for his very valuable services, but John Dickenson intended to find out.

Probably no one would ever know for sure what motivated Rex and Melinda to embark on their elaborate plan to do harm to Hailey and Ben. No evidence of economic or financial gain had surfaced. The likely explanation, based on the available evidence, was simply that Rex and Melinda were psychopaths. Psychopaths with unnatural sexual urges, and with the wherewithal to do and take whatever the hell they wanted. Rex saw Hailey and he wanted her. Maybe for himself, maybe for his sister, maybe for both. He, or they, took her. She wasn't their first. But, unlike the others, she got away. This enraged Rex and Melinda, leading them to work patiently on a long-range and elaborate plan to get her back. Then Hailey and Ben began their relationship, another stroke of luck for Rex and Melinda. They had nothing against Ben personally, but hated his father, the retired dentist, ever since years before when, as a county supervisor, he had the audacity to attempt to block the development of their Scott Valley property. It worked out for them anyway, because their project was ultimately approved, thanks to a little political pressure, but Rex and Melinda never forgot. That was inherent in their psychopathy. They never forgot. They would get their revenge. No hurry. Wait till the moment is right. And didn't this all come together beautifully? They developed a plan to get their revenge against Hailey, and then to take out Ben to destroy his father, whom they detested. Also, harming Ben inflicted more delicious hurt to Hailey. It was meant to be.

Things had gotten better in those three months for Hailey and Ben. And for Bebe and me, too. We finally moved into our new house, and it was great. Definitely worth the wait. Bebe was happy. She loved her little house with her own window. And, for the first time in her septuagenarian (in dog years) life, she had a yard large enough to give her room to run. But still, something was missing ...

I was standing in the checkout line of Raley's grocery store when a headline from a tabloid caught my eye. The mainstream media furor had all but disappeared, but the tabloid headline read, "Famed Airplane Crash Victim Rex Randall Ryder The Third Found Decapitated in Dubai!" The headline was on the front page, adjacent to another headline that read, "85-Year-Old Elvis a Hospice Patient in New Jersey!" I usually skim the covers of those tabloids when I'm at Raley's; I can't help it. It gives me something to do while waiting in line, and invariably makes me laugh. But I never actually bought one. Does anyone actually buy those things? This time I did buy one, and hurried home to read it.

Before unpacking the groceries, I set the magazine on the kitchen table and opened it to the page with the article. I brought Bebe in and sat down to read it, my heart actually pounding. I read it out loud to Bebe:

The body of a decapitated man found early yesterday morning in a posh Dubai hotel was positively identified by authorities as that of Rex Randall Ryder The Third, grandson of the famous 1940's cowboy movie star Rex Randall Ryder. The deceased, along with his sister, Melinda Ryder, were believed to have been killed in an airplane crash over the ocean. Their private jet had filed a flight plan for a Paris, France, destination, but the airplane mysteriously veered off course and disappeared from radar contact. It was believed to have crashed in the ocean, but no wreckage or other evidence of the aircraft has been found. According to Dubai authorities, besides having been decapitated, Ryder's body showed signs of horrendous brutality. Whether the injuries to his body occurred before or after the decapitation is thus far unknown, according to a report.

Authorities also stated that another person, an African-American female, was found alive in the hotel room along with Ryder's body. She was reported to have been cuffed or chained to a chair with her head covered by a hood, in fair condition but with some bruises. She is not considered a suspect in Ryder's murder, but is in the custody of Dubai police, suspected of the crime of "cohabitation by an unmarried woman," which under Sharia law can be punished by imprisonment.

Staff and other eyewitnesses at the Dubai hotel reported to the police that the hotel accommodation, an opulent four-room suite, had been booked in the name of Melinda Ryder, sister of the beheaded man. When they checked in, their entourage consisted of the Ryders, the African-American woman who was found confined to a chair, a white American woman who authorities believed to be the Ryders' bookkeeper, and four large men who appeared to be bodyguards. They had checked into the hotel the previous day. In the early hours of the morning of the discovery of Ryder's body, eyewitnesses heard loud noises coming from the hotel suite, including shouting and screams. The police were called, but before they arrived at the scene, the four large men had hurriedly departed from the hotel with Melinda Ryder and the bookkeeper, who appeared to be hostages. They sped away in two black SUV's and have not been apprehended.

This newspaper's Dubai correspondent interviewed two high-ranking knowledgeable officials in Dubai's police bureaucracy who asked to remain anonymous, fearing retribution. Both officials, interviewed separately, appeared certain that the killing of Ryder and the abduction of his sister and the family's bookkeeper were related to, and possibly ordered by, Mexico's notorious *La Peninsula* cartel. The officials also believed that Melinda Ryder and the bookkeeper were to be sold as slaves to a Sheikh in a remote and clandestine eastern region of Abu Dhabi.

Sharia law in the UAE is very harsh and prescribes severe punishments for activities not considered criminal in the west, although the government is taking steps to relax these draconian laws. Flogging and stoning are legal punishments under Sharia law. For example, alcohol consumption is illegal and punishable by 80 lashes. Human rights organizations claim that female rape victims who report the crime are often convicted of false allegations, punishable by years in prison. There was a reported case in 2013 of a 24-year-old Norwegian woman who reported an alleged rape to the police and received a prison sentence for perjury, illicit consensual extramarital sex, alcohol consumption and false allegations. But the laws are enforced selectively, and often are not applied to non-Muslims. Slavery has been outlawed in Dubai for several decades, and prostitution is illegal. But human trafficking, forced prostitution, and similar depravities exist in Dubai's underbelly even as its wealth, modern technology, skyscrapers, and luxury hotels attract investors, tourists, and expatriates.

Bebe listened intently as I read the entire article. When I had finished reading, we both sat in silence for a long time. Then Bebe asked, "When are you going to Dubai?"

Acknowledgments

Thanks to my wife Ann for her support and patience. When at age seventy-four I started writing a full-length novel, *The Septuagenarian – An R-Rated Thriller,* she thought I was crazy. Now that I have finished my second one, she still thinks I'm crazy, but a little less so.

After I retired from my day job as a Superior Court Judge in 2008, I began writing as a pastime, starting with short stories for my grandkids, and then columns for our local newspaper. Not until 2016 did I think about attempting a full-length novel. There is a saying that everyone has a novel in them, so I thought, why not? But there is a further saying, generally attributed to Christopher Hitchens, that "Everyone has a book in them and that, in most cases, is where it should stay." Not taking that wise advice, I have now finished this, my second book.

As with the first book, I am grateful to my friends, Dave and Kaye Caulkins, and to fellow retired Judge William Davis for being the first to read the manuscript and give me the encouragement and confidence to show it to others, and ultimately to publish. They also went through the time-consuming and painstaking task of editing and critiquing the manuscript.

Thus encouraged, I sent the manuscript to other friends for further review and critique. They are Kent Goheen, Gary Sundberg, Mike Grifantini, Sherry Coonrod, Bill Cushman, Andrew Marx, Tom Raper, and Mel Chambers. Their valuable contributions are much appreciated.